M. J. FA

is the pseudonym for Molly Keane. She was born in Co. Kildare, Ireland, in 1904 into 'a rather serious Hunting and Fishing and Church-going family' who gave her little education at the hands of governesses. Her father originally came from a Somerset family and her mother, a poetess, was the author of 'The Songs of the Glens of Antrim'. Molly Keane's interests when young were 'hunting and horses and having a good time': she began writing only as a means of supplementing her dress allowance, and chose the pseudonym M. J. Farrell 'to hide my literary side from my sporting friends'. She wrote her first novel, *The Knight of the Cheerful Countenance*, at the age of seventeen.

Molly Keane published ten novels between 1928 and 1952: *Young Entry* (1928), *Taking Chances* (1929), *Mad Puppetstown* (1931), *Conversation Piece* (1932), *Devoted Ladies* (1934), *Full House* (1935), *The Rising Tide* (1937), *Two Days in Aragon* (1941), *Loving Without Tears* (1951) and *Treasure Hunt* (1952). She was also a successful playwright, of whom James Agate said 'I would back this impish writer to hold her own against Noel Coward himself.' Her plays, with John Perry, always directed by John Gielgud, include *Spring Meeting* (1938), *Ducks and Drakes* (1942), *Treasure Hunt* (1949) and *Dazzling Prospect* (1961).

The tragic death of her husband at the age of thirty-six stopped her writing for many years. It was not until 1981 that another novel—*Good Behaviour*—was published, this time under her real name. Molly Keane has two daughters and lives in Co. Waterford. Her latest novel, *Time After Time*, was published in 1983 and her cookery book, *Nursery Cooking*, was published in 1985.

Virago publishes *Devoted Ladies, The Rising Tide, Two Days in Aragon, Mad Puppetstown, Full House,* and *Taking Chances. Loving Without Tears* and *Young Entry* are forthcoming.

TAKING
CHANCES

M. J. FARRELL

With a New Introduction by
CLARE BOYLAN

PENGUIN BOOKS – VIRAGO PRESS

PENGUIN BOOKS
Viking Penguin Inc., 40 West 23rd Street,
New York, New York 10010, U.S.A.
Penguin Books Ltd, Harmondsworth,
Middlesex, England
Penguin Books Australia Ltd, Ringwood,
Victoria, Australia
Penguin Books Canada Limited, 2801 John Street,
Markham, Ontario, Canada L3R 1B4
Penguin Books (N.Z.) Ltd, 182–190 Wairau Road,
Auckland 10, New Zealand

First published in Great Britain by Elkin Mathews & Marrot, Ltd., 1929
First published in the United States of America by J. B. Lippincott Co., 1929
This edition first published in Great Britain by Virago Press Limited 1987
Published in Penguin Books 1987

Printed in Great Britain by
Cox and Wyman, Reading.

TO
DIANA

INTRODUCTION

Nothing puts history in perspective so firmly as fiction. M. J. Farrell wrote *Taking Chances* in 1930, a period when women's lives were so unthinkably complicated and endangered by manners that some still hunted side-saddle. Yet there are two abortion attempts in this ironic study of misplaced passion, and a lot of heavy sexual goings-on, referred to, with no irony at all, as "light behaviour".

In a recent profile in *The New Yorker*, the novelist, now revealed as the octogenarian Molly Keane, called herself "a great old breakerawayer". At twenty six she was already a rebel, cutting her teeth on her own society, the privileged hunting community of the Anglo-Irish landed gentry. Keane showed not just the beauty of their sheltered world of big houses and predatory play, but the riveting selfishness which made their prolonged loyalty the exclusive preserve of their (often unpleasant) pet dogs.

Irish Society and government was, in fact, less narrow half a century ago than it is now. The puritanical Irish Constitution, into which are enshrined legal prohibitions on both divorce and abortion, was not drafted for another seven years, until 1937 (although the cruel Censorship of Publications Act, which virtually exiled writers like Kate O'Brien and later Edna O'Brien, was already a year old). The real difference between then and now is that writers—especially women writers—rarely told all. Keane was the exception. Within her own rarified "divine" world of

dainty manners and bloody sports Molly was at the same
time an eager participant and a starkly unstockinged
camera lens. Rarified living conditions can limit understanding, but for the exceptionally intelligent they sharpen
the perceptions and offer rich material to record. The
nakedly black humour that delighted a new reading
generation in Molly Keane's *Good Behaviour* and *Time After
Time*, was, at this early stage, softened by youthful
enthusiasm, but already she was so caricaturing her own
way of life as to anticipate its decline.

The world so vividly brought to life in *Taking Chances*
(and all the novels of M. J. Farrell/Molly Keane, with the
exception of *Devoted Ladies*), has now almost vanished,
though survivors still cling to crumbling manor houses in
mounting discomfort and with dwindling funds, eccentric
but valiant exiles, like the remnants of the Raj. It was a
world where servants were faceless while dogs were ''little
people''; where a good day's hunting earned a girl the
ultimate accolade: ''That girl of Rowley's is a proper bit of
stuff. In fact I think she's a real live human being.'' Molly
Keane is adamant about the fact that their world was not
based on wealth (her own family, she says, was only
moderately funded and the need to augment her dress
allowance was her literary spur), but on a knowledge of
horses and easy access to cheap land and domestic labour.
Whatever the reason, times change and people too, but
when a new and very young novelist—Irish and female to
boot—pokes her pen so provocatively through the social
fabric of her own world, one realises that people do not
change with the times: it is people who change the times.

Farrell was not the only outspoken female literary voice
of the thirties. What made her place in English literature
unique is that her comic tone, nudging delicately between

irony and parody, was elsewhere only being employed on
stage and screen, and then the writers were always male. It
is no surprise to learn that she later turned to stage drama
and that subsequent novels (such as *Spring Meeting* and
Treasure Hunt) were first seen as drawing room comedies in
the West End. Molly stuck her neck out, not just by placing
her support firmly on the side of the "bad" girl, (and
allowing her, in spite of flimsy morals and a singular lack of
contrition, to more or less have her own way) but with a
hard-bitten line in home truths aimed at the most
vulnerable parts of society's sacred institutions:

Your honeymoon—you thought vaguely of your honeymoon all
your life: of its joys or horrors, as the mood took you. But what you
had never visualised were its dreadful moments of boredom,
moments when you delivered yourself of words with travail
unmitigated.

Taking Chances is not solely a comedy. It is also a love
story which veers between shrewd assessment of the politics
of passion and youthful poetic licence. There are also
occasional glimpses into the heart's core, reminiscent of the
intense intellectual heart-searching of Rebecca West. As
Farrell intuited the vulnerability of her own rarified world,
so she observed the integral flaws in the theory of love.
Again and again she returns to the incompatabilities of
love's central elements, of intimacy and adulation, of
loyalty and passion:

Her love and faith in him were far greater than that evasive trick
of intimacy, the secret of which is born between two and is rarely
discoverable—especially by the one who loves most.

Stories are not the author's main concern. Her fiction
conforms to a pattern of plot and setting, handled with

consummate skill. Her real obsession is with people and places, with location and dislocation. From behind the heavy furniture of behaviour, she retrieves the real meat of literature, the agony and the absurdity, for the entertainment, invigoration and discomfort of the reader.

In the midst of ardour, irony is at hand. The lovers confront one another with violent emotions but the cypher of reality is—their dogs. In *Taking Chances* Molly's delightfully naughty heroine, doubting the impact on the man she desires of her *risqué* wardrobe, confides to her bad-natured little dog: "Squiff, if only he could see me in my just—nothing-at-alls. Squiff, you immoral dog, you can always be seen in your just—nothing-at-alls, that's why you get off so strong." She defines the charm of her romantic hero, Rowley, in terms of the fullest range of attraction, offering one of those phrases which have become collectors' items to her huge number of fans, "dogs gave him the same helpless surrender as women". In a moment of real pain when the one truly sensitive character discovers that a gesture of friendship is really an invitation to treacherous conspiracy, it is the stoic suffering of his faithful hound we are shown;—"blind victim to his god's caprice"—when the promised outing is peremptorily reversed.

The storyline of *Taking Chances* is remarkable mainly as a blueprint for a pattern that Molly Keane has made her own. Most of Keane's central characters are members of the landed gentry, self-absorbed and taking their superiority and their privileged lives for granted. Into their sealed world comes an outsider, in some cases an innocent who becomes their victim, but in nearly all of her novels, including *Taking Chances* it's a survivor who knocks them off balance and exploits their relative *naiveté*.

Taking Chances, set in the fictitious Irish county of Westcommon, introduces us to the languid Sorriers of Sorristown house—handsome Sir Ralph (Roguey), lovely Maeve and clumsy, stuttering, younger brother, Jer—who have taken their minds off the vital business of hunting to see Maeve spectacularly married to neighbouring squire, Major Rowley Fountain. The year at Sorristown has only as many days as 'the hunting season, and suffers no interruption of this vital pursuit, even when misery and vengeance rebound from their selfishness as when Roguey's amusement with a village girl results in unwanted pregnancy and blackmail.

The outsider who arrives to disturb their smug mutuality, is Mary Fuller, heiress, scatterbrain and *femme fatale*. Mary has arrived from London with a mountain of luggage and her ratty little terrier, as an unlikely bridesmaid for virtuous Maeve. Mary is one of Molly Keane's dazzling creations, vulnerable and ruthless and with an unsettling appeal. She is shrewd but scatty, devastating though not beautiful—''Mary, whom you looked at once, wondering whether she was pretty, and twice to know that she was so lovely that you must take a third look and love her to distraction and sacrifice ever after.'' She has a Raymond Chandler line in dialogue and a sense of survival so imperative as to threaten all with whom she is involved. Keane pits Mary's animal survival instinct against the elegant self-sufficiency of the Sorriers in a contest of manners and expectations versus emotions and determination. As in most of her emotional confrontations, there are to be no clear winners—but she makes no secret of whose side she is on. Keane rejoices in her naughty heroine, shaping her with a mixture of youthful adulation and witty provocation, and clearly indulging her own ''breakerawayer" instincts at the same time.

The glamorous heiress doesn't just confide in dogs—she has gone to them. Experience has led her to believe that all men want ''the same *one* thing'' but she amiably concludes: ''Perhaps its *just* as well when the world's so hard on sweet young things who can't pay their poker debts.'' She responds to a question on ''What's the divinest thing in life?'' with the hoarse and swift response: ''The first cigarette of the day!'' She is an adventuress, who employs all available assets, especially her dramatic body ''being not so much immodest as unselfish on the subject'' and she toys not just with love but with its uncertainty:

She knew, they both knew, that there is an utter moment, a brief, lovely interval, which time past, love, no matter how pitifully we bolster up its semblance, trembles and dies. But the utter moment had not come yet. Not *just* yet, Mary thought, reaching towards it blindly, with her lovely head thrown back bravely; a hell of a rake she was

Molly herself must have been something of a headliner. By the time *Taking Chances* was published, her literary life was no longer a secret, and its knowledge earned her some disapproval from the stricter brigade of local mothers. Writing novels was bad enough; writing about intimate relationships, and with a sense of humour—''very *mal vu*'', as Molly puts it. It is probable that this minor notoriety pleased Molly more than it upset her. Two years later she was again to rattle the mothers when she met and fell in love with her future husband, Bobby Keane. She lived with him for five years before they got married. (''In those days it wasn't done, but of course it *was* done,'' she smiles.)

She was an eager debutante but a reluctant writer. Young Molly Skrine (her maiden name), had first put pen to paper ten years earlier when she wrote a hunting romance for Mills & Boon to boost her dress allowance. "Pure as cocoa," she says deprecatingly of that literary debut which earned her fifty pounds and was used to pay for a great party in the Shelbourne Hotel and a pair of hunting boots. The same description might apply to pure Maeve, the Irish beauty who suffers a nasty martyrdom at the point of Molly's caustic pen. Keane manages to make virginity seem a kind of short-sightedness which turns marriage into Blind Man's Buff.

Soon—in a few hours—they would be together for always, and each day would be a day to love each other more. And the nights? But Maeve's nice thoughts stopped short there in a mysterious, hallowed glow.

Mills & Boon would never have sponsored Molly's boots in return for this ironic exercise, for the good girl is destined not for joy unconfined, but for—"the vitriolic, futile importance of a slighted woman".

As a writer, the young M. J.'s attitude to her own society bore comparison with their view of the fox. There is respect and even affection and indulgence, but he is legitimate prey. She has been described as having a "ruthless affection" for her characters. In *Taking Chances* we are shown Mary after her first successful Irish hunt: "Nearly crying with excitement ... while hounds broke up their well-deserved fox." The outsider, equally triumphant in romantic pursuit leaves Maeve, "painfully jealous, as all unimaginative women are, and proud as only the pure in heart are proud".

Molly Keane was, herself, something of an outsider. Although her social credentials were impeccable, her mother, a published poet and "literary recluse", refused to indulge Molly and her sister with the clothes, lunches and parties necessary to "launch" a girl. Molly believes that her sister Susan's romantic prospects were permanently damaged by the gown she was compelled to wear to her first dance—"A sort of tennis dress".

She herself was saved by a friend called Daphne whose mother included her in party invitations. Later she found a livelier life with the Perrys of Woodruff House in County Tipperary and in spite of her parents' disapproval, she more or less went to live there (returning home only for dull intervals of novel writing). The move proved to be a happily fatal one, for it was there that she met her future husband and became friendly with John Perry, a son of the house, who later collaborated with her on plays. In spite of her mother's indifference to hospitality her social life progressed "frightfully well" and she became familiar with most of the great Irish houses. One of the great pleasures of her fiction is her vivid evocation of the life in these houses.

Only the recent novels tell the full story, the bitter cold, the horror of the nursery and servants' quarters, but earlier works stirringly recreate the elegant houses with their magnificent settings and their imprint of unimaginative aristocracy.

Always watching over Sorristown with love and brooding, are the mountains, beautiful with a secrecy like death, and kind as solemn mothers.

All this one saw by turning from the unlovely, orderly chaos of an ugly room . . .

Molly herself did not fit into the category of "unimaginative aristocracy" and her bright mind was at work not only on the people she knew and the poignant truth of the failure of intimacy in their social skills but on the potential for loveliness in their comfortable surroundings. In *Taking Chances* she manoeuvre's Sorristown into stylish Mary's management and lovingly details its transformation.

Now, under Mary's guidance, the room, like a girl of accepted ugliness dressed suddenly in the right clothes, had acquired an exciting beauty. To-night, long curtains of wood-smoke blue and rainbow flame swept a chord of rich colour, shutting out the thought of the night. . . Two wide, low sofas of impossible depths and redundancy flanked the enormous wood fire at the precise angle for warmth and comfort, their hollows wadded by loose cushions covered in silver and blue and flame-clouded silk. The heterogeneous collection of furniture that had been vomited by some god of disorder about the room was gone.

My Ireland was a very different one from Molly Keane's. I shared with her a fascination with houses, but mine were city terraces with the cinema for social life and respectability as the highest aspiration. We shared also the national characteristic (now fast disappearing) of being inadequately educated. Molly was taught by a series of governesses and then "finished" at a wholly farcical-sounding French boarding school in Bray, County Wicklow. She was a reader "but not in any organised fashion". This handicap may turn to advantage in the novice writer for it can liberate an early imagination from self-consciousness. There is just one grave error of speech in *Taking Chances*: the wife of a local tenant farmer makes a reference to "horrid" behaviour—a word never used by the native Irish; the local terminology would be "desperate" behaviour. But a delightful, natural Irishness permeates her perfect prose, giving it texture and a piquant individuality. When Rowley marries Maeve, out of duty more than love "his old stud groom confided afterwards to a friend that marriage had made a great wreck o' the major; he was as cross now as ye wouldn't believe". And when old Aunt Edythe, who rules Sorristown through her weighty purse, encounters Mary in one of her famously shocking outfits ("not so much a dress as an inspired indiscretion"), the visitor is momentarily discomfited by "a look in her eye that would make a quiet cow in a secluded field blush for her forgotten bust-bodice".

It is not surprising that the disclosure of Molly's second life as successful novelist caused disquiet among the rural gentry for not only was her material frequently wittily scandalous but her characters were sometimes real and readily identifiable too. She happily claims to have no imagination and says that she has always written about her life. If this is true, then Molly, at twenty six, must have been a disturbing dinner guest, determining the manoeuvres behind the manners.

She also saw the detached manipulations of those distanced by age from sexual engagement. The self-immersed young in *Taking Chances* barely notice their older and rather more colourful relatives, who plot the lives of the young from a distance and who are as full of lively malice and unhealthy interest as any of Keane's more recent, splendidly bad old things from *Time After Time*. The dowager aunt develops a fascination with Mary's capacity for disturbance: "Aunt Edythe peered greedily over the bannisters at the silver storm of Mary's flight ... Almost, she snuffed the air that youth had breathed."

Her oblique yet encompassing view of behaviour and intentions also gave Molly Keane a premature wisdom. There is an almost Wildean precocity in romantic judgements such as the following: "There are few lengths short of which a man will stop but a woman's compliance is as limitless as are her subsequent reproaches." As in

Rodin's visionary sculpture, "*The Gates of Hell*", love's loss
is most imminent when its consummation is at hand. There
is a ring of jaundiced truth to this image of Mary victorious
in love: "lost in a hopeless void, realising the utter
remoteness of passion fulfilled". Yet to define Molly Keane
as cynic would be to grossly underestimate her powers as a
novelist. Even the most astutely ironic work suffers a
limitation of dimension and is divided from the best of
fiction by the latter's encompassing humanity. *Taking
Chances* is not as great a book as *Good Behaviour*, but it shows
all the promise of a resounding talent and a natural
authority in the difficult management of theme and plot.

Farrell set herself a difficult task, to establish a vanished
way of life and at the same time to expose it. As Anita
Brookner was later so devastatingly to do in a number of
her novels and especially, *Look At Me*, she elected a silent
witness, one caught up in, but not involved in, a glittering
world. Jer, youngest of the Sorriers, is more sensitive than
his brother and more intelligent than his sister. He
worships Maeve, who has been a mother to him since his
own died, and is in love with Mary, but kindness compels
him to cede passion to compassion: "He cared for Mary's
hopeless self that he would never trouble her with the love
that was in him for her enthralling body." In a world
where the important things are "having a good leg for a
boot" and knowing how to put a horse into its fence, Jer is a
foreigner because he is afraid of horses. A plain, almost
invisible man, his intelligence is masked by a severe
stammer. He sees everything—not just the secret liaisons,
but the small gestures, the eye engagements, that signal
future entanglements. More painful, he sees beyond the
romantic intrigues to "a reality which hurt like a bruise".
Irresistably drawn into the involvements of the beautiful

and selfish, he is the disillusioned go-between. Ploddingly clear-sighted, he performs love's dirtiest labours, while anticipating its loss: ''Where is romance? It is where we are not and in all things out of reach.''

Although his affections are unconditional, his perceptions are so acute that he sees right through the handsome heads and beautiful faces to the primitive workings of the minds within. He watches his sister, Maeve, in love—''so mildly confident in her right to the biggest happiness in the world'' and suffers for her as confidence crumbles in a blind struggle to respond to her sophisticated new husband:

''It's a bad thing,'' Jer thought, ''to care about someone so much that you learn something about their natures. The more you know about them the more afraid you are of them. Maeve is getting like that with Rowley. If only she'd crash along and be herself, and not study him. I wouldn't like to bet on her being happy now.''

When lewd old Aunt Edythe, excited by the destructive presence of Mary, plots a course of rejuvenation, it is not the ''restrained artistry of her inspired make-up'' that Jer notices, but ''the cobweb fine stockings, through which the bones of her legs and ankles showed as many-angled as those of a hungry little bird''. Whereas the others are merely repelled by ''that which is hateful to indecency in the thought that their old should not forget, as utterly as though they had not known them, the lusts and passions which are to youth by right of youth'', Jer percieves a cruel, prophetic dimension to the tough old bird's punitive physical regime:

Bad enough she'd been as her old bullying self—bad enough indeed but now she was sickening—Orange juice and violet rays and massage—Jer shuddered. The vulgarity of it, and the pity!

Was this all a bright, violent past left you when your clear mind went faintly cracky with age? This, and the greedy excitement that flashed sometimes into old dim eyes and shook in swollen, gouty fingers?

With sudden, terrifying apprehension Jer looked from Aunt Edythe, scented and powdered and bedecked, to Mary, her lovely head stooped over her writing, the back of her neck such a swift line; unalterably young, her clothes so soft and ordinary and careless. God forbid that she should grow old dreadfully like this other, who had been wild and sweet and witty, and loved to distraction too, in her hour.

More than half a century spans the distance in years between the writing of *Taking Chances* and Molly Keane's most recently published novel, *Time After Time*, but there are unmistakable and engaging similarities in the characters of both novels' lively older ladies, who are full of plot and poison. *Taking Chances*' Aunt Edythe and the health-conscious April of *Time After Time* share not only "a punishing regime of diet and exercise" but a past that is rich in blame. Whereas Aunt Edythe was undoubtedly a young girl's unkind caricature, Aprile shows the unflinching Molly enjoying a joke at the expense of her own age group and in some ways at her own image as well. The novelist is a self-confessed health fiend, with a love of life and an unswerving loyalty to her routine of exercise and healthy eating. It is characteristic of this perfectly mannered, deeply compassionate, ruthlessly funny writer that she should turn the sharpest of her wit on herself rather than abandon a good jest.

Taking Chances is more than a tribute to an era past, it is a toast to an extinct species—the fabulous heroine. There are no more Marys—fast-talking, chain-smoking, hard living, perfuming the air with adventure and romance. There are only old ladies like Aunt Edythe who remember and ever-young ones like Molly Keane who restore memories and stir imagination. To her, and to Virago who have ordained a standard for nostalgia, we of the guilty, smoke-free generation give thanks.

Clare Boylan, Wicklow, 1986

CHAPTER I

SINCE James I. granted lands in Ireland to a
soldiering Sorrier there have been Sorriers at Sorristown. Eleven generations of the breed have ridden
and fished and shot over the land granted to their
ancestor.

Like all families forming part of the English
garrison in Ireland, the Sorriers have had their ups
and downs. But for the most part a streak—not of
cunning exactly, but of something more acute than
shrewdness—has enabled them to hold on to their
possessions and prosper in a manner rarely found
inherent in the Irish landed gentry. It was this
acuteness which raised the Sorrier of the Union to
a baronetcy, and the same quality was evident in
the late Sir Harcourt Sorrier's timely sales of much
of his property, before there broke for Irish landlords
the evil days of the Land Acts.

The present representatives of the family do no
discredit to a handsome race. Tradition says that
the Sorrier men were handsome and bold, and the
women of the family charming and virtuous crea-
tures. Tradition must be quoted, as the numerous
family portraits which frown or simper from the

walls of Sorristown are of a mediocrity which
hardly supports the theory of persistent good
looks.

The third baronet and his sister, who stood together
before their door in the first chill of an October
evening, waiting, Roguey eagerly, Maeve with a
different depth of urgency, for the sound of a car
coming up the long avenue, in looks at least did
credit to their breeding. As they and their younger
brother were the last of the old Sorrier line, so
perhaps were they beautiful with the stored beauty
of generations.

Roguey, a landed proprietor of some importance
before he left his preparatory school, added to his
brilliant fairness and long, stupendous lines an assurance of manner which had in it an insolence, almost
a challenge, at variance with the changing, un-
decided look about his mouth.

Maeve loved her elder brother with a passion of
devotion from which self had, from her earliest days,
been utterly obliterated. To live with Roguey and
keep house for him; ride the horses that Roguey
would not ride; fish the best salmon streams behind
Roguey; nurse him or his dogs when he or they
required her ministrations—this was all that Maeve
required of life. At the age of eighteen she had
taken the reins of the household out of the careful
and tenacious grasp of the aunt who had ruled at
Sorristown and brought up Roguey, Maeve and
their brother Jer since their mother died—a sweet
but ineffectual mother who had not long survived
her husband's tragic death.

How often Maeve had heard her Aunt Evie

describe that dark happening! The dreadful evening when Hubert Lande and Harry Falconner, two
dear friends of poor Ralph Sorrier, came riding up
the old coach drive to warn Sorristown of the long
procession that followed a dead man home through
his own great gates.

"Oh, dear, dear!" Aunt Evie had said. "And
only that very morning she had asked him not to
ride one of the young horses, and so it was poor old
Surefoot that killed him. Perhaps if she hadn't
interfered he might be alive still. Surefoot came out
on her head into a road over a two-foot bank.
(*Do* be careful, Maeve! *Never* let a horse get into
the habit of jumping stickily.) Then, as I was telling you, it was dark by the time they brought him
home. We saw the lanterns coming up the old
coach road—it's the shortest, you know, from the
Castle Fountain lane. They had laid him in a
farm-cart—on straw, of course. I can remember
quite well his boots had to hang out over the tail-
boards, he was so tall. And someone was leading
Surefoot—*poor* Surefoot! And Amazon, a hound he
was very fond of, was coming along behind the cart
with her head under his feet. Oh, it was all so
dreadful! I can never forget it; nor the throngs
of country people who followed the ' bold Baronet,'
as they called him, home. Jer was born that
night—poor little baby! We never thought he'd
live. *She* just smiled at me and said I was to mind
you and Roguey and Jer for her, and then she
died."

Maeve was thinking of this story as she and
Roguey, the present Sir Ralph Sorrier, waited at the

head of the old coach road, while little pools and wreaths of mist washed coldly nearer to them up the sides of the river valley below the house.

But beyond sad thoughts, warm like packed coals round her heart was the thought that Rowley, Rowley for whom her love passed all bounds, soaring out into infinite regions beyond even her love for Roguey, was coming—would be here at any moment now.

Maeve and Rowley were going to be married. Two months ago that had been decided. The announcement that a marriage had been arranged, to take place early in November, between Major Rowland Arthur Fountain, of Castle Fountain, Co. Westcommon, and Maeve, daughter of the late Sir Ralph Sorrier and Lady Sorrier of Sorristown, Co. Westcommon, had long since appeared in the *Morning Post* and the *Irish Times*. For the last months Maeve had spent much time in answering, with laborious politeness verging on stolidity, many letters of congratulation upon her engagement. For, though Maeve was the dearest and most charming of girls, the consensus of opinion held that luck was mostly on her side. Rowley was perhaps the best-liked man in the countryside.

" Awfully late, isn't he ? " Roguey turned to his sister impatiently, his brown forehead crinkled in a frown, his eyebrows up in his hair. " Let's go in and have tea—unless you'd *rather* wait, of course. I don't mind." He got down from the stone balustrade where he had been sitting, and stooped to pick up a small and ferocious dog.

" Right, Roguey. Yes, we'd better start tea. I

8

expect the train is late or something. We won't
wait for Jer, either."

"No, he's shooting Loughlin's bogs with Jerry
Conroy—bound to be late."

Roguey idled behind his sister in the big, dark
hall. Then the Demon—that fierce, small dog—
put up a black kitten from behind a brass Indian
tray: the Demon was a terror on cats and on other
dogs, when roused. This hunt ended in the black
kitten being marked to ground up a fir-tree, some
hundred yards from the hall door steps. Roguey,
his tea forgotten, was giving an excellent imitation
of the horn's "Wind—'im—in," when a large
car pulled up almost beside him.

"Hullo Rowley!"

Roguey turned to greet the car's occupant, his
young face alight with pleasure.

"Been having good sport? My God, what a car!
Is it a wedding present? Maeve's in the house.
Do you want to see her? No, come round to the
stables while there's light."

"Of course I want to see her." Rowley climbed
out of the car, stripping off his coat. His soft
tweed clothes, dull yellow shirt and shoes hallowed
by age were as much part of Rowley as his quick,
decided movements.

Without being tall, Rowley had a clean length of
limb that was pleasing. Every line of his body
expressed strength, activity. His light, intelligent
eyes were curiously expressive, but their animation
was immediately falsified in the sulky jut of a
rather heavy jaw; and the strong mouth was not
greedy only because its owner was accustomed to

9

get what he wanted, and only cruel when he was provoked. About Rowley there radiated something so compellingly attractive, so provoking of interest, as to be nearly uncanny. Women had loved Rowley helplessly; men delighted in his friendship; dogs gave him the same helpless surrender as women; and the worst horse had a most wholesome respect for his ways. Rowley never gave himself away, but would rag others up to a point that was nearly malicious.

Now he walked quickly through the hall and into the library, where he knew, without having asked Roguey, that he would find Maeve.

On the hearthrug Maeve was sitting, her slender legs and round knees hunched within her long arms. Her back was to the door, and her yellow head was bowed to the fire-light, which etched out the mooney lines of her stooping neck and soft cheek and chin.

" Roguey "—Maeve's voice was still and deep and rather toneless—" ring the bell, Roguey: I quite forgot Jer was to have an egg for his tea."

" *Maeve !* " Rowley came across the room and stood over her, " Hullo, Maeve ! " His hands under her arms, he pulled her up to her feet, close to him, determinedly.

" Oh, it's *you*, Rowley ! " Happiness rising in her, strangling in its intensity, Maeve stood quite still in his arms, waiting for his kiss. She was not provocative, but in her helpless quiescence there was a surge of passion. When his kiss came she sank with it, the curve of her back bending against his arm. His head bent down too, Rowley kept his mouth hard on hers.

Roguey, seeing them together, shut the door softly behind him and went across the hall to stare out into the evening with something hungry and unsatisfied about his young face that was not quite good to see.

"Hullo, Roguey! Who owns this t—t-toppin'——" Jer struggled to finish his sentence, the cruel impediment in his speech the more apparent for his eagerness to know who the owner of the big Bentley might be.

"Slap yourself, Jer," Roguey advised casually. This exercise was calculated to relieve Jer's stutter, and its performance was always insisted on by his elder brother and sister.

"Oh, the *car*!" Roguey divined the subject of his younger brother's curiosity before the slapping process could produce the desired effect. "That's Rowley's. I suppose it's some sort of a wedding present. I left him in the library with Maeve ten minutes ago. I looked in, but they were a dam' sight too busy to see me."

A shade of anger at his brother's tone of jeering boredom crossed Jer's face. He distorted his mouth and slapped himself, finally producing the remark that Maeve was engaged to be married and could do what she liked, he supposed.

"Did you see Jerry Conroy?" Roguey asked, paying no attention to his brother's remark.

"Yes, I was shooting with him."

"And what did he say?" Eager to know, Roguey was equally unwilling to ask the question.

"He t-told me just what he told you. And you'll have to give it to him, Roguey. C-can't have a

scandal with Maeve's wedding coming off, c-can
you?"

"Oh, *hell!*" His face clouded with anger,
Roguey turned away from the door and crossed
over to the library. Jer could hear his voice from
within the room inviting Rowley to join him in a
drink; heard Rowley's refusal, and Maeve saying:

"Ring the bell, Roguey. I forgot Jer was to have
an egg for his tea."

Darling Maeve! How Jer loved her! It made
him a little cold and sick to think of Maeve belonging to anyone as utterly as she was to belong to
Rowley. She was his sister, and Jer loved her with
something of the same flaming ardour which was in
Maeve's love for Roguey. It always thrilled him
that she should remember things for him—such
things as eggs for his tea, after a long day in the
bogs, or giving him first turn in the bathroom when
he was tired. There was a great deal of the small
boy in Jer still, in spite of his twenty-one years.

When he came into the library he shook hands
with Rowley, almost shyly, and, picking up the
Demon, subsided into a chair and into silence, while
he contemplated Maeve's deft, lovely movements
among the tea-things, and the look of nearly stupefied
satisfaction in her wide hazel eyes, which glanced
so often and so helplessly over to where Rowley sat,
discussing with Roguey matters of horses and hounds
and coverts and the foxes therein.

"Did you have a good day, Jer?" Maeve asked,
arranging Jer's tea-cup and the boiled egg in its
shining silver egg-cup. "More snipe in than last
day we were up there?" As her brother struggled

to answer she murmured mechanically : " Slap yourself, Jer," and relapsed into inattentiveness long
before he brought forth an answer to her question.

" Maeve, you haven't seen Rowley's new car yet,"
Roguey said, half-way through tea. " Are you going
to honeymoon in her? Rowley, you've got to come
out and have a look at this Equis colt. Maeve,
have you picked your bridesmaids yet? I won't
arm Carol Lumsden down the church. Jer can
have her—he's only an usher."

" I heard from Mary Fuller to-day," Maeve said—
" she's coming."

" What's she like? "

" Oh, she's lovely! And so rich! She's coming
over the week before."

" Can't be rich *and* lovely," Roguey asserted.
" What's the snag? her ankles? or does she give a
horse a sore back? "

" She's perfectly t-t-toppin'," Jer asserted with
scarcely a stagger.

" Keep quite calm, everybody. She won't *look*
at Roguey. She's engaged." Maeve lit a cigarette
slowly from the match Rowley gave her, then met
his eyes for a long moment. Jer attended pointedly
to his tea.

" How stinking of you, Maeve! You might have
got hold of a possible girl for me," Roguey protested
at last. " You know those new loose-boxes aren't
paid for. Sorristown needs an heiress badly.
What's she engaged to? "

" I forget his name—a guardee."

" If Roguey's any dam' good, he'll take her off
him," Rowley asserted. " You ought to get married

now, Roguey. You'll go to the devil altogether, yourself and Jer, without a woman in the house."

Roguey laughed.

Jer, who could hardly bear to think of Sorristown without Maeve there, scowled heavily.

" I'm sorry, Jer," Rowley said in a quick aside to his future brother-in-law. " I'm a beastly roost-robber, I know, but you mustn't be too hard on me."

" Paddy Doyle told me to-day "—Paddy Doyle had been stud-groom at Sorristown for upwards of thirty years—" that when Miss Maeve'd be married an' out of it I'd be aiquil to an ass in a bog." Roguey's imitation of Paddy Doyle was entirely successful. " Good Lord! isn't it awful to think we only have Maeve one month more? Jer, let's murder Rowley, shall we? "

It ended, of course, in a senseless rag; and in the Demon, nearly hysterical, being pulled by Maeve off a prostrate Rowley and held choking and gasping in his collar, while Roguey, Jer and Rowley fought in inextricable confusion on the hearthrug.

" Oh, do stop it, chaps! There's Venus come in at the window, and she's pinched the chocolate cake." Maeve indicated the hastily retreating form of a large hound puppy who had taken advantage of the noise and an open window to add one more crime to her already crowded record. She now bolted across the lawn and disappeared under a large Portugal laurel.

" I'm going out to have a look at your car, Rowley. Coming? "

Together Maeve and Rowley went out. The lines of the big car loomed gigantic in the dusk.

"Oh, Rowley, how awfully cracking!" Maeve was deeply pleased. She was flooded with lovely thoughts of the times she and Rowley would have together in that big car—driving to meets; homeward drives in the darkening evenings with the stinging memory of a good hunt hot and close with them; wonderful times, with no partings, but with the same fire and bath and food and bed waiting for them both: the times when they would be together for always.

Yet, being deeply shy, Maeve could only say again: "Rowley, it is marvellous," and ask questions about the driving and controls, barely listening to his answers.

"Little ass! You don't want to know a bit," Rowley laughed at an inept question. "I think I *must* kiss you. Can we be seen?"

"Yes. Don't. You can't now, Rowley."

"You don't mean that a bit." He looked at her strongly. "Darling Maeve, you do want it—say you do?"

Half an hour later Rowley's big car slid down the drive of Sorristown. The giant white shafts of his head-lights struck the silver of the beech stems to marble, black and white. Rabbits, their wild, silly eyes dazed by the glare, blundered grotesquely away before the blinding terror of light. Rowley drove over one, and thought with pleasure of the fox that would pick up the corpse before morning. The supply of foxes in the Sorristown woods was a strong one. He thought of Maeve—Maeve white and lovely, the gold of her smooth hair and the gracious curling lines of her body. It was her beauty that cried to Rowley, held him, stilled him, would not be denied. Rowley was certainly going to marry Maeve for love. His loneliness at Castle Fountain had really very little to do with it. He was not disturbed by the almost negative acquiescence which was all he knew of her love for him. He would teach her passion. It would be fun. Darling, beautiful Maeve! He had no doubts at all about the happiness that was there for them to take and hold and keep together.

CHAPTER II

ROGUEY and Jer were sitting by Maeve's bedroom fire eating oranges and talking while Maeve had her bath. They were a companionable trio, and did things with great pleasure in each other's society.

Now there was only a short while left to Jer and Roguey before Maeve would be taken away from them: translated to that far, indefinite sphere of marriage. They felt, though neither would have admitted it to himself or his brother, a mournful appropriateness in snatching at these dear, private moments. They would talk, building bright plans for the future, when Maeve would be living twelve miles away from them at Castle Fountain, while all the time a regretful heaviness that they clumsily tried to conceal from her weighted their thoughts of the months to come.

Jer felt it most—that was because he loved Maeve; while Maeve loved Roguey; and of the three of them Roguey loved Roguey best of all.

It was a nasty business that the pair of them were discussing this evening as they awaited Maeve's return from the bathroom. An affair of a pretty girl and her brother, one of Roguey's tenant farmers, who had rounded short and nasty on the Baronet, and was prepared to dig out all there was to be obtained as purchase money for a sister's (always rather tottering) virtue.

" If you want to shut his mouth, Roguey, you'll have to give him——" Jer stopped and gabbled the air helplessly.

" Slap yourself, Jer. Yes, I suppose he must get it. Mount Spring's about the best farm I've got, too. Curse these women ! "

" Don't talk like a c-cad." Jer filled his mouth with orange and regarded his brother resentfully over his bulging cheeks. " If you must have that sort of fun, have it. But don't cut up over the c-consequences."

" Shut up ! "

" Where are you going ? "

" Going to get a drink."

" You were t-tight at dinner-time."

Roguey swore, his lips whitening. Jer's assumption of priggish airs was as unendurable to him as only the strictures of a close relation can be.

Jer dabbled his fingers in Maeve's jug, wiped them on one of her towels, and, thus freed from the sticky thraldom of orange juice, lit a cigarette. He did not like smoking, but Maeve hated the smell of oranges in her bedroom. He waited for her to come back, brooding sombrely over the fire, his cigarette held awkwardly and his heavy shoulders stooping forward. Jer was big and clumsily made. Sometimes he suffered severely from asthma. He was very like many of the dark-faced, duck-bodied Sorrier ancestors whose portraits made the dining room such a gloomy place. His stammer lent a nervous sullenness to his manner and a portentous-

ness to his least word which he resented cruelly.
Jer was permanently on the very point of getting a
job, or perhaps of going up to Oxford—at such a
time as suited his brother's pecuniary convenience,
and when such matters as the payment for the new
loose-boxes should be satisfactorily concluded. Jer,
who did not come into his own money for another
two years, was quite content to remain at Sorristown fishing and shooting—he hated horses—and to
allow so small a matter as his future to take shape
how it would.

Maeve came into the room. Her prim, warm
dressing-gown could not quite spoil the lovely strong
lines of her body. Her eyes and cheeks were bright,
her yellow hair a glory in the lamplight. Jer,
watching her comb it out with a green comb, fell
into a restful stupor of pleasure.

" Where's Roguey?—Slap yourself, Jer—I thought
he'd come up."

" So he did, but he went down again just
now."

" Oh, did he? " Maeve peered uninterestedly at
her own reflection before she came and sat near the
fire opposite to Jer. She kicked off her slippers and
warmed her large, graceful feet.

" This time next month you'll be married to
Rowley," Jer said at last in funereal tones.

" Yes, Jer." Maeve's assent was almost reverential. " You and Roguey will be keeping house by
yourselves then. I wonder how you'll get on."

" Oh, I expect it will be all right! " Jer said with
desperate cheerfulness.

" Oh, of course! Anyway, Aunt Evie will love

19

to come back and fuss over you both. But, Jer, you will look after Roguey as well as you can, won't you? I know it seems queer asking you—you're so much younger; but you always *were* the sensible sort of person who came in to meals in time, and remembered the dogs' dinners, and so on. You will, won't you, Jer?—Slap yourself, Jer—You really will?"

" Will what?"

" Mind Roguey."

" Stop him getting off with such as Lizzie Conroy and drinking himself silly, d'you mean?"

" Oh, Lizzie Conroy! That's nonsense." Maeve dismissed Lizzie Conroy in a flat voice of infinite tolerance. " But I *do* think Roguey's drinking more than he should. We must stop that, Jer. It's so bad for his nerve, to drink."

" His nerve isn't much to boast about now. He was jolly shaken by that fall last week. Doyle said so."

" Ah! what do you know about nerve?" Maeve spoke with the patient contempt of a brave rider for one who is no good. " And as for discussing Roguey with the servants, I think you might find something better to do. That, and assing about with Jerry Conroy, is about your form, though. Perhaps Jerry Conroy told you Roguey's nerve was gone, too?"

Jer grimaced hideously for nearly a minute. Maeve had left the fire and gone over to her bed before he managed to say: " No, we had other things to talk about, as it h-happens."

" Sorry, Jer. I didn't really mean that a bit.

20

Only you know it *worries* me leaving you two here all by yourselves."

Maeve, aware that any word of hers could touch Jer almost to the point of tears, strove in her mind for less troublous subjects. They discussed her wedding: which aunt was to have which room. Maeve told him about the under-clothes that had come for her by the day's post; and Jer, opening the drawer she pointed out, examined the garments critically, remarking, without much originality, that they would be damnably cold.

" Oh, no! They're lovely! " Maeve got off the edge of her bed and bent over his shoulder to fold the pile flat again. " Mary sent them over."

" When is Mary coming herself ? "

" The week before the wedding."

" These things are just like Mary, aren't they? " Jer indicated the exquisite, flashing heaps of layered colour, flame, cyclamen, nude, in the drawer. Then he shut it slowly, kissed Maeve good-night with solemn unction, and left the room.

CHAPTER III

THE dwelling-house of Mount Spring farm is a
two-storied, unlovely building. On a day of hopeless storm towards the end of October the rain
washed in green pools about its surrounding manure-
heaps and beat with long, wet fingers against the
dark, uncurtained windows. The yellow-dashed
walls of the house were flaked and crumbling, but
its new slated roof was tight and weather-proof for
many a year to come.

To one side of the house lay an abortive attempt
at a garden. A few spruce firs shot up, irrepressibly
healthy, among the rank grass; and hunched thickly
against the house was a hydrangea bush, its heavenly
blue flowers an exquisite protest of colour in the
drab squalor of the place. Six young turkeys
balanced in a swaying, misogynistic line on the fence
which divided the garden from the farmyard. The
rain washed off their black, tortoise-like backs; it
seeped with soft penetration into the heaps of
manure, and trickled in rivulets to join the flat
pools that lay in any hollow spot.

A girl came out of the house—a pretty girl. She
stood bareheaded in the rain, listening with almost
distraught eagerness to the sound of a car passing
on the road below the house. She pressed both
hands against the door-posts, holding herself forcibly

from running out to the gate; and, as the car went by, she turned back into the ugly house, her knees shaking, her breath coming cruelly, in the reaction from her anticipation.

"Lizzie!" An aguish voice of penetrating refinement called to the girl. "I wonder are you wise, dear, running out in the wet? Don't be taking any chills now, and you in the state of health you're in."

Lizzie Conroy turned quickly away from her mother—a piteous gesture, helpless to conceal the thickened lines of her young body. She sat down, stooping herself together, in a chair near the coldly burning fire and stared sullenly into vacancy.

"I wonder at you, Lizzie, I do really." Mrs. Conroy spoke in mournful protest. "Haven't ye brought down enough disgrace on yourself and annoyance on your family, without ye'd go gadding out o' the house at every old motor-car passes on the road? It's horrid behaviour. And look-at here, me girl, you needn't be thinking your gay Baronet'll be down these parts looking for you. How likely, indeed! Oncet a man gets what he wants, he don't want it any more—or not from the same woman." Mrs. Conroy sniggered in enjoyment of her epigram, before continuing: "I will say for him he treated you very well, considering all. You're in as tight and snug a place with as good land to it as any in Ireland, and ye may thank yer brother Jerry and meself for that—only for us fixing him so tight ye'd be the way y' are and not one ha'penny the better of it. Such a lady you're getting, we may all slave ourselves into the grave before you'd stir a finger to do a hand's turn for one but yourself."

Without speaking, Lizzie got up from her chair, and with a glance of venomous animosity in her mother's direction walked out of the kitchen and up the steep staircase to her own bedroom. Here she sank down again in exactly the same attitude as she had taken up in the kitchen, and continued to gaze, with the fixity of unimaginative despair, at the wall, bare save for a tawdry and dreadful picture of the bleeding heart of Jesus.

Crouched in her chair like a sick person, Lizzie was thinking of other things than the bare, untidy room. Her body hardly felt the dank chill of the place, so far away was her mind in a trembling, bright past. She saw a man and a girl walking in summer fields, joking and teasing each other; the man with easy assurance, the girl with shy, new-found delight. Easy meetings, growing more frequent; and with each repetition increasing in intimacy, increasing in difficulty. No teasing and nonsense between them now: nothing left but the one fierce, stark thing, which she had desired too much to fight against it with either art or conviction. Not ignorant, but young, greedy and helpless, she had given—given till desire failed. Then came the days of pitiable waiting, of terrified realisation; letters—the dreadful letters she had written to him; her family's realisation of the full state of things; her mother's deft twisting of the sordid matter to their best advantage; and now this inexperienced, awful thing, coming daily irrevocably nearer. Lizzie waited through the weeks and months in a dull stupor, a miserable mental twilight, shot through by futile hopes, scourged to sickness by daily disappointment.

"He'll come to-day," she would think in the mornings, and wonder whether the wearing of a new jumper would inevitably call forth her mother's acid comment. Through the day she would wait, hope rising feverishly at the passing of each car on the road; each hope meeting its inevitable small, painful death, for Roguey never came. He had done handsomely by the Conroys in the matter of payment for his pleasures; any further re-adjustment of the matter was away beyond thought. The thing finished for him, he shut his eyes easily to the fact that the consequences, however well paid for, were hardly pretty.

Below stairs Mrs. Conroy put up the lace curtains with unaided nimbleness and skill. This done, she chased her turkeys into a house and proceeded on a round of inspection through cow-byres and horse-boxes, eggs being the object of her search.

Within one of the boxes her son, Jerry, was engaged on the early education of a good-looking young horse. Mrs. Conroy—unlike most women of her class—was entirely without fear where horses were concerned. She surveyed the sweaty, white-eyed youngster on which Jerry had just put the breaking tackle with an eye that saw beyond his present ragged appearance.

"That'll make a good one, Jerry," she observed.

"Ah, he might." Jerry spoke with a casualness that did not conceal from his mother an enthusiasm for the horse in question. "This old box is very crampy," he continued. " We had better stabling in the old place."

" Ah, go on—you an' the old place! Had ye better land in it? Wouldn't the cows stand an' stiffen on the hills before they'd pick a blade of grass in it? We did right well getting this farm out o' the sir, whatever little inconveniences are put past us on the head o' the matter."

" Well, whatever he done for us, he didn't kill himself doing it. Stand over now! " This to the young horse. " And it could be the sir'll get the dirty end o' this stick yet. Wait awhile now till ye'll see! "

CHAPTER IV

PERILLA MARY FULLER, accompanied by a very
much waisted, very morose little terrier—by name
Mrs. Squiffy—stood among her mountains of luggage
on the cold, deserted platform of Rennis Station.

High above the ugliness of steel girders and iron
footbridges there shone a star, set slanting and
beautiful in the smooth, grey pearl of the evening
sky. The porter, who now appeared at the door
of the signal-box and approached Mary, was not of
a poetic turn of mind, otherwise he might have
perceived the close affinity of loveliness between the
girl, her white beauty wrapped in soft grey fur, and
the serene star. As it was, he approached shyly
and said to her:

" The train for Sorristown 'll not be in for an
hour yet. Will ye come in to the fire an' heat
yerself, Miss? Ye should be famished with the
cold."

" I beg your pardon? What did you say? I've
got a buzzing in my head from getting salt water in
my ear last time I bathed—it makes me *just* a little
deaf." Mary's voice had a reedy hoarseness infinitely attractive.

Blushing, the porter repeated his invitation.

" No train for an hour? " Mary questioned,

horror-struck. "How far is it from here to Sorristown? Can't you get me a taxi?"

"A what? A hackney car? Well, ye could
hardly," the porter informed her funereally. "Every
car in the place is gone to a wake."

"To a *what*? *Why* did I ever leave England?"

"Ah! what about England?" the porter interrupted almost harshly. "We have only to do with
the little Ireland that we has. But where you med
the big mistake, Miss, was to let the through train
from the junction go from ye."

Mary made a face, more to herself than at the
porter, and expressive of her extreme dislike for
reminders of past errors. "There's someone looking for you," she said. And as the porter removed
himself from her vicinity, she regarded with interest
Rowley's back.

She liked immediately what she could see of him:
his weathered hat, dilapidated, pale tweed coat and
good flannel trousers. A minute later, when he
came up the platform towards her, she found herself
positively hankering after his tie—she was a collector
of these. When he spoke—which he did with
pleasant assurance—everything about her seemed
for a fraction of time arrested, spinning for a second
wildly in unknown space, before dropping back into
a normal plane.

"What? I've got a buzzing in my ear, it makes
me *just* a little deaf—I got water in my ear when I
bathed," Mary told him huskily; while the porter,
murmuring "Oh, God!" faded discreetly into the
waiting-room.

"How beastly for you!" Rowley regarded the

slim, shining thing with eyes of interest and sympathy. " They told me you wanted to get to Sorristown. Can I drive you? " He added casually: " My name's Rowland Fountain. Maeve was expecting you to arrive this morning. Did you miss the train? "

They progressed out of the station to his car—the new car, Maeve's dream car. Mary got in and sat there beside him; not very talkative; tired after her long day's wrestling with the unknown vagaries of an Irish railway. Rowley arranged a fur rug round her in an unprovocatively fraternal manner and produced his cigarette case.

" No, thanks. Thoroughbreds, aren't they? I only smoke gaspers." Mary produced a rather crumpled packet from her expensive and beautiful snake-skin hand-bag and straightening the third last cigarette which it contained, lit it at the match Rowley gave her.

" Can't really afford to smoke anything better," she told him as they moved out of the station yard. " I'm so permanently broke. I was awfully relieved when you offered to drive me—hiring cars is such an expensive game."

Rowley glanced with grave approval at her exquisite, close-wrapped fur coat and the little soft hat she wore.

" Very lucky I had to come and see about a horsebox to-day," he said.

" Yes, awfully lucky for me. Irish trains are terrible, aren't they? I wish I'd brought my car over, but it didn't seem worth it for such a short time."

" I thought you were going to stay on after—after Wednesday's ceremony, and hunt. Maeve thought so."

" I don't know, really. It depends if I like Roguey. I hate riding a person's horses unless I do; it makes it so awkward if you cut them. I *love* Jer. Perhaps he'll mount me."

" Jer doesn't ride, you know."

" Oh, I forgot! What a pity! I think he's so nice—Jer. He never stammers talking to me. He's a darling. And he's so cracked about Maeve. I haven't got any brothers, but if I had one I'd like him to be like Jer."

Mary was silent; but in her silence Rowley could feel her quick thoughts running on, and wondered, with a warm interest, what next she would say. It was not alone that she had a face and voice to throw spells, but there was all about this girl, breathing from her, an atmosphere of charm, secret and afar. She was exciting. Things, one felt, would happen round her. Like the lady who rode to Banbury Cross, " rings on her fingers and bells on her toes," Mary was a factor for disturbance. She was, Rowley felt sure, a person to be distinctly loved or disliked, never a person to be just tolerated. Remembering Roguey's new loose-boxes, Rowley smiled and then frowned. She was not, he hoped, for Roguey. He looked down at her sidelong, wondering. An impartial judge, he felt that the lines of her, beneath that fur coat, could not be otherwise than sure and sweet. Was she pretty? No trick of colouring enhanced her rather pale fairness, but there seemed to burn within her a secret flame of never-ceasing possibility. Her mouth, kissed by the many, would still be utterly desired by the few. Her body won, herself, the essence of her beauty, would still remain afar, uncaught.

Rowley summed her up with easy approval: " Attractive—very. B'Gad! if I wasn't in love with Maeve she'd—interest me. Too pretty to be good, with that mouth. And almost too good to be true. I must start her talking again. That's an easy voice to listen to."

" Have you ever hunted over here? " he asked.

" No. I've always wanted to; but now I'm terrified." She laughed, looking out of the car at the big blind banks at either side of the road. " I simply can't imagine *any* horse being a safe conveyance over these fences. I wish I was safe back in my own country."

" Make Roguey give you his old mare, the ' Moth.' She'll introduce you to this country in the right way."

" Oh ! " Mary's eyes regarded him gravely from under the brim of her pulled-down felt hat before she laughed, and laughed again, she did not know why. " I think I'm going to like Ireland," she said.

" Yes, you must. We all want you to like Sorristown. Jer will be heartbroken if you go too soon."

The car turned in at Sorristown's big, impressive gateway; the tyres whispered quietly on the smooth surface of the drive. Mary, with a sudden change of mood, an access of wild panic such as children experience with a strange party drawing inevitably near, leaned forward, clutching hot fingers together in her lap.

" I *wish*," she whispered—it was a thin wail—" I *wish* I hadn't come."

Rowley, sitting beside her, pretending he hadn't heard, suddenly and disturbingly echoed her wish from the very depths of his being.

CHAPTER V

JER and Mary were very fast friends. She was really more Jer's friend than Maeve's—one of the reasons why Maeve had asked her to be a bridesmaid at her wedding.

Jer sat in her room helping her unpack on the evening of her arrival at Sorristown. He criticised her clothes. "What a lewd dress! The aunts will spit fire and blood if you wear it here."

"Desperate collection of old ladies you have got together," Mary sighed.

"Yes, of course. Roguey and I are the last male Sorriers—at present. But d-didn't you like Rowley?"

"What, Jer? I've got a buzzing in my ear—— "

"I know, Mary. You told me once, an' each of the aunts twice and every one else six times over. I said, didn't you like Rowley?"

"He seemed rather nice, Jer. He and Maeve won't hit it for very long, though."

"Well, I know that too." Jer nodded, sadly and wisely. "But it was cute of you to spot it at once. Maeve loves him too much to see straight, but she won't k-keep him."

"He's awfully in love with her now, Jer."

"Yes, he's in love, but Maeve's in earnest."

"Isn't he?"

33

" Oh, at the moment.   But she won't k-keep him."

" You know so much for one so young—the difference between a week-ending and a never-ending passion, for instance." Mary aimed rolled-up stockings into a drawer, missing it badly several times.   " I think hunting is like love—the same sort of excitement.   You're uncomfortable and cowardly waiting at some covert, and then suddenly you're swept into madness; you can't help yourself, you *must* get on——"

" Till? "

" Oh, till the blindest fence of all.   An' then it's even money on your chances of a really crashing fall. Marriage is a bit of a toss-up for virgins who have the importance of being virgins on the brain.   Don't you think so, Jer? "

" You're making me so miserable about Maeve, Mary.   Suppose she hates it? "

" Oh, she won't.   Cheer up, darling, and go and turn my bath on.   *And* tell me which dress will cause least vibration among the she-male haggery downstairs."

When Jer had gone about ten minutes, Mary set out for the bathroom.   At the end of the passage, Jer had said it was; but which end?   Maeve's room was on her right.   She put her head in, and seeing Roguey, still in his hunting-boots and a friendly tweed coat, sitting over the fire, she advanced, because to retreat was so obvious.

Roguey came forward.   They had not yet met, these two.

" How d'ye do? " he said.   " This *is* Maeve's room, but she's not up yet."

Mary transferred a large sponge from her right to her left hand and shook Roguey's gravely.

"Oh, how do you do? I was looking for a bathroom. Jer turned my bath on, but I don't know the way." Exquisite as a past dream, fragrantly fair, Mary caught her slim, embroidered wrap together and raised misty eyes to Roguey's. "I'm *jus'* a little bit deaf," she explained, as he did not answer her at once. "Did you say you'd show me the way?"

Roguey, looking down at her from his great, fair height, pulled himself together, stammering:

"Yes, rather! Come on, down here!"

During their progress down the dusky length of the passage he found nothing more to say. At the lighted door of the bathroom she asked for a cigarette. Roguey produced his case and lit one for her clumsily. In her bath Mary found that, along with the dampness round his eyes, subjects for consideration. Used to swift work, his early show of interest did not thrill her. She was, as a matter of fact, totally unaware of the unsafe propensities of a scanty kimono when its wearer, with a poorly drawing cigarette in one hand, and bathing apparatus in the other, stoops over an awkwardly held match.

"And this," thought Roguey, as he stalked stiffly back towards his own room and there stuck his foot in his boot-jack, "is exactly where I take it." Was she, he wondered, pretty? The realisation that he did not even know added to his immense impatience to see her again.

Mary, once more in her room, with the steam of her bath still curling up her hair, gave to Roguey almost

35

as much attention as she was gracefully bestowing on her nails and fine eyebrows.

She had now seen this brother of whom Maeve had always spoken in terms of reverential adoration, and whom Jer had scarcely ever mentioned. Tall, good-looking and blessed with a leg which could not be other than his bootmaker's joy (an attribute in a man held in chief esteem by Mary), Roguey yet lacked something wholly—an essence, a quality, which accounted, she supposed for the quiescence of her curiosity concerning him as a man. It was not because she had thrilled him so immediately that she realised that never could he thrill her. And this, since she had decided before her departure for Ireland that Roguey would make an excellent and suitable husband, was a pity.

Pausing in her ministrations to her own loveliness, Mary gazed for a reflective moment at a framed photograph which stood on her dressing-table. It was of a young man, well-bred, pleasant to look upon, totally uninteresting. " Don't know why I brought *you* here." She picked up the picture and pushed it into a drawer. " Poor Tony! You *did* want me, didn't you? But you're broke and I'm broke. Besides, it wouldn't 've lasted—at least for me. Don't know about you, Tony—you wouldn't have it that way. Decent of you, I must say. I'd *so* much rather it was you than Roguey. But he can pay up my debts and mount me; you can't pay your own or mount yourself. Poor Tony! Never mind, darling. I'll always remember some of the times you've kissed me. I think this Roguey person looks stuffed." She resurrected the photograph, looked

36

at it again, and put it away petulantly. "So do
you," she said; "and you all want the same *one*
thing. Perhaps it's *just* as well"—she twisted her
smooth shoulders to grimace funnily at her charming,
narrow face in the tilted glass—"when the world's
so hard on sweet young things who can't pay their
poker debts." She stood up, wrestling her so nearly
naked body into a garment, which was not so much
a dress as an inspired indiscretion, wound a string
of jade beads round her neck, and as the gong
sounded in the vast distance of the big house, slipped
out of the room and down the wide, dark passage—
a silver, lovely pirate craft, sailing into strange and
uncharted seas.

At the foot of the staircase she saw Roguey
waiting—for her, she felt no doubt on that score.
Cocktails, he told her, his eyes on her shoulders as
he talked, were in a room apart, owing to Aunt
Edythe's rabid dislike of their consumption. You
couldn't be too careful with Aunt Edythe—she had
all the money in the family and was as old as a
bush.

In a darkling room where several dogs slept,
curled tightly in their baskets, Maeve and Rowley
were standing by the fire, while Jer silently mixed
the drinks on the ledge of a bookshelf. Mary, coming
forward a little blindly from the lighted hall, stumbled
and nearly fell across the dark and silently protestant
form of a cocker spaniel, which lay in obliterated
gloom upon the hearthrug. Rowley it was who
caught her under the arms as she crashed, saving her
from a baddish fall. Having done so, he released
her with a swiftness that proclaimed him too aware

of her, despite Maeve's cool, beautiful presence so near them.

Her smooth green dress was like water falling in rhythmic beauty over Maeve's perfect body; her golden hair curled flat and close round her ears; and her slow voice crooned loving reproach to the indignant spaniel and expressed relief at the narrow aversion of Mary's fall, all on the same note of flat unconcern.

"That's the second time you've saved my life to-day," Mary said to Rowley. "Oncely, from cold and starvation; twicely, from a broken neck. I hope you'll be in hand the third time."

"Why must there be a third—third time?" Jer handed Mary her cocktail and watched her drink it with the same unaffected pleasure with which he watched Maeve brush her hair.

"Things always happen to me in three's," Mary explained. "All my life is spent having triplets. No, I don't mean that either."

"Anything in reason, but I'm afraid that disaster's outside my province."

Rowley's laughter struck Maeve as a bit uncalled for. Having caught an allusion to triplets, but not quite followed the rest, she smiled uneasily, hating such subjects, and suggested joining the aunts in the drawing-room.

In the drawing-room four elderly ladies of the Sorrier family, and the husbands of two of them, awaited the coming of their young hosts.

Aunt Evie—she who had endeavoured to bring up Maeve, Jer and Roguey in the way they should go—was a comfortably stout lady with a naughty

enough twinkle in her brown, bird's eyes to promise
that a measure of humanity survived the past days
of her careless youth. Given the right company
and when on her day, Aunt Evie could be most
singularly ribald. And she did love a naughty
story! "Oh"—and her brown face would crease
itself into a thousand wrinkles of delighted appreciation—"how *nice!* How *rather* nice !" She adored
Jer, approved strongly of Roguey, and stood in
slight awe of Maeve, whose unfathomable singleness
of spirit was a matter entirely uncomprehended by
her aunt.

Then there was Aunt Ruth, who was just a silly.
No one ever bothered about her. And how her
husband, an elderly, white-faced ass, had ever come
to marry her was one of the surprises from which
the unmarried ladies of the family had not, in the
passage of years, recovered.

Aunt Amy was a darling, gentle and untidy, with
a divine gift for painting horses and dogs, and the
quaintest, quietest way of contributing odd and
pointedly relevant remarks to nearly any matter
under discussion. She had long endured a confirmed
hypochondriac as husband, loving and cherishing
him in health and imagined sickness with perpetual
sympathy.

Great-aunt Edythe almost confounds description.
Tiny and sick in body, her undefeated spirit still
swayed matters to her liking both in her family and
among her associates. A despot and a tyrant, she
was only not a bully because the obedience of others
fell automatically before her purposes. Her money
they thought would go to Roguey, but no one could

be quite sure about this, for Aunt Edythe, although acute dissection of the affairs of others was to her a chief sport in life, kept implicit counsel in regard to her own.   She adored young men of parts, and liked girls if they were pretty enough or daring enough to recall to her a taste of her own youth, when she had been one of the record-breakers of her generation.

When Mary came into the room she glanced at her, crosswise and again : quick, darting looks ; appreciative, penetrating and amused.   Mary came straight to her, and sat down on the sofa beside her.   " Uncle Harry sent you his love," she said.

Aunt Edythe wanted her dinner badly at the moment.   She also sniffed a faint tang of alcohol about Mary.   She made no reply, but looked at Mary's dress as though she divined how much, or rather exactly how little, Mary was wearing underneath it.

"Jer," Mary said later, " she has a look in her eye that would make a quiet cow in a secluded field blush for her forgotten bust-bodice.   Don't you think so ? "

" She's a queer one, right enough," Jer replied.

But at the moment Mary had felt defeated and, like the cow, had nearly blushed.

Dinner was a good but dull meal.   Maeve, softly, deeply in love, talked radiantly to those on her either hand.   Mary, sitting between Roguey and the asinine uncle, did not talk at all.   She looked at Roguey occasionally, and occasionally listened to the uncle's restful, unceasing flow of anecdote ; and through it all a thin, irresistible current pulled her eyes across and down the table to where Rowley sat,

grimly intent on the entertainment of Aunt Edythe.
" I'll never know him any better," Mary thought.
" I mustn't. How lonely! " She felt cold. The odd
intimacy of their meeting and the drive from the
station became suddenly the trivial things their
proportions warranted. Maeve sitting there, good
and sweet and fair and happy, loomed, a lovely
insuperable barrier, between their further knowing
of each other. Mary, meeting dear Jer's eyes across
the table, perceived that he was amusedly directing
her attention to the neighbouring uncle, whose
story was held up at an exciting point for the want of
an obvious question.

" What?—I'm *jus'* a little bit deaf. Oh, I see!
Did she really? How utterly grim! "

" Mary! Oh, I believe it's port, not deaf—deafness—*deafness*," Jer stammered hopelessly.

" It's not. It's the journey." Mary faced
Roguey, lifting heavy, intoxicating eyes to his. " I
know you'll forgive me for not being bright."

Roguey's face lightened suddenly, as though an
intense illumination flooded through him from
within. As he leaned towards her, all his dark-
faced Sorrier forbears on the wall seemed to frown
in awful unison. Aunt Edythe, echoing their
unspoken thoughts, indicated by a cough and a
shiver that in her opinion it was more than time for
the gentlemen to be left to their wine.

Mary pinched Jer's little finger as she joined the
file of ladies on their way out of the room. " Do
they go to bed early? " she asked.

Jer nodded encouragingly and closed the door
softly on her shining back.

" So your Uncle Harry sent me his love, did he, indeed? " Aunt Edythe, now full-fed and seated in the most comfortable chair in the room, addressed herself to Mary's pale profile.

" Yes."

Mary, who was at the moment endeavouring to assemble a large Egyptian cigarette and a green holder of immense length but inadequate breadth, gave up the task in despair. Very little more and she could have cried.

Aunt Edythe indicated a seat beside herself and said surprisingly:

" Dear me! Your uncle was a most fascinating man. Is he as naughty as ever? "

" He's in his bath-chair a good deal, and I think Aunt Lucie is rather strict with him."

" Always was, always was. A woman with a mind like a cess-pit. She'll choke one day with her own poison." Aunt Edythe spoke with venomous reminiscence. She stopped and sighed. " Well, well, I'm a silly old woman. Is that this week's *Tatler*? Let's have a look at it." She went through the pages, dabbing a hawk-like talon on this snapshot and on that.

" I knew his father—a *devil* to his wife. Yes, that was a very old scandal. . . . Now, *he's* absurdly like the old man—Blotto, did we call him? He *was* a man to ride, and such a *wonderful* weight! . . . Now tell me "—she had turned back to advertisements—" do you wear these belt affairs that go *zip* at the side? No? Well, I really think I must buy a pair before I die."

" Don't you do it, Aunt—oh—Edythe." Jer had

come into the room and leant over her shoulder. "Maeve got stuck with one of that breed once, and the zip patent went back on her, and we had to cut her—cut her out of them."

"Had you, indeed, my young friend? Great fun for you, I've no doubt." Aunt Edythe rushed the rest of the advertisements and concentrated her waspish attention on a page of society chit-chat.

A long way off, at the end of the big room, Mary saw the other men coming in. Oceans of green carpet, islanded and rocked with much furniture, was between them, but she knew at once the certainty of Roguey's approach to her, to her only, and knew too that the same dim mood of loneliness which at dinner had nearly made her cry was again upon her.

Roguey came and sat beside her in earnest silence. Complacently aware that the aunts would view his action with speculative interest, he was for once totally unmindful of even Aunt Edythe's criticism. He only wished—wished savagely as the time went on—that the old witches would get up and go to bed.

Ten o'clock from the silver chimes on the mantel-shelf. Ten o'clock in a heavier boom from the hall. Thank Heavens! Aunt Evie was collecting her work together. Aunt Edythe was tearing the advertisement for corsets that go *zip* out of the *Tatler*. Roguey got up to look for a glass of water for Aunt Amy, and when he gave it to her glanced idly at the piece of paper on which she had been scribbling. She had been drawing a funny thing—a girl-faun. The thrown-back head and grace of carriage, bold but with a wildness that was nearly shy, were Mary's. Roguey picked up the bit of paper when Aunt Amy wasn't looking and put it deep down in the heart of the fire. He understood the perfect caricature just sufficiently well to dislike it.

When the aunts, armed each with a shining silver candlestick like an evening star, had gone up to bed; and the two uncles had slunk in murmurous accord towards the warm limbo of the study, forgetful of, and equally forgotten by their young relatives, Jer put a plaintive tune on the gramophone. Sitting down beside Mary, he held her hand, explaining that he did so because the tune was of such touching beauty and melancholy as to make the strongest weep.

. . . "Why am I lonely? . . . Why am I blue? . . ." a strong, perfect man's voice wanted to know. The silly words set to a tune of tears-without-hope, world-without-end, laid their sad charm on the room.

Maeve, sitting opposite to Rowley, met and held his eyes, a world unspoken in hers. He knew what she was so helplessly promising—something most precious that he would hold for ever in loving gratitude, something so sure as to admit of no doubts or possibilities. For without doubts, possibilities— exquisite, perilous hazards—are not; and there is a wild, immeasurable ecstasy that does not go with safe, generous love. Rowley, smiling back into Maeve's young, confident eyes, knew this with a dull perception that nearly hurt him.

The song was over, and Mary got up.

"Can I go to bed, Maeve? I'm so hopelessly tired. No, *don't*, please, come up with me: Jer will—will you, Jer?"

" I'll bring two oranges up to your room and talk," Jer asserted, rather than promised.

"Right! Divine plan! Good-night." Mary shook hands prettily with Roguey. "Good-night." She smiled at Rowley and Maeve and took herself off to bed, heavily shadowed by the worshipping Jer.

Roguey, on his way to the study for a good-night drink with the uncles, suddenly changed his plans, and went off with two little white terrier people to draw the newspaper cupboard below the stairs—a covert which seldom failed to hold a good rat.

In the drawing-room, Rowley, left alone with the loved one, immediately announced, with more decision than tact, the enormous importance of his immediate return to Castle Fountain.

"All right." Meave made no attempt to detain him, other than suggesting that he had better wait till Roguey came back to give him a drink.

"Don't want a drink a bit. Darling. . . . Good-night, darling Maeve."

Maeve, who loved Rowley so awfully, stayed in his arms a little closer, just a moment longer, than he'd have kept her. On her way up to bed she laughed unsteadily, catching at the bannister of the wide stairs. You can be unbearably happy.

Driving homewards, Rowley thought of Maeve resolutely. Yet in the big car there hung a faint, pagan air: elusive, exciting, almost not there; a snare and a delusion to befool the memory; as unreal as the husky echo of a voice whispering, " I'm *just* a little bit deaf."

45

CHAPTER VI

IN the dining-room at Sorristown, Roguey, the rat-hunt concluded and the two little terriers to whom he never failed to show sport, and who adored him with fierce jealousy, closely beside him, poured himself out a drink.

" Just a spot." He carried it over to the dying fire and lit a cigarette. God, what a girl! Never was before, never would be again, anything *quite* like. He finished his drink and wandered upstairs. Perhaps, if her door was open and Jer was still in there talking . . .

The door was open, and Jer was still in there talking. As Roguey came up the corridor he heard him say:

" Roguey? Yes, he used to be pretty good. They say he's no dam' use now, though. He had a couple of nasty spills point-to-pointing this year. He wants to be half t-tight now before he'll ride a hunt."

" Oh, Jer, how unkind!"

Roguey couldn't help hearing them. As he went on up the passage to his room, his loathing rage of Jer and Jer's remarks gave way with stunning suddenness to a sick realisation of the brutal truth, so carelessly spoken by his brother, so carelessly accepted by Mary.

We are, even the strongest of us, very largely what others think we are. This was almost terribly true of Roguey. He sat down on the edge of his bed, a light, horrid sweat of anguish breaking out over his body. What Jer had said was true—a truth he had not faced and could not bear. But to hear it from Jer—that damned little coward Jer, who wouldn't get up on a horse, who couldn't bear jumping a fence—and that she should hear it from Jer, was a bitter matter. Maeve, anyhow, did not think it of him, could not think it of him. To assure himself on this score, Roguey knocked at Maeve's door.

Maeve was in bed. Her golden plaits lay straight across the sheets, giving her a pathetic air of extreme youth.

" Hullo, Maeve! "

" Aren't the aunts ghastly? " Maeve was pursuing her own thoughts. " At least, in a body they are. Did I tell you I got a letter from the Bishop to say he'd come the night before? We must get Mary to put some more clothes on that night."

" I thought she was wearing a hell of a dress to-night." Roguey regarded the ash of his cigarette with abstracted eyes. " Are you sure she's engaged, Maeve? She wasn't wearing a ring."

" Oh, it's off. She told me."

" Maeve, I think she's marvellous. Crashing. What horse shall I give her on Thursday? "

" Give her Brown Trout."

" No. Dirty, common old brute: he's no sort of ride."

" Give her the Moth."

" She might be too hot for her."

47

" Well, Roguey, give her my old Tranquillity, then."

" That old plug! She can't go fast enough to warm herself."

" Well, I'm sorry." Maeve laughed softly. " You're in a bad way, darling. Mind Jer doesn't cut you out with her. He's well away. Anyhow, you've nothing else in the stables fit for a girl to ride— unless the little horse you bought from Conroy. How did he go for you to-day? "

" Stinking awful! "

" Put you down? "

" No, he didn't actually fall, but he never put a foot right all day."

" I never knew why you bought the horse. That beastly fellow Conroy never does have a right one."

" What's the matter with the horse? The horse is all right. Dammit, I hope I'm proof against Conroy's sticks! Well, he's not everyone's horse, I know that, but he suits me all right."

" So long as you're pleased——"

" Oh, I'm pleased, right enough. Matter of fact, though, he's a rotten ride. He's a dirty brute: you'd never see a hunt on him. You'd better ride him on Thursday, Maeve, and see how you like him."

" If you don't like him, I certainly shan't." Maeve meant to say: " If you can't ride him, I can't," and her meaning penetrated soothingly to Roguey.

" No. What's more, I wouldn't let you ride him. The horse isn't fit for you. No, he's unfit for a

48

rough-rider. But he'd be a grand horse if you could once get him right."

Roguey talking about his horses was a very different matter from Roguey riding his horses. Before he left Maeve's room he had talked himself into feeling a brave man again, and this comforting belief quite enabled him to forget, if not to forgive, Jer's " imputations on his 'ossmanship."

CHAPTER VII

SORRISTOWN is one of those rare places that have and hold an inexplicably strong attraction for those whose lucky ways are set for them, even for a short space of time, in such good and fair surroundings. Contented people, one felt, had always lived at Sorristown. Men who loved sport, and their wives, who placidly forgave them their lapses from the stricter paths of sobriety and virtue, had there dwelt together in harmony.

Standing with one's back to the stone, creeper-covered house, with its long rows of tall windows, one could imagine little girls in frilly knickers and red umbrella skirts bowling hoops along the smooth, wide paths which led from the house to the walled garden. One could see them in later years, foaming dreams in laces and ribbons, join their brothers and their brothers' friends in elegant competition on the shelved, green stretches of the archery terraces. Their marriages with the neighbouring county gentlemen are chronicled in the family archives— pointed lettering on yellow paper telling of the matrimonial achievements of Amelia, Jane or Mariella.

Old books on sport in Ireland give generous space to the prowess in the field of generations of Sorriers. As a family, they rode straight, shot straight and drank hard; while the dallyings of Roguey's ancestry with the daughters of their tenants had produced in the county a type of good looks that persisted astonishingly.

Roguey was a good specimen of the males of his race. For him there was nowhere in the world such a place as Sorristown. Sorristown, the old grey house with its windows winkered with creeper, looking through its beech trees out over its river and across the best of a fair hunting country to the blue of hills afar off. Sorristown with its salmon fishing; its woods—famous covert for cock—horses in the stables; dogs in the kennels; served by retainers old in the ways of the place and ripe in deceit—such is Sorristown: a rare paradise for sportsman or woman, a place to take and hold you for its own.

" You always say you're so poor," Mary said in genuine bewilderment to Maeve. " In England you'd be beggared if you had a place like this. How *do* you do it, Maeve? "

" We are beggared, really. But the place has run itself now for so long it just goes on of its own accord. I suppose Roguey ought to cut things down a bit. But you can't sack any of the servants-- they've been here too long."

" Your old stud-groom, Maeve? He can hardly walk."

" Poor old Doyle! He's no great addition, certainly. But he wouldn't take himself off if you paid him to go. He does nothing, of course; but he's a marvellous feeder. Look at those youngsters." Maeve indicated a yearling, a two-year-old and a nice three-year-old colt in the field below the avenue railings, where they leant together. "He *can* do young horses. He'll come toddling out here three times a day to them with this and that and the other. But if he only looked at the worst weed, I think it'd put up condition."

They went on to the garden, where Maeve delivered messages to an old man crooked as a notched stick, whom they found reviling his underlings and all their works as he thumbed and poked in a house full of well-grown flowers. He explained at length the impossibility of executing every order Maeve gave him, and stoutly refused to yield up the secret of his hiding-place for the apple loft key.

"He's a cross old devil," Maeve said, retiring worsted, "but he *can* grow peaches. I'm terrified of him."

A round through a farmyard of terrific size and untidiness brought them to the sacred precincts of the stable yard. Here, in the last loose-box visited, they found Aunt Edythe on an unescorted tour of inspection round the horses. "The sort of awful thing Aunt Edythe *does* do." Maeve very nearly showed annoyance.

"And how is *this* bred?" Aunt Edythe shot out a bony forefinger towards a bay four-year-old colt upon which she had gazed during three minutes' damning silence.

"By Eskimo out of a mare by Eagle's Pride," Maeve answered, pleased at even so slight a show of interest.

"Any more like him?"

"No."

"H'm—you're *lucky*." With which she took

herself out of the box, announcing her immediate
intention of returning to the house for lunch.
" Come with me, my dear," she said firmly to
Mary, adding across her shoulder to Maeve, " I
sent that young man of yours round towards the
garden to look for you."

As Maeve set off alone for the garden she felt
bound to admit to herself that Aunt Edythe could
be rather sporting when she chose. " And the old
girl's the best judge of a horse in the country—old
crabber that she is."

On their way to the house and lunch Mary found
little or nothing to say to the awesome presence by
her side. The sight of Roguey riding towards them
on a rather peacocky-looking horse came as something of a relief to her. When you are of that lucky
type to whom custom has nearly staled the sensation
of being a permanent centre of attraction, the effect
of a companion who obviously cares and thinks
nothing about you is disintegrating. Mary hailed
Roguey's arrival with a pleased shy smile. Aunt
Edythe, hobbling back towards the house alone,
laughed—a witch-like chuckle. " A bad, naughty
girl," she thought; " and about the only girl for
you, Roguey, my lad. But she'll not have you—
not she."

Back in the stable yard, Roguey was taking Mary
once more through each box, the sheet on the
occupant of each being duly turned back for her
inspection. Even when you love horses and know
a little about them, the inspection of the same stud
twice within ten minutes is something of a strain.
Mary, who knew very little about a horse, but whose

gift of manners was a divine thing, did not even
hurry. She heard again the achievements of the
battered brigade, again the hopes which centred
trustfully about the youngsters.

" Now "—Roguey posed the question to her with
anxiety—" what horse shall we give you on Thursday? "

" Something that knows more about jumping
banks than I do," Mary suggested. " Are you really
mounting me, though? Bar all jokes, it's most
terribly kind of you."

" As a matter of fact, I think I'll give you the
Moth. She'll carry you flying. She takes a little
bit of a hold for the first couple of fields, but you
leave her head alone and she'll come back to your
hand. And she *can't* make a mistake. She's a
wonderful ride."

They stood side by side in the Moth's box, while
Mary inspected her for the third time, and on this
occasion with a more personal interest. A little
weedy bay mare was the Moth. She stood 15·2
and looked all ends and no middle, but she was a
poem in front of her saddle, and the strong, humped
jumping quarters promised good things. She was
over in front and boasted a pair of badly fired hocks,
but her lean, long head was the gamest thing that
ever looked through a bridle. Mary said she
seemed a useful sort.

" She's not pretty, but she's undefeatable. Fast,
too, mind you. She's won three point-to-point
races with good horses against her, and ran into a
place twice."

" Did you ride her? "

"I didn't ride her when she won." Roguey spoke shortly. "It's half an hour past lunch-time."

.   .   .   .   .

In the little room where they had drunk cocktails the night before, Jer and Maeve, Roguey and Mary and Rowley now sat, luncheon over, and their duty to their elders done.

Rowley was silently examining the proofs of Maeve's photographs which had arrived by the morning post. Maeve was directing Jer's attack upon a small packing-case, and Jer was paying no attention to Maeve, while Roguey sat in silence, a dog in his arms and his eyes fixed unwinkingly on Mary's legs. They were indeed wonderful legs, slenderly strong, and her brown shoes were of an undeniably good breed.

"These are terrible! Simply shocking! In your photographs, Maeve, you never look as if you had enough sense to come in out of the rain." Rowley placed the proofs in Mary's greedy, outstretched hand.

"Oh, what agony!" Mary laid them down one by one. "This is the gem, though you look as if you were giving birth to a coil of barbed wire!"

"Yes, I'll give that first prize." Roguey had them now, but he didn't keep them long. Mary was much more interesting to look at. "You'll have to push Mary out of your wedding group, Maeve. She'll kill you stone dead."

"You'd look quite handsome if you only had Carol Lumsden beside you."

"What's my fellow bridesmaid like?" Mary wanted to know.

" Like? *Like?* She's engaged to a parson."

" Oh, that won't be much fun for poor Jer!"

" Is it me?" Jer looked up from the packing-case, his face distorted in all directions. " I'd sooner make love to a—to a—a—corrugated-iron roof." He managed it at last.

" Carol's very nice. I like Carol awfully," Maeve said in a flattening voice. " Look, Rowley, what a topping present! Aren't people *kind?*" She pulled a hideous gigantic glass-and-silver rose-bowl out of its packing and regarded it with unaffected liking.

" What is it? Not a baby's bath? How too previous!" Mary leant over the end of a wide sofa on which she was lying, to look. But Maeve, a blush struggling up to her hair, was packing her present away without another word. Presently she carried it out of the room.

" Mary! Oh, you always were lewd!" Jer stuffed straw packing into the fire.

" Mustn't be low with Maeve—Maeve doesn't like it." Even Roguey reproved her.

" Oh, I *wasn't* low! I wasn't, really. I *didn't* mean to be." Mary hated to be disapproved of. She sat up straight on the sofa, and her eyes, nearly full of tears, met Rowley's. One of his closed expressionlessly. " He's much too human for Maeve," Mary thought at once, and in her mind the thread of their companionship, broken last night, knit itself together once more. When he said to Roguey, " What are you mounting Mary on on Thursday? The Moth?" she knew that neither had he forgotten that drive, and the same perilous thin thread of intimacy vibrated to a strange point of excitement between them.

" Come and look at that four-year-old, Rowley." Roguey got up and threw the end of his cigarette into the fire. " Coming, Mary? "

" Well, and you swore you'd come ferreting with me." Jer was like an aggravating little boy of six, to whom a treat has been promised. " You know you did."

" Oh, let her alone! Do come, Mary! "

" I must go with Jer." Mary spoke in a sort of panic, because Rowley's eyes had just said: " Come with us."

" Oh, let her off, Jer! " Rowley laughed.

" Of course, if she likes." Jer was sullen.

" But I do like—I mean, jokes apart, I do *want* to come ferreting. Just wait for me to get a hat." She was up, out of the room, gone: swift in her movements as a flame.

She returned inside five minutes, wrapping a scarf the same strange colour as her eyes round her neck; pulling down an uncompromising *béret* over one eyebrow, she stuck a cigarette in her curling mouth and said to Jer, " I'm ready."

Never had Mary known an occupation so cold or so tedious as ferreting with Jer. First the walk, up through the grey, dull November fields—that wasn't so bad. Jer told her all sorts of interesting and scandalous things on the way—anecdotes of the countryside, almost Biblical in their directness. " You see that fellow, Mary? " Jer pointed out a distant figure stooping over his slow ploughing. " That's James Cavanagh. He married a wife, and

57

then got frightfully fed up with her for not having
any children. Once he told her what he thought of
her, and she rounded on him good and proper and
said in any case it was his fault. So he rushed out
of the house in an awful temper and down to the
village and got hold of a young virgin. . . . Well,
in six months' time he brought the girl proudly to
his wife and said: ' *Now*, was it my fault? ' She was
livid. She yoked the ass and cracked off to Father
Doyle and asked him what he was going to do about
it."

" And what did he do? "

" I don't know what he did, but anyway they've
got a young son now, and all is c-con-concord."

Yes, the walk hadn't been too bad, but the silent
Jer waiting for a shot at a bolting rabbit was not
half such an interesting companion. Mary shiv-
ered, shoving her back into the shelter of a bank,
smoking endless cigarettes that burnt brown and
crookedly and tasted acrid in the cold wind. Damn
ferrets, especially ferrets that refuse to come above
ground. Jer was so eternally patient, though his
eyes looked red and sore in the wind, and he seemed
just as cold as Mary, yet, when the five o'clock sun
had almost vanished behind the last cold rim of
Ireland, and Mary thought that tea, blessed tea,
could hardly now be far off, he cheerfully suggested
prolonging the agony by a protracted wait for
pigeons coming in to roost. Jer was a single-
minded sportsman, and it never occurred to him
that Mary, whom he so loved, could be otherwise,
or less keen than Maeve, who knew as much—more
—about fishing and shooting than himself.

The way home, though, Mary adored: back down long hills in the greying light, walking up the cold grey aisle of beeches towards the big lighted house, with its promise of warmth and food, the hope it held of something else—a nearer, forbidden excitement. But as they rounded a corner of the avenue, Rowley's car, · with a still-faced Rowley driving it, came towards them, slowed down, but did not stop, passed them and left them in the darkness.

Mary felt as an engine may feel when a ruthless, unsympathetic hand fumbles its gears—the same jar, the effort to pick up way. She had not realised how much she had counted on seeing Rowley— Rowley whom she hardly knew, and only knew was not for her—again, soon again.

CHAPTER VIII

Aunt Edythe dictated letters to Aunt Evie, who wrote with diligence and without comment or complaint. The two sat on either side of the drawing-room fire—a fire that burnt lavishly in a much-polished, elaborate steel grate, yet failed to lend any but an impartial air of comfort to the great room.

The Sorristown drawing-room, venerated with severe respect by generations of Ladies Sorrier, still held itself apart in chaste isolation from the rest of the dog-ridden, comfortable house. No dog ever wished to curl itself on those glacially repulsive chairs. The multiplicity of small pieces of furniture formed a very labyrinth where the unwary one seeking vengeance of a cat was not unlikely to meet with horrid accident.

Though the room was large, the only true spaciousness about it was the outlook from its great, clear glass windows: very high windows, and embracing, it seemed, all the mountains and all the wide sky with a gesture of vast graciousness. The silver beech trees parted meekly before that window, sweeping away in ordered wings to right and to left, so that Sorristown's widest window might look out on the lovely Ireland that lay before it. Below was grass, shaven and shorn—wide lawns of surpassing green; flat first, then sloping down to meet the thickets of rhododendron that flung in due season their joyaunce of clouding colour up towards the grey house, and downwards then, till they met the rougher fields, through which the great salmon river ran.

Solemn and glorious is the river that flows through Sorristown. No prattling, tattling stream, this majesty of water; yet when the S's of its course bend most steeply and the faster water races, catching round rocks and lining out in swift currents, then is a joyful loveliness, a wildness to grip your heart. Like stilled dark wine are the slower waters, whereon lies a calmness that is sad and of the ages, and of the place and for ever. For years past remembrance Sorriers have preserved these waters that they love, and killed their kingly salmon there in due season. For Sorriers are a family of fishermen, and learn young to throw a pretty fly over their famous waters, and grow up wise in the lore of the river—that lore that is not learnt so much as bred in the bone.

Beyond the river again rise the low hills—near and friendly, their small houses so plainly to be seen, and the little fields on their slopes fenced with such elaborate artifice as to make you smile for the poor carefulness of those who work in them. And last, but always watching over Sorristown with love and brooding, are the mountains, beautiful with a secrecy like death, and kind as solemn mothers.

All this one saw by turning from the unlovely, orderly chaos of an ugly room and looking out through wide windows at the country where that first soldiering Sorrier had wisely built a house wherein to found the family of which this story tells.

Aunt Edythe, of course, was not a Sorrier. If anything, she inclined to despise the breed into which she had married. But though she was very rich, Aunt Edythe's poverty in such matters as love and reverence was great indeed.

Aunt Evie, who loved those three children of her upbringing, Maeve, Roguey and Jer, bore with the old lady's ways principally for their sakes. Better than any other she was able to conceal their shortcomings and embellish their more gracious actions in a manner likely to find them favour in those important old eyes. She loved Sorristown too, and knew, better than most, how, for all the gracious care bestowed on its upkeep, the old place was hungry for money—always more money. Money was lavished and swallowed there, and though Roguey was rich enough, perhaps, it was of Roguey's children and the continuance of Sorristown that Aunt Evie thought in the moments when the dreadfulness of the oldest relative tempted her to throw down the edifice of indispensability that she had been these years in building into her relations with the ancient whose tyranny had never yet been overpast.

To-day Aunt Edythe sat and dictated a letter to one who, like herself, had seen riotous days and now, like her too, lived in the excitements and loves and appetites of a world that had forgotten her.

" DEAREST MILLICENT " (Aunt Evie wrote),
    " Evie and I are at Sorristown for the wedding of poor Ralph's only daughter—a delightful girl (you may remember her at Bodmin as a small child), but

dull, my dear. Her mind—as is only to be expected
in conjunction with so much bodily beauty—is a
garden, and a garden planted entirely with Madonna
lilies and potatoes. (The Peruvians, by the way,
were a perfect sight at Bodmin this year. Next June
you must be there.)

"You would remember John Fuller—young devil
that he was! I cherished almost my last passion
for him in '92, though I was an old woman even
then. And didn't he play up to me! Well, we
were all fools once, my dear. But I will be shocking
Evie if I'm not careful. Anyhow, what I was going
to tell you is that *his* daughter is here as bridesmaid.
A stronger contrast to the bride would be hard to
find. She reminds me of no one but myself at the
same age, and I was not considered a beauty, was I?
the dam-fine-woman type was so heavily in demand.
But I quite see that I was born out of due time
(though I made the best of my defects); for to-day,
judging by this Mary, I should be IT.

"I'm nearly as much in love with her as I was
with her father thirty years ago. Her legs, her eyes
(made for fun), her mouth, her lovely clothes—the
creature quite goes to my old head. As I told you,
I see in her again myself. The boy Roguey (and a
good boy, too, mind you) is quite fascinated, but
there is another complication about the affair that
is more exciting——"

Here Aunt Edythe glared through her lorgnette
with horrid intensity in the direction of her aman-
uensis.

Aunt Evie looked up after a pause: " Yes—' the

boy Roguey,' " she repeated. " What comes after that? " With a sixth sense she perceived, though why she could not tell, that Aunt Edythe had said more than she intended to say, and the long years of her companionship had not left Aunt Evie deficient in the art of steering clear of minor troubles.

" —is very like his poor father, but if possible rather more of a fool," Aunt Edythe continued with hardly a stagger. " And not near such a good man to ride over the country," she went on, a stern eye on Aunt Evie, whose pen wavered for once in its obedient course.

"—a very weak horseman," continued Aunt Edythe, in her firmest voice. " I watched him ride a little school on a young horse yesterday, and, my dear, I was quite shocked. But there *are* no good men in these days. When you and I remember Pongo Steel and dear Dickie Ashton-Tufton "—got that, Evie?—" Yes, compared to *them* these ball-dancing, cocktail-drinking young asses are poor stuff. However, I suppose Roguey is neither worse nor better than the rest of them. Can any of them drink, or ride a horse, or make love as they used to do, I wonder? Maeve I consider has picked a real prize——"

Aunt Edythe broke off again, holding out her imperious little claw for the unfinished letter. She read it over, chuckling with delight at some forgotten conceit, and added to it a few lines, the production of which contorted and agonised the patient Evie's expensive fountain pen.

" Now,"—she folded the missive, licking the flap
of its envelope with a grim eye on her companion
—" now, my dear," she continued, " have you
written for that belt affair I told you of? *No ?* But
I desired you to do so at least two days ago. Well,
you can do it now.

" The Lady Edythe Sorrier desires Messrs. Rib-
bingham & Stayson to send her on approval . . .
a pair of—what d'you-call-ems? "

Aunt Evie shook her head. She was for it now.

" Well, how very tiresome of you, Evie! It is
extraordinary to me how stupid you can be. Fancy
losing the advertisement, when I actually took the
trouble to tear it out of the paper for you! Well,
really. What is to be done about it? "

" I will look through some of these old *Tatlers*,"
Aunt Evie suggested. " There is sure to be an
advertisement for it in one of them."

But the search proved unavailing. Belts and
corsets there were in plenty, and of almost every
conceivable variety except those whose fastening had
so completely taken the imperious old fancy. Aunt
Edythe grew more fretful. Then she grew rampant.
Then she sulked. And the moments towards post
time wore onwards.

Times of stress have sometimes their flashes of
illuminating inspiration. At fifteen minutes before
White, the old butler, was due to collect the letters,
one of these blessed flashes came to Aunt Evie.

" I have no doubt at all," she said, " that *Mary*
has at least half a dozen of these garments."

" Not her! " Aunt Edythe grunted coarsely.
" Wears as little as she can help under her clothes."

" Well, in any case the children haven't come in yet, so we can't ask her." Aunt Evie sighed.

A sudden excited curiosity leapt into Aunt Edythe's eyes.

" No," she murmured, " they won't be in before the post goes. How very unlucky that is! Very tiresome indeed. Really, Evie, I see no reason why the child should mind if we took a look through her things to see if there is such a garment among them. Indeed, why should she mind? I was talking to her about them the first night she was here. Yes, that will be the best plan, Evie, and you can explain to her how you carelessly lost the picture."

" Really," Aunt Evie murmured faintly, " really, I don't like the thought of exploring through her drawers."

Aunt Edythe fixed her for a withering instant with an eye of scorn. Then:

" Don't be a dam' fool," she said as she rose to her feet and proceeded to thread her way through the furniture to the door.

Seldom had Aunt Evie seen the old lady mount a flight of stairs with such surprising agility. She fairly flew up the steps and along the dark passage towards Mary's room.

Aunt Evie followed with hesitating dislike. Uncanny, the fascination the very thought of Mary seemed to exercise over the old lady. More than uncanny. There was something vampire-like about it. Aunt Evie, mild and unimaginative as she was, almost hated following her into that room of Mary's.

How quiet and waiting the room seemed to be! It was all Mary's. It was aloof from them, like her.

66

It smelt cool and sweet and held itself away with disdain from their prying eyes.

Aunt Evie coughed uncomfortably, her dislike to being there growing every moment more intense. But the lust of the thing had its grip on Aunt Edythe now. She peered about her eagerly, seeing with greedy eyes the bottles on the dressing-table. Picking up a lipstick, she smeared a little on the palm of her tiny hand and laughed excitedly; unscrewed the lid from a box of rouge then, and buried her claw of a hand in the scented depths of a vast green powder-puff.

"In *our* day, Evie, we weren't quite so frank about this sort of thing, eh? Were we, eh?"

"I don't imagine you will find corsets on her dressing-table." Aunt Evie quite failed to keep the frightened disgust out of her voice. "Do hurry!" she urged nervously. "I am sure the servants will be here in a moment to light the fire."

But Aunt Edythe paid no heed at all. It *was* a sort of lust, this passion of curiosity which was on her. The old slow blood had flown to her cheeks. She was the sickening travesty of a girl in whom a greed for soft, lovely clothes, exquisite scents, and all that art can do for loveliness is only natural. But to see this knuckly little hand running down the length of a dim silk stocking, and to see old eyes gloating with a kind of shamed secrecy over the fragile wonder that was a nightdress, and to hear the cracked scream of jay-like laughter with which an intricate garment for evening wear was voted *too*, too puzzling, m' dear—all this was little short of sickening.

67

" Well, they're not here," Aunt Edythe said at last, sliding shut the long, shallow drawers, so old and beautifully fitting. " To tell you the truth, I never thought we *would* find such a respectable garment in *that* young lady's wardrobe."

She opened the wide doors of a mahogany cupboard, picked up a shoe, and held it to the light. " Exquisite," she pronounced. She spread her gouty little hand down inside the long, narrow foot and pinched the slender waist of the jewelled heel between her thumb and forefinger, puzzling fruitlessly over the looped intricacy of the fastening.

" *Please*, Aunt Edythe," Aunt Evie protested from the doorway now, whither she had retreated step by nervous step. " *Please* come away. I know we'll be——" Caught was what she meant to say, but she could not quite get the word out.

And caught Aunt Edythe was. Though not by Mary, nor yet by one of the servants whose entrance Aunt Evie dreaded. But as she leaned, mumbling curiously, over Mary's wadded satin nightdress case, there was born beneath the eiderdown an eruption swift and vengeful, and a small snarling white dog darted a snake-like neck and set her teeth good and proper in Aunt Edythe's arm.

Aunt Edythe, who had dealt with dogs all her long life, was less upset by the onslaught of this one than most ladies of her advanced years would have been. Mrs. Squiffy, having done her sacred duty, retired now to the centre of the nightdress case, whereon she screwed herself down with fierce subsiding growls, darting wicked eyes at the retreating intruders. Of the two, Aunt Evie was far the more perturbed. Aunt Edythe treated the incident as faintly comic, and entirely refused to be as shaken as she ought to have been by it.

.   .   .   .   .
.   .   .

It was not until after dinner the same evening that the word went forth through the house that her Ladyship's spectacles, tortoiseshell with a purple ribbon, were lost. Her Ladyship without her spectacles was a burden and a trial to all. With them there was some hope of keeping her quiet at a crossword puzzle.

The house-party wandered aimlessly round the downstairs rooms without the least expectation of recovering the lost property, each being thoroughly convinced that the spectacles were safe in one of Aunt Edythe's own pockets. Nor were they found when Jer went up, last of the lot, to bed. He knocked at Mary's door on the way past, and found her sitting over her fire eating an orange in rather sullen silence.

" Well," Jer said.

Mary gave him some of her orange and continued to eat without speaking.

" D'you know, I found those specs," she said at last. " I found them before dinner."

" Why didn't you say so? " Jer was plainly taken aback.

" Because, after all the fuss she's made to-night, she'll look pretty silly when I say I found them in one of the drawers in my chest of drawers. I did, really."

" But how did they get there? No, really, how could they have? "

69

"Why did Squiffy bite her? She scolded me awfully about it, and said it was because she put her off a chair in the drawing-room. Squiffy was on my bed when I came in. Of course she'd been there all day. Jer, I hate old women who come spying round. She has a funny sort of interest in me, you know, and why should she have? It's—it's so queer. She oughtn't to take any notice of us, she's too old. D'you know, Jer, after all, I think you'd better hand her in the specs to-night and say you found them somewhere. It might be better. Do it now, will you? Suppose"—Mary screwed her head round fearfully—"suppose she came to look for them when I was asleep. That would be too awful."

Jer left Mary's room, frowning and puzzled, and walked straight across the corridor to Aunt Edythe's.

"I found them—I found them in the conservatory," he improvised.

Aunt Edythe, sitting up in bed very straight, swathed in white and blue shawls, received the news and the recovered spectacles with indescribable hauteur.

"*About* time you tore yourself away from that young woman and went to your bed, I should think," she remarked to his retreating back.

Dumb with rage, Jer shut her door. He felt exactly six years old, and caught out at that.

70

CHAPTER IX

MARY was putting on her hunting clothes. Although she had dressed herself many times and often for hunting, she could never be utterly sure that things would go right. It was exciting, like a game. So many things *might* go wrong, and even one thing wrong was enough to put you out for the day.

Her garters; there was one boot—she never could remember whether it was the left or the right—into which it was most fatally simple to put your garter back to front. And then dangerous work round the back of your calf with a pair of nail scissors, or else the blessed perfection of your boot smudged for the day.

Her tie. This was sometimes a bit of a toss-up with Mary, but the result was usually creditable. Her veil, though, had a fatal habit of showing a forgotten tear at the last minute; and this, of course, one never discovered till the very latest second of departure.

To-day her hectic efforts, seconded by Jer, who had deserted his own food, got her down to breakfast only half an hour behind time, looking distinctly good, if not so placidly assured in her rightness as Maeve.

Maeve rode astride, and rode with sober brilliance. She looked almost less vulgar than any woman riding

astride has the right to look, and she had a quiet and
excellent way of getting the greenest horse over
the country.   On a good horse she was undefeatable.
Her leg for a boot was very nearly the equal of
Roguey's, and the boot on it to-day did her credit.
She was still wearing a checked tweed rat-catcher
coat when Mary came down, and her closely-done,
tidily-netted hair was as yellow as butter in the light
of the morning.   She and Roguey were absurdly
alike.

"Hullo!" Maeve greeted Mary, looking up
smilingly from the preparation of the dogs' break-
fasts.   "You poor thing!   Did you have a dreadful
battle with the boots?   I sent Jer up to help, but I
knew Roguey would only talk, so I kept him."   She
looked at the clock as she passed by with the dogs'
dishes in her hands.   "You've exactly twenty-five
minutes.   Can you do it, do you think?   I don't
want you to choke yourself, but we've only sent the
horses on as far as Castle Fountain."

Mary felt inadequate and untidy, although when
she left her room she had been conscious of the
unalterable excellence of her appearance.   Now she
looked with liking at Maeve's precise white linen
stock with its plain gold pin, and felt that it looked
cleaner somehow than her own silk one, brooched
with a tiny fox's mask in brilliants—the gift of an
elderly swain—a gift such as Maeve would never have
accepted.

Aunt Edythe did not come down to breakfast,
and the other aunts had finished and departed at a
more seemly hour; but a couple of uncles stayed
behind to keep Mary and Roguey and Jer company,

and to discourse on the wind and the weather and on the prospects of finding foxes and the prospects of scent to hunt them with. Through the discourse of their fox-hunting memories Roguey looked after Mary's needs, feeding her from the large shining dishes on the sideboard, and paying less than no attention to the dictatorial maundering of his elders.

Jer ate his own breakfast in silence, contemplating Roguey's assiduous attentions with scorn. Roguey was in a sweat, Jer knew, because he had given Maeve the old horse he really liked, to-day, and must ride both first and second horse, two in which he had neither confidence nor liking. One was a flashy, showy sort of brute that could hardly be stopped or steadied for the first three fields of a hunt and couldn't last three miles even on top of the ground; the other was the hot little horse of Jerry Conroy's.

"Roguey," Mary said, "shall I like the Moth? I know I will, of course. But tell me."

Jer felt her getting away from him. He was so out of it over the horses and the hunting that it hurt him fiercely, sometimes. He hated listening to all Roguey's awful horse-buck, which a question like Mary's loosed so disastrously.

"Yes, you'll like her," Roguey assured Mary with the confidence which we all feel in our own horses when someone else is going to ride them. "I wouldn't put you up on her if I didn't think she was the very best. But, y'know, she's a ᵽrare sort. Fast, y'know. She'll go and stay. I've never got to the bottom of her yet. An' there's no fence too

73

big for her an' no fence too trappy for her. Maeve rode her into an awful stone-faced place one day, out with Toby's harriers, and when she reached the top of it damned if there wasn't a big stile down the other side. Well, she stood on top of the fence counting the steps in the stile, and then she walked down them, one by one. No, dammit, that's a fact. Now, where's Maeve? Maeve'll swear to it. No, I'm not lying, Mary. Now, Maeve "—Maeve had just come back to the room—" now, Maeve, didn't the Moth walk down that stone stile near Bryanstone with you? "

" Well, she *fell* down it "—Maeve looked up from turning down the wrists of her thick chamois gloves —" if that's any use to you, darling."

Maeve was wearing her dark grey hunting coat now, and her hard hat sat primly above her yellow hair and pure forehead. Lilies don't grow round fox coverts or in the fields we ride over, otherwise you might have thought, to look at Maeve, that you had indeed seen but a bright lily blow. Her loveliness had the same chastely, folded, devout serenity, the same sharply devised, unreachable purpose—beauty in all good innocence.

If Maeve had no more purpose than a lily, who has not known that cold thrill of entirely unsordid rapture that a bright lily growing gives one? Is not that purpose enough?

" I don't want to hurry you," Maeve said, " but I do think we ought to be making a move soon——"

Mary scurried up to her room to mess about with lipstick and veils. Before she went Jer gave her a piece of the marching chocolate that he took with him to eat shooting, and lent her a yellow silk handkerchief.

"Bye-bye, darling Jer. How I wish you were coming to take care of me! I'm so frightened I can hardly bear it. Be good to Squiffy." Mary, still struggling with her fur coat, ran down the steps of Sorristown and fell into the car beside Roguey.

"Oh, how hateful hunting is! Why *do* we? There's a button running into my shin now. It's like hell! Oh, dear! Oh, my God! Oh, it's bust off now. *Oh*, how lovely! . . ." Mary subsided. A minute afterwards she raised her hoarse voice to demand of Maeve in the back of the car what she thought the divinest thing in life.

Maeve, who knew, said: " I don't know."

" The first cigarette in the day," Mary answered, lighting it.

"You're right, too. Give me one, will you? " Roguey wanted her to light it for him, but perversity being one of Mary's names, she held the wheel and let him light his own.

They were late arriving at Castle Fountain, and drove straight into the stable yard, where the open doors of boxes showed that some horses had gone on. Maeve did not even show temper when she learned that Rowley had left some ten minutes earlier.

" He was as knocked about not to wait for yees," his old groom told Maeve with immense tact; " but sure he had to be out of it; he's to ride a brown horse o' Joe Murphy's to see would he like it, and he went on to meet it. He says the horse should carry yourself, Miss."

"Do I know the horse? What's it like?"
Maeve was watching Mary mounting with pre-
occupied and uncritical eyes.

"Well, now, a hell of a nice quality animal
altogether. It's like nothin' only a horse ye'd see
on paper. It's like a horse was painted."

Maeve stuck her toe in her stirrup and mounted
her fidgety old horse (nearly sixteen-two he stood)
from the ground. Roguey was still fusing round
Mary and the Moth at the mounting-block.

"Thanks, Cullen. Ah, shut up, silly, old fool!"
as her horse walked a step and stopped with his
back well up and a cunning, aged eye swivelling
back towards the toe of her boot.

"Lead him on a step," Maeve said. "Such
nonsense!"

"Hullo, Maeve! Are you going to be kicked
off? Oh, so am I. Aren't fresh horses poisonous?"

Not even when Mary ramped up behind her, *very*
nearly setting her old rogue to it good and proper,
did Maeve say a word beyond a courteous assent to
her question. It was Roguey who said:

"For God's sake don't ride the Moth on that old
lad's tail. He's put better people than Maeve out
over his head for a dam sight less."

"I *am* sorry. I *am* a silly, aren't I?" Mary took
rebuke so sweetly she was a joy to scold, just as she
was to look at and to love. Roguey thought how
good it was to be going out hunting with her, and to
have given her a real good horse to ride.

She sat straight enough on the Moth, anyway,
bang in the middle of her saddle, and rode with a
long stirrup and a long rein, very pretty looking.

No possible comparison between her and Maeve. Maeve—one would say it as the highest praise— looked an excellently-turned-out young man, and an exceptionally nice horseman at that. But Mary—Mary in her blue habit, her eyes bright and her hair a glint of joy behind her veil—was a thing to rave about. If there is a divine essence of what a girl *should* look like on a horse, Mary had it.

Though, indeed, she was far from being an excellent horse-woman. She talked the wildest love and nonsense about her horses, but would often ride them unkindly, as much from carelessness as from ignorance. However, a thing that looked so lovely and was always so brave as Mary was, could never be short of mounts. Nor was she often left to hunt by car and on her feet. For if men have been known to swear that never again should she ride a horse of theirs—the last one lent her having been ridden right out, and abandoned to a strange stable miles from home—the same man would fall again, and forgive her for her charmèd ways. Mary's own horses were not infrequently laid up, all three of them together. Still, she got more days into a season's hunting than fall to the lot of more careful and deserving girls.

To-day was thrilling. For to-day she was to ride her first hunt over an Irish country, and was, so she had been assured (and in conviction on that point, whether it be mistaken or no, lies the reason why most of us ride a horse bravely or badly), mounted on something that really was the very living best.

Mary did not think about Roguey at all. She supposed she was grateful to him for having given her

77

a horse, but other things were so much more deeply exciting than Roguey and Roguey's love. The way they were riding was more exciting—the look of the fences off the road and the dim, pale country beyond.

" We'll draw that covert to-day," Roguey said, and Mary looked across to a black little tangle of a wood. On the steep bank beyond it, strong-going gorse sloped down to the brilliant thread of a little river, full to the top of its rotten banks with November rain.

They had left Rowley's big demesne fields behind them now, and the country that stretched on either hand was more enclosed. Banks, Mary saw—tall single ones, over which her curiosity was not un-mixed with apprehension. Big stone facers, solid and kind, plenty of room on them, and an odd loose-built stone wall. No two consecutive fences quite alike, and scarcely a strand of wire to be seen; the going mostly grass, though here and there a field of plough showed up rawly, white gulls stooping and wheeling above it, dim like sawn-out pearl in the grey, soft air.

Riding along the wet, winding road, Mary felt secretly, radiantly expectant. Why was it? What was it? Something lovely and forbidden was to happen soon. Something she had in all the fuss of departure forgotten. What was it? Why did Maeve's square grey back put a halt to her happiness, jarring her with a little pain like tears? Even the gulls seemed to wheel with a more pensive and melancholy humour as Mary, passing their fields, remembered now why she mustn't—she mustn't *ever——*

78

But just beyond this most present and absorbing thought, there, without reason, ran still between herself and Rowley that tiny dangerous thread, and along it excitement thrilled in queer snatched particles. And the thread was so taut. And the thought humming along it, the lawless thought crying from her wild heart, was: *All* right. But I'm going to see him soon—soon. It hummed and flamed perilously down and up that faint, compelling thread of intimacy and danger. And Roguey riding beside her, and Maeve on ahead, were nothing in the world beside that secret excitement.

They were late arriving at the meet. The hounds had moved off down the road towards their first draw, and the last of the field had left. Bright-faced girls in tweeds and rain-coats were starting their cars. One or two hardy spirits, pushing off on bicycles, called greeting:

"Hullo, Maeve! Roguey? He's going to Kenny's knock first."

Mary stared at the bright girls, thinking how pleasant they looked, and one of them was so pretty—*marvellously* pretty! They were too polite to look at her much, and did not, in any case, have time for much looking, for the Moth took Mary down the road towards the other horses in a way that meant having her among the hounds soon if matters were not adjusted. Mary adjusted them severely.

The field regarded with faintly thorny curiosity, this peerless-looking stranger, something of a passenger, they thought, on Roguey's old Moth. But such a lovely passenger! She was Maeve's bridesmaid. Oh, *yes*, of course. But what a contrast

to poor Carol—the other bridesmaid! But that was
so like Maeve. She was talking to Carol now,
introducing Mary, and Carol, who was plain and
shy, and to whom Jer would prefer for his love-
making a corrugated-iron roof, found no words for
this dangerous flame who looked at her with kind,
blank eyes before she rode away with Roguey at
her side.

The field was crushing down a narrow lane now,
and far ahead in the crowd, riding with two other
men, Mary could see Rowley in the distance. She
had never seen him on a horse before, but knew
at once and unflinchingly that so much excellence
could not be other than Rowley's back. Near to
him the intimate, exciting thread seemed broken and
lost. Mary plunged into talk with Roguey. How
far to the covert? Just across those two fields—
oh, yes.

Now there was a pause, horses fidgeting, while
slowly, one by one, the field jumped a pole across
the gap at the end of the lane. A little boy riding
a corky pony was jumped off and put up again with
chaff and encouragement.

The Moth, fresh and fidgeting, bucked over the
pole, jumping it off her fore-hand in the disintegrating way in which the best of Irish horses will
jump timber from a stand. Mary shot forward in
her saddle, but survived, laughing. Looking at the
back of the little boy who had been jumped off, she
felt that matters might indeed have proved worse.

Down the long grass field she and Roguey cantered, and the joy of riding a thing that was such a
lovely mover as the Moth bit into Mary's whole

being with gladness. She did not see that she was beside Rowley till she heard his voice saying " good-morning " with grave insistence.

" Well, I'm *awfully* glad Roguey's given you the old mare." He spoke as though it really mattered, more than anything—almost. He should not have done that. For now all the gladness that had come to Mary from riding the Moth forgot its origin and rejoiced again in this secret, unacknowledged intimacy of theirs.

But he was only near her for a minute. A voice—it was the Master's—was saying: " Rowley, slip up to the top of the covert, will you? And tell Roguey I want the field to stay on the road." And he waited with his hounds, grim on his fidgeting horse. He was a little, nervy man, and as brave as a lion over the country, though as a huntsman not quite a star. While Rowley rode off to his station, one whipper-in was cramming his sticky horse into a distant thorny gap.

The hounds, eighteen couples of them, fresh as larks, their desperate keenness only just within discipline, faced the covert and their huntsman's horse.

" Steady, Villager—*Villager*——"

Mary heard the old villain rated again before the huntsman turned his horse's head towards the covert, his excellent voice leaving a thrill in the air as his hounds stormed into that dark-green, broken sea of gorse.

Lovely, lovely, *lovely!* Up on the hillside Mary watched and listened, thrilled to her heart's core. There, with a wild country round her, a good horse

under her on which to get over it, and a right pack
of hounds shaking the bushes in as good and holding
a bit of covert as there was in the country.

Every minute the hounds were nearer to finding
their fox, though Mary did not know this. She never
learnt anything about hunting a fox; even now,
when she saw them busy as bees, their sterns feathering together like a fleet of clustered, winking white
sails, as they drove out in a line that still they could
not quite speak to, she was all unprepared for the
holloa from the far side of the covert that sent her
blood racing through her.

"Steady now, for God's sake!" It was Roguey's
voice from the gateway off the road across which he
had put his horse. "There's not one hound out of
covert yet."

Then the short, tingling notes on the horn, and
the first six couples of hounds came flying to them,
topping the fence out of the covert, casting themselves over the good grass field, a moment hesitant
before they flung themselves on the line, their
voices the proudest music mortal man can hear.
The rest of the hounds were on now, straining
forward to their leaders, while Rowley, the Master
and the first whipper-in had as sweet a start with
them as the most designing could devise.

Down past the covert swept the field, cursing and
jamming their horses into the first fence. Roguey
deserved a prize for having kept them where he did
till hounds got well away. But had he realised what
scent would be this day in the open, he might have
unleashed their ardour a priceless minute sooner.

Mary felt lost and forsaken and hopelessly caught

up in the crowd. The little Moth pulled her badly, very nearly galloping on into the first fence below the covert. It was little more than a gap, however, when they jumped it where not a few had jumped before them.

What a crowd! How dazing and beastly it was! And what about the hounds? Mary liked awfully riding on top of them, though she never had an idea what they might be doing. There they were, right in front of her, the wrong side of that black-looking fence which bounded the field she was in now. There, at least, were the three red-coated backs of the men who had got well away with them. Quite good enough for Mary, who set the Moth going straight across the field, oblivious of the fact that the rest of the world (headed by some wily one who knew the bit more that is so often fatal) had turned and galloped right-handed and for the moment away from the hounds.

Arrived at the bottom of the field, Mary saw that a small but heavily swollen river ran below that black and evil fence, and a wide ribbon of emerald bog girdled the river with its traitorous green.

The Moth knew something about bogs, and far more than Mary did about the sort of fences one does *not* jump, so, though Mary stuck in the spur on one side, and kept a whip to her ribs on the other, she declined utterly to have anything to say to either bog, river or blind and (as it happened) wired fence. There are moments when Fortune favours even the extremely foolish. And in one of those moments Mary was aware that the hounds had crossed the river again back to her. In the field below that in which she battled with the wisely reluctant Moth, they were feeling for the line of their fox again. Now they had it and proclaimed it right, driving across the field with music good enough—every hound on, the best of them snatching it from the best. Over the next fence with a crash; turning short where their fox turned inside it— never over-running his line by an inch. *God*, there was a bit of scent this morning!

Now was that, or was it not, a cattle-gap in the fence that divided Mary from the very field they were in? It was. Mary, abandoning the present contest with the mare, pointed her nose towards the gap and set her going again.

How much, or how little, of that hunt Mary would have seen unpiloted must remain a matter for conjecture.

But when her almost unbelievably glorious position was reft from her, and that before she had time to jump even one fence, regret was not by a long way the feeling uppermost in Mary's mind. No, the sight of Rowley and Major Anthony Countless, the Master, on the right side of the river (from which the whipper-in was still struggling to extricate his horse) filled her with a lively gratitude to the Providence which keeps an eye on bad girls.

"*Not* there," Rowley said, catching her, as she was ramming the Moth into almost the only un-jumpable place in an otherwise sound and pleasant bank. "Here you are." He squared up the good little horse he was riding to the fence and popped him over handily.

The Moth made no mistake about getting to the

84

top of that, and none at all over the ditch on the
landing side—in point of fact, she jumped it a great
deal better than Mary did.

" *Oh !* " said Mary, righting herself. After all,
it *was* her first experience of an Irish bank, and the
Moth just flashed to the top of her fences, hit them
bang in the middle, and sailed out over whatever
might be on the far side in a manner that was stylish
but took a bit of sitting on.

All grass, this bit of country was, and it carried a
tremendous scent to-day.

Never will Mary forget that, her first hunt in
Ireland. Only three people counted in the world :
herself and Rowley, and equally with Rowley that
little fellow, the Master, who seemed to see, no
sooner was he in a field, the best of all ways out
of it, the quickest way to get to his hounds—an
artist, he was. Though to-day there was not much
scope for true artistry. It was a day for taking the
fences just as they came, and no time to wait and
choose the handiest way out. For twenty minutes
without a semblance of a check hounds fairly flew
on across those good grass fields, while Rowley and
Major Countless set their horses well alight over as
nice a bit of country as one could dream about.
And Mary, tighter in her saddle now, just sat on the
Moth, who took her along better than best in their
wake. No fence to stop you, and every one a bit
different from the last. A narrow bank, now with a
big jump up but no ditch on the landing side, now
with a safe and solid double, on top of which the
cautious might roost for ever if they would : a weakly-
bushed-up gap in the corner of a field—but it might be

a strand of wire hidden in it. Seeing Rowley hotting his horse into this obstacle, Mary did the same by the Moth, who left it nearly as far below her as her rider did the saddle. Now a big, stone-faced bounds fence, taking a real good one to reach the top. Rowley *just* got up—a rattle of his horse's hoofs on the stones, a bit of a scramble, and he was there all right. But the Moth would jump this sort of thing all day. And Mary, for once sitting right, had, as they dropped off it, the good feel an undefeatable stylist like the Moth gives one over such a fence.

Anthony Countless, who had cut out to the left and given the unprepossessing boundary quite a brilliant miss, was now in the same field with his hounds and just on their left. Heads up and sterns down, they stormed now into the first bit of covert they had touched since leaving Kenny's Knock—gorse bushes and thick briars masking an old sandy quarry hole in fastnesses impenetrable.

" In, for a certainty." Anthony was off his horse and forcing his way through the brambles.

" On your left, Tony—there used to be a crater there." Rowley was on the ground, too, giving both horses to Mary to hold. But there was no doubt now about where their fox had got in—three couples of old hounds were marking, keen as wolves, above a big sand-hole, its fresh stopping scrapped out by badgers, in all likelihood. Well, " twenty minutes, *and* they flew," is not a bad epitaph for the first hunt of the day.

Mary, through her efforts to frustrate the two led horses in rubbing their sweat-itching heads im-

partially against the Moth and herself, and checking
the Moth's refined dislike of their proximity, knew
that her blood sang through her veins—not blood
any longer, but wine and life. And the sound of
Anthony's hunting horn (and he could blow a
horn!), and his voice (which was good, too), and
the hounds' voices, thrusting each other aside,
scratching like terriers in the sandy earth as though
they meant having that fox out themselves—she
knew that to these things fall the hottest, most
glorious moments Life can give : effort, a spice of
danger, and the warm feeling of very nearly child-
like content that comes when a hunt (even if to luck
belongs all the credit) has been seen the best. There
is no equal for the sensation that was with Mary now
as Anthony came stamping out of the little covert,
and she heard Rowley's voice and the crack of his
whip, as he rated the hounds on to him away from
the open earth where they still scratched and
growled.

Anthony said : " Thanks very much," and took
his horse from her without so much as seeing who or
what manner of female it was who gave it to him.
He mounted and rode across the field, his hounds all
on now.

Rowley came out of the covert. He was laughing
when he took his horse from Mary, and still laughing
when they greeted the first members of the field to
arrive on the scene.

" No," he told Maeve, who appeared less hurried
and bothered than most of the others, " we took
some catching. Oh, yes. . . . Oh, Tony found a
way across the river three fields below the covert.

Yes, the obvious thing for you was to go back to the
bridge. Yes, but fancy that fox crossing the river
twice. Must have been severely headed. But, my
dear, I'm *rather* proud of my chief bridesmaid!"

"I was wondering where you'd got to," Maeve
said to Mary, not so much crushingly as inquiringly.

"Well, she'd got to the hounds—somehow. At
any rate, when Tony and I got over the river she
was with them."

"*No?*" Maeve was frankly and generously delighted. "How *brilliant* of you! Really, wasn't it,
Rowley? I suppose you saw them turn short that
time when all we clever people rode for the bridge.
Did you?"

"Yes," said Mary.

"Well, I *am* glad you saw it! I love a short dart
like that, don't you? And the little Moth carried
you well? Roguey!" Maeve called him. "I
must tell Roguey." She rode away from them.

"*Little* liar!" Rowley said. Only Mary was meant
to hear, and no one heard but she. They were
riding up a narrow road which they had crossed
in the hunt. "Remember *that* spot?" Rowley
showed her where they had jumped out, and laughed
at her again, "I thought you really *had* come unstuck
there."

"*No*, I don't sit very tight, *do* I?" Mary was
adorably confidential about the matter. "Only
I did love it, though. My dear, I was so thrilled!"
She made another confession. "I *love* jumping
fences," she said. "Do these hounds *always* go so
fast?"

"It *rather* depends on what sort of a smell there is."

88

Rowley looked at her, and then, because he was enchanted, rode away. But he left behind a truly special secret in Mary's eyes.

Roguey fell back to talk to Mary as hounds and hunt jogged slowly back to their next draw. How clever she had been (and Mary had only been silly, and knew it). And Rowley told him she'd ridden the mare the best, too. Roguey was so pleased! Well, and did Mary like the mare? But of course he wouldn't have put her on anything that he didn't know to be a bit above the best. Yes, it had been bad luck getting thrown out of that hunt. A fast thing. Never saw the way they went after they crossed back over the river.

And Mary, riding a nice quiet horse now, warmed up and happy after that good little hunt, the edge of her secret hidden behind her eyes, was sweet and accessible to him and garrulous like a child. Lovely it had been. Never again did she want to jump anything but banks, or ride any horse but the Moth. What was this covert they were going to draw now? Tomashogue. Tom-a-shoke. What a *name*! Would they find a fox there?

They did not find in Tomashogue bogs, nor did hounds ever look like finding. But as hunting gates were non-existent, Mary had plenty of fences (banks with wet ditches, principally) to jump, which kept her more than happy.

The hounds drew on up the long, narrow bogs that lay below a ridge of hills. Not very continuous covert in the bog, but here dry, secret ledges where a fox would love to lie up undisturbed, and there strong-growing gorse, elbowing out in straggling

triangles into the white bog grass and spiky clumps of
rushes. Snipe, singly and in wisps, got up, their
flashes of white cutting the grey air, small swords of
light. And the hounds drew on, conscientious, if not
very keen about it. It was not an easy place to find
a fox, nor from which, when found, to get any but
a good one to go.

Anthony's distant back and infrequent voice were
remote, and unactual to all those who had not, like
him, the alert responsibility of finding and hunting
a fox upon them. But of every yard his hounds drew
Anthony was aware, a confident eye on an old reliable,
a warning rate of a youngster a shade unsteady, a
hearty note in his voice for a keen young hound.
And as the long notes on his horn drew them out of a
covert drawn blank, his mind was casting on, busy
with the details of the next draw on his list.

It was three o'clock before they found again, and
scent with this fox now was not what it had been in
the morning. Still, they hunted him nicely for
thirty-five brisk minutes before a couple of guilty-
looking cur-dogs, young horses galloping, and cattle
well over the line, complicated matters severely.

Anthony, holding his hounds on, was lucky to hit
off the line of his fox over a lane-way.

Some time behind their fox now, hounds hunted
on slowly across a boggy valley, scent vanishing in a
field of cold plough across which they could not
show a line. Nor did they, with a sudden bright
sun in the sky, get a touch of their fox again.

After four o'clock, and at the end of the day's
draw, they were on the road for home. The Master's
back, bleakly distant and somehow totally expressive

of his state of mind, still worrying and puzzling over
that fox which had beaten his hounds and himself,
made Mary—who would just as soon hunt a red
herring in a string as a fox, anyway—laugh and say
to Roguey: " I *am* sorry for his wife to-night."

Mary had enjoyed that hunt awfully, too. Not
quite so lovely and grand as the morning's dart,
perhaps. Still, the Moth had given her a much
more sedate and pleasant ride, and she was getting
the right feel of jumping a bank now.

Roguey had not materialised very conspicuously
in the first thirty minutes, when hounds had run
on a bit, but in the slower stages of the hunt he had
been there all right, with a complicated tale of
having been held up by wire earlier.

Mary hadn't thought about him. She had followed
Maeve, who had looked back and said: " Come on,
Mary," when hounds had first opened in covert.
Maeve knew a point from which to get a good start
when hounds left this covert, *if* (all considerations
duly weighed, and having successfully and un-
ostentatiously procured her start) she made the best
use of it.

How nicely Maeve rode a hunt Mary did not
realise; but it was pleasant to find yourself always
just somewhere near enough to hounds, and still
rarely in danger of a bad mark from their huntsman. Funny how Maeve would slip out of a field
when other people were riding over it; and hounds
twice turned and came to her as if by magic. Such
an easy magic, Mary thought, little knowing how
these artists think and remember and decide all in
a flash, their quick minds cutting through the hurry

and indecision of those who hunt their leaders—
brave enough to jump a house or a mill-stream,
only if someone else will take a cut at it first.

Yes, Maeve was a champion, and so very quiet
about it. Quick and quiet, and with the determination that is bred of sound judgment first and un-
shakable nerve second. And of course to-day she
was mounted the very best. The old horse with the
wise eye and the big knee who had been so near
kicking her off in the morning knew all there was to
know about his job, and a bit over in case of
accidents. He was indeed of the *élite*, the really
extra. To be on his back when he cocked his old
ears at the first whimper from a hound in covert told
you the stuff he was made of, and the thrill went
through him to you as you picked up the rein of his
plain snaffle and waited during those tense, expectant minutes between a find and the start of a hunt.
And whatever the going, it seemed the same to this
plain old horse, who galloped through dirt or on top
of the ground at his own good pace, which was not
perhaps of the very fastest order, yet he could stay
at it for ever. Then, any place, in any fence that he
was stuffed into, he'd stand back and look at it,
wiser than a man, and, throwing his heart over first,
get himself and his rider to the top and out into
the next field like the undefeated old champion he
was.

" Good old man ! " Maeve said, as she got off
him that evening at the cross roads where Rowley
had left his car.

The fugitive sun was sinking low, but there was
no frost in the air. Grey and quiet the sky, and grey

the straight road down which the hounds were jogging very quietly towards their distant kennels. The horses with them, one man leading two, and another one, with a side-saddle on its back, were set for home now, their hearts in their tummies, the warmth from their bodies fogging in the colder evening air, blurring upwards.

A car came past the hounds, slowing up. Mary heard the rate of the second horseman, whose led horse was awkward as he put the hounds over the road, and in the distance came the voice of the whipper-in who rode on with them. She saw his arm out and whip-lash down, and the hounds pressing close round his tired little horse as the car passed.

" Good-night."

" Good-night, sir."

They jog-jogged out of sight.

Nothing now but hounds' close footprints and the sharper outline of hunters' shoes in the mud. And in the faint sky the first pale paring of a new moon gleaming dim above the black, purpling hedges of the empty road.

Mary sighed. Oh, how tired she was! And an argument between Maeve and Roguey and Rowley was going on round her. Why *do* people plan and argue? Can't they just be glad in the faint tiredness of their bodies and the warm peace of their hearts? Why all this brisk argument? It was about the ride home. There stood Rowley's car, its great lines sullen and heavy in the dusk. Who was to drive home in it?

Rowley said:

" Roguey can lead Mary's horse, and my man can take yours, Maeve. I'll drive you two girls to Castle Fountain."

That would not do. It meant taking Maeve's old horse three miles out of his homeward road if Rowley's groom was to take back the little horse Rowley had ridden to-day. Maeve was quite determined this should not happen. So, finishing her sloe gin and remounting, she said with sweet and final obstinacy:

" No, *thanks*, darling. You drive Mary as far as Castle Fountain, and Roguey and I will ride back there. Really, I do mean it."

" Oh, please, no!" Mary said. But she slid, a little stiffly, off the Moth and watched Roguey knot up her martingale and slip the rein through the bit ring, ready to lead her home, all in an unprotesting dream. She was tired, too tired to argue. Anyone could do just as they liked, and—and that big car looked so dark and safe. No, dangerous it looked—that was it. Whence came the thrill.

" Good-bye, Roguey; thank you awfully. Maeve, I'm a pig——" Mary stood, one foot in the car, the collar of Rowley's big coat turned up like a cowl round her pale hair, and her face gentle in its tired-ness. She disentangled a bare hand from the cavernous length of one sleeve and waved it politely to Rougey. Then she climbed in and sat as still as a mouse by Rowley's side. The big car nosed heavily on before its power came to it for shouldering the miles away.

" Tired? " Rowley said to her.

" *Yes*." Mary pulled her mind up sharply. It

94

shouldn't be a thrill just to tell Rowley you were tired.
But it was. Oh, wonderful. . . .

"Almost home now." Rowley was staring out
through the wind-screen intently on the road before
him. His mind was so far away from his driving that
he must give to it all the intention he had. "We'll
have a drink then," he said, "before the others
arrive—you and I." He shouldn't have said that.
Again how well he knew it! That was the last
thing he ought to have said—dammit! the very
last. But he was all caught up—caught up in this
queer spell of intimacy and faint excitement. It
had to do with the gentle but rakish loveliness of this
absurd girl sitting so unaffectedly quiet beside him.
And it wasn't her beauty, either. Had she been
ugly as sin, to him she would have remained equally
exciting. Out of the question, though—all this
warmth and enchantment and nonsense. He put
it from him, trying to find a cause for annoyance,
something to set his teeth into. Then, looking
round at her suddenly, he laughed. He couldn't
help it. He was smitten with the remembrance of a
wise little horse, and a foolish girl whipping and
spurring her into the traitorous green enamel of a
really soft bog.

"Why did you charge a bog *and* a river *and* two
strands of wire this morning?" Rowley asked her,
still laughing.

"Oh, *don't* laugh at me! Because I'm *rather* a
silly—I suppose that's what you want me to say.
Mary wriggled with quite genuine discomfort inside
his big coat.

Rowley felt as when one rags a child and the child

blushes and may even cry. Mary had blushed. It was almost as much as he could bear. If she were to cry, he would have to stop the car and comfort her.

" *Rather* a brave silly," Rowley said. " I told you—I was awfully proud of my chief bridesmaid. But she mustn't be too rash. It's a fatal combination to be rash *and* lovely. Now I'm paying obvious compliments," Rowley said, " and we haven't *even* had that big drink yet."

The car turned in at the gates of Castle Fountain. And now Rowley knew, without any hesitation or doubt, that the very most important thing in the world was just going to happen.

Mary was coming into his house: into his own Castle Fountain, that comfortable, unimposing old house, why designated castle the Lord only knew. He was taking her in, all alone. It was terribly important, almost a solemn moment, and fraught through with that excitement which, unconfessed and unadmitted, held them both so strangely together. Mary's nearness and tiredness lent it all a warm, cherishing touch of ecstasy. As he stopped the car and turned to her, Rowley felt that the right and urgent procedure of the moment was to lift her out and carry her in—into *his* house. The door should shut on them both together, with the world of things and people left outside. Because of that thread of understanding and intimacy. Because, without any doubt, they belonged.

Of course he did not carry her in, or do anything so silly and natural. But it was fun to see her in his house, all the same; to say, " This is my house,"

and hear, " What a nice house you live in," coming
in her husky, purposeful voice; to expound its
geography to her with an entire absence of the
constraint which Maeve still contrived to maintain
on these occasions. Then to hear again her voice
in the hall saying " Rowley? " and laughing because
she was lost. " Oh, *here* you are! " with all the
relief of a child finding the friend it has stupidly
mislaid.

She was in his room, wandering towards the fire,
touching things as she passed with strong, friendly
little hands. " What a lovely horse! . . . Is this
you? . . . Oh . . ." Mary said, and was silent,
standing before an expensive and excellent photograph of Maeve.

" Will you have a drink with me?—you must,"
Rowley said.

Mary came over to the fire, taking her glass from
him. She didn't say, " There's too much whisky, or
too little soda, or no thank you *really*." She took it
like a good child prepared to drink its milk.

" Oh, how lovely it is here! What a heavenly
thing to drink whisky is! " was what Mary said.
" Thank you *so* much! Now if I had a cigarette
I'd be good, *really*. Oh, *thank you!* " She fell
comfortably silent.

Rowley was silent too, looking at her, watching
her drink and smoke and lean back in her chair—
so tired and quiet, the good child she had promised
to be. He wondered a little what her thoughts were,
guessing she was sensible enough not to think very
much, but to take things as they happened to her,
and let them go again before they grew stale and

G

profitless with long keeping. At the moment silence was good, so while it was good she kept it; small and wise and lovely, sitting there by his fire. Hardly a word even for his cross little dog that made friends with her—a waspish little devil of a terrier that hated Maeve almost as much as it hated its bath, but came to Mary with unbidden interest. The warm silence thrilled closer round them.

"Oh, *here* you are, people!"—it was Maeve. Her cheeks were cold and bright as apples from the sting of air and exercise. She was every bit as tidy now as on the moment when she left Sorristown in the morning. She leaned over the big fire, warming her hands briskly, and smiled at Mary and Rowley, but especially, of course, at Rowley.

"I'm simply ravenous for tea, darling," she said to Rowley. "Why didn't you and Mary start? You really shouldn't have waited for us."

Rowley said: "Oh, I'll ring for it," and walked across to the fireplace and pushed the bell.

"I *must* wash first," Maeve said to Mary. "I expect you'd like to, too. Come on." Maeve's tact was so ponderously obvious that Mary almost giggled, but followed her, nevertheless, with meek obedience.

"This is to be my room," Maeve said, stopping at the end of a long corridor. Her hand fitting possessively round the big oak door-handle, she swung the door open and clicked on the lights.

"What a nice room!" Mary said politely.

"Yes, I really think it is *quite* nice." Maeve stood in front of the bright hot fire that Rowley's

careful old housemaid had lit because of her coming,
and surveyed her prospective bridal chamber with
satisfied, calm eyes.

Green walls it had—cool, water-green walls—
and white spotless woodwork. A beautiful old
painted French bed took up a large share of one
long wall. Mary would have covered it over with a
pale brocade, one of those exquisite pieces of stuff,
where sprigs of slim faint rosebuds slip dimly into
worn oblivion. Maeve liked white linen bedspreads,
sheer and smooth as glass; filet lace and monograms
and elaborate stitchery, Maeve liked; and a great
swelling bag of an apple-green eiderdown. There was
a stiff painted couch too, with apple-green cushions,
and a new basket for Maeve's spaniel with a green
cushion and folded blanket, all complete and ready.
Vaguely patterned chintz curtains, green and mauve
and unassuming, were pulled across the two wide
windows. The rest of the furniture was old, gleaming walnut wood, its lovely dark knots twisting like
long snail-shells in the shaded light.

Mary had never so nearly liked Maeve as now,
when she stood, for once slack and unpurposeful,
looking round this room where she was going to
sleep with Rowley—this room that she had made as
lovely as she knew how to make it. And she was so
shining and lovely herself, so fit for happiness!
Maeve had taken off her hunting-coat and hard hat.
She was pouring water that steamed out of a bright
brass can into a smooth green china basin and adding
bath salts in a little glass spoon. Mary unconsciously
envied her this gift for making pretty ceremonies
out of each tiny, unimportant thing she did. Mary

would have slushed bath salts in, digging into the
loose pink crystals with wet, careless fingers.
Maeve's ways were far more quiet and gracious. . . .
Lucky, Rowley was! . . . Maeve had put on a soft
tweed coat now and pulled her yellow hair out over
her ears. She looked so young and trusting, so
mildly confident in her right to the biggest happiness
in the world. For her Mary felt sudden wild misgiving. Misgiving for Maeve, whose lot was fixed
and sure—the thing was absurd.

Maeve picked up her hunting-coat and looked
round the room with grave proprietary eyes which
somehow upset Mary's pity.

" Ready? " she said, and, putting off the lights,
preceded Mary down the stairs and back to Rowley's
room, where tea was laid now on a square oak
table near the fire.

Roguey was there. He was finishing off a drink
as they came in.

" Now, Mary," he said, " have some tea. Are you
hungry? Are you too hot? You'll be cold if you
sit there. Now, have an egg. Oh, you've got to
have an egg! Yes, you must have an egg—of course
you must."

Poached eggs, faintly orange and milky white;
toast, butter, tea—thin, scalding China tea; red
jelly in a white pot; cake you didn't want but ate
because Roguey bothered you about it; the lights
and the hot fire and the begging, insatiable dogs—
Mary was aware of it all through a kind of haze that
fogged her about. In the haze were voices insistent
as signals through a fog. The voices said: You're
not to cry. *Silly, silly*. Of course he must sit beside

Maeve. Of course he *wants* to. Listen to Roguey
—what's the ass saying? You must pay attention, or
you'll *cry*. She turned to Roguey, desperately
trying to catch at something ordinary and sensible
that would keep her on the tracks.

"Oh, *yes*, Roguey, I'd like to hunt in Ireland
always now. It's so wild. I think it's romantic.
No chicken farms and market gardens, or anything
beastly. Yes, I'd love to. Couldn't I bring my
horses over here? Wouldn't it be *fun*? Would you
keep them for me?"

"'Fraid you wouldn't get very far on English
horses in *this* country," Rowley put in suddenly. He
was not laughing at her any more. He was annoyed
and upset. Mary could see that. Why? At the
idea of Roguey keeping her horses?

"They're *very* good jumpers," Mary defended her
stud at once. "Except p'raps my darling Rattles.
He puts me down twice a day regularly. But I do
love him so terribly, all the same." She looked about
her for a light for her cigarette, and relapsed then
into a dream of riding her horses over an Irish
country.

"I could take a house here," she planned, suddenly excited as a child. "I'd like to have a bit
of fishing too—it would keep Bee quiet in the spring"
(Bee was the tolerant cousin who lived with Mary
and went about with her sometimes, drawing a
royal income for her pains)—"and I could hunt.
How many days a week could I get?" she asked
Roguey.

"Four or five days if you had the horses to do it."
Roguey was radiant. He thought of houses crying

aloud for tenants, and all seemingly in the most central places from which to hunt. He promised to let a rod on his own water to Bee. He would find horses for Mary. All things should be made quite too easy.

Maeve was silent She did not altogether like the idea, she could never have told just why. She did not know enough about Mary to disapprove of her distinctly. But though she was too fair to condemn, her instinct mistrusted this loose, divine creature, who sat there in the firelight making her exciting plans quite as though she meant to carry them out by the week after next at the latest. Maeve never entered into such wild schemes. It seemed to her an overdone form of amusement. She looked over at Rowley, and was not displeased to see him sullen and bored, taking no part in the discussion, which had now advanced so far that it demanded an ordnance map should be spread upon the floor for the furtherance of matters.

Roguey talked ceaselessly, and Mary interrupted him whenever she felt like it, studying the map in between. Maps, which she could never read, had a bewildering fascination for Mary. In all her twenty-seven mis-spent years she had never yet quite given up her personal contest with them.

"What have they done in the drawing-room, Rowley?" Maeve said.

"What have they done in the drawing-room, Rowley?" Maeve said again. They were difficult words to repeat, too. Because they only meant: "Take me away from these two, darling. Then you can kiss me and not be bored and bad-tempered

any more. *P.S.* I love you, Rowley, so much—
you don't *know* how much."

So for Rowley to say: " 'Fraid they haven't done
anything since you saw it on Tuesday. The painter's
had 'flu, you know," came to Maeve as a cold shock
of disappointment. But she only thought: " Something is worrying him, poor darling! He'll tell me
all about it soon—he always does." Here Maeve's
love lied as brazenly as love always does lie. For
Rowley had never yet discussed an immediate and
personal problem with her. Had never, indeed,
found very much to say to Maeve; partly because
he had not many words, partly because her love and
faith in him were far greater than that evasive trick
of intimacy, the secret of which is born between two,
and is rarely discoverable—expecially by the one
who loves most.

So, because Rowley remained dumb and inaccessible to that shy, daring advance of hers, Maeve must
decide that he was, of course, tired, or had things to
do. At any rate, those two young idiots, Mary and
Roguey, should not remain at Castle Fountain to
disturb his peace any longer than Maeve could help
it.

" Roguey," she said, " we ought to get back to the
Aunts. You know we really should."

" Oh, don't go yet! " Rowley said briefly. And
when, at long last, Maeve succeeded in getting
Roguey on his feet preparatory to departure, he
said: " Have a drink, Roguey? " It really seemed
as if he had forgotten the anxieties for Roguey's
temperance which Maeve had so lately imparted with
loving secrecy,

" *Maeve*, have a drink? "

" No, thank you, Rowley." But he *knew* she never did drink whisky. How forgetting and unintimate of him to offer it to her! Not like Rowley.

" Mary, have a drink? "

Mary shook her pale head. Her eyes were dark with secret thoughts—her own, her very own. They stayed with her for all the miles home.

" Good-night," Rowley had said. " Don't do it again, will you? " Quite quietly in the dark he said it as he put her into the car beside Roguey. Mary knew he was thinking of a bog and a river and a wired fence. Sitting beside Roguey, holding herself away in stilled excitement, she thrilled with gratitude to her own helpless silliness that had given her this. Given her—what? *This.* In the silence (for once Roguey was silent) of the drive back to Sorristown both Mary's hands were warm in the large gauntlet of one fur glove, and one hand was preciously curled inside the other. When they got back to Sorristown Mary intended to look at the strangely important hand which Rowley had held quite an instant longer than he need have done.

In the back of the car Maeve was suddenly aware of a feeling of matronly indulgence towards those two young things in front. Perhaps, after all, if Roguey cared very much about Mary, it might not be such a bad thing for them to marry. Mary was not—no girl in the world could be—a fit mate for any man so nearly peerless as Roguey. But she was pretty, she was rich, she cared about the right sort of things. Above all, if Roguey desired her it was right and fitting that he should have what he wanted.

Maeve decided that Mary must certainly be her first guest at Castle Fountain. Matters could then be arranged in a seemly and suitable manner—Maeve herself would see to it. Her own love for Rowley gave her a boundless sympathy for all lovers. And when she brought off this thing for Roguey, there would be the greater joy of having done it for him herself.

Maeve was very sweet and almost friendly with Mary all that evening. She knew why Mary's strange little face hid a secret surprising rapture to-night. Her love for Roguey all uncertain and un-happy now, soon it would be proud and sure like Maeve's own love, that had once, too, been dim and surprised. Of course Mary must love Roguey. You saw it in her slow eyes looking down at her own hands, and in her quiet, careful movements. Maeve felt very gentle and sympathetic towards this girl, who would know soon the wildest, deepest happiness there is to know. Because—of this Maeve was sure—Roguey loved her.

CHAPTER X

WHY Rowley went to Sorristown that afternoon,
the day before he was to be married to Maeve, he
could never afterwards decide—or not satisfactorily.
For Rowley hated to admit, even to his most secret
self, that he had done anything—the smallest thing
even—because he could not help it. He had many
good reasons to give instead—last matters. about
to-morrow's ceremony that must be settled with
that ass Roguey: any but the real reason, that ten
miles away from Mary he was helpless not to see
her. He cursed himself fifty times over for coming
and wasted nearly an hour messing about the stables
with Roguey before he set off for the river, where,
Roguey told him, Maeve and Mary had gone. " I
don't want to see them—don't want to see either of
them," Rowley thought as he walked along. Then :
" My God ! I'd give my living soul not to be getting
married to-morrow——" The thought of it brought
him back on his hocks a bit. He had half a mind
to go back to his car and return to Castle Fountain
and stay there till he had to meet Maeve in the
church—Maeve, his virtuous and loving bride.
Then he remembered that in any case he must dine
at Sorristown that evening, and so, and so—well,
there was no harm done if he saw her again, just

once again, with the safe gap that Maeve's presence made between them.

He thought of yesterday, and how brave and silly she'd been, stuffing the Moth into her fences and surviving falls by miracles only. And afterwards how quiet she'd been when he drove her home— how silent yet communicative. "Yes, Rowley, yes," like a good little child; and she was not good, he guessed, nor yet a child. But her lovely staid gravity was as much her, as little affected, as those enchanting moments when the spirits of the Bacchantes ran wild in her and she spoke with a tongue not lewd only, because she was wild and sweet and witty, and, to look at, the direct subtraction of all morality. Well, hell! if this was how he felt, it was time to take a pull, and none too soon at that. Rowley, walking along the river bank, determined to go as far only as the next bend. Then, if he did not see Maeve, he could with decency return to the house and his car and get away from Sorristown till the evening. Roguey had said she wouldn't go further up than the Sally Stream, and he was at the bottom of the pool now, the silver race of its waters shouting in his ears, but no sign of Maeve.

Tall spikes of rain stabbed like lances into the dark water of the heavy stream; Rowley, looking at the sky leaning darkly above, ran till, just as the shower broke in earnest, he gained the shelter of one of the huts Roguey had built along his fishing. Rowley pushed open the door and sat himself down on the end of a rickety bench to wait the passing of the storm.

Sitting there alone, he played with himself the

hopeless game of bringing her image before him, tricking it out with every lovely, slowly-remembered thing about her. The tilt of her head, listening— she *was* a little bit deaf, " *Jus'* a little deaf," he could hear the hoarse voice explaining. The clean, lovely lines of her, like a little ship she was, so set and balanced—a pathetic pirate ship that sailed and raided other craft of all they had, and, finding none of her takings good to keep, threw them on the waters and sailed away so much alone. A child-ship, greedy and helpless and hopeless. A lovely ravager, twice forgiven by the poor stupid craft she sacked and left behind her—always behind her.

Hurrying, stumbling footsteps running down the uneven path woke Rowley from his queer dream, to see herself standing in the doorway, rain in her hair, plastering it down to her wet, cold cheeks; her wet clothes, heavy with rain, soaked and draggled round her; all about her an air forlorn and terrified. Yet Rowley, seeing her looking for once nearly plain, loved her suddenly with double intensity.

" Oh, *what* shall I do? Do come and help, quick! She's fallen into the Tinkers' Hole and I *can't* get her out, and I can't get her to swim round." There were agonised tears in Mary's voice.

" *What?* Maeve? " Rowley flung his cigarette among the heaps of jackdaws' nests that littered the open fireplace, and was out in the rain running beside her, racing for the Tinkers' Hole, that deep pool with its straight, greasy walls of rock.

" No, no, much worse—Squiffy! She was hunt-ing a water-hen, an' she must have gone in. She's swimming and swimming and she can't get out."

108

" Poor Mrs. Squiffy! " They could see her now, the little sharp head clefting the dark water, could hear the futile whining and the sorry splashing noises of her passage round the steep edges of the pool.

" I've tried, I've *tried !* You can't get down that way. Oh, do be careful! Please! Oh, oh, *Rowley !* " Mary knelt, straining down, terrified, watching him climb down, down—leaning over the dark water, saw him miss Squiffy badly—heard his voice " Poor Squiff! Darling, *was.*" He had her now, hauled up by the scruff of her neck safe on his ledge of rock, safe in his arms. Poor little Mrs. Squiffy, so nearly a goner, now so tired and limp!

" Mary, have you got a belt? "

" Yes." She took it off her jumper and threw it down to him, where he made it fast in the cummerbund of his silk hanky wrapped round Squiffy's skimpy little tummy.

" *Now*, Mrs. Squiffy! " And with Squiffy a limp rag round his neck, her four legs pathetically arranged on either lapel of his coat, Rowley climbed up again to where Mary waited for him.

" Oh, poor Squiffy, mother's darling! Precious, was water *awful* cold? Did swim like hell, darling? No one helped. You were marvellous, Rowley; thank you so frightfully."

Rowley had no idea she was such a baby about things, really. She laughed and very nearly cried. She must carry Squiffy—no one but she. Squiffy was so very nearly exhausted, she mustn't walk a step. Idiotic and quite adorable, she carried her back down the narrow path, back to the door of the hut, where, with a jar of helpless surprise,

Rowley saw the glow of a fire, leaping within, licking its way up the wide-built chimney.

"Oh, but how?" Mary stopped short in the doorway.

"Must have been my cigarette end—I threw it away among the rubbish in the grate when you called me."

Rowley hoped, hoped with a sort of despair, that she would not go in to the warm, safe shelter of the hut. He said to himself: I can just not kiss her, walking back in the wet. In there by ourselves it won't be possible not to. I mustn't let her go in. He had reckoned without Squiffy—Squiffy, who struggled out of Mary's arms, and hopping stiffly to the ground, selected the warmest corner by the fire and, there ensconced, proceeded to lick herself dry.

"Wise one! We'll just dry ourselves together." Going into the fire-lighted room Mary took off a sopping coat and flung it—a pathetic little soaked heap—on a corner of the bench. She squatted over the fire like a Girl Guide of ten, stoking it carefully with pieces of stick. "Don't bother about us— Squiffy and me," she said to Rowley. "We can look after ourselves now. If you were looking for Maeve, she went up to the house about half an hour ago."

"Oh, can't I come in?" The fawn-feeling in Rowley was uppermost. He didn't care, wasn't serious—he just wanted to be near her. "You needn't be selfish about that fire—after all, I did light it, and—I'm awfully cold. What a sopping coat!" He picked the coat up and hung it from a

nail in the wall. " So's your jumper." He touched
her shoulder, and Mary stood upright, facing him
in the glow and gloom. The rain was falling again
outside—a sure, kind curtain between them and the
rest of the world.

" Not very wet," Mary said helplessly. Her hands
were shaking, the world was shaking and rocking.
One moment she felt just a silly, the next she was a
divinity—a divinity because his arms were round
her. She must open her eyes to see if his were
looking at her, and because of what she saw in
them must put down her face against his arm.
Only the whisper of a kiss passed between them,
only the faintest first promise of love, and they were
apart. He was bending over Squiffy, drying her
with his silk handkerchief, and as Jer's step came
carelessly down the path towards the hut, Mary
was searching the pockets of her jersey for a damp
packet of cigarettes.

" Hullo, Jer! " Rowley felt caught. It was a
terrible, sneaking, illicit feeling. He hated himself,
but at the back of it was an excitement, a glad
knowledge that he had yielded to his own desire,
because in giving way he had found his feet set
surely on a path of forbidden, secret, delicious
discovery.

Mary, never unequal to an occasion, said : " Oh,
such ghastly doings ! I nearly drowned Squiff, and
I got soaking wet. You'd better come in or shut
the door, Jer, and if you *have* a cigarette on you,
I'll love you for ever. I do now, but still——"

" You'd much better go on up to the house,"
Jer suggested, with loving practicality.

" When I've just discovered this marvellous fire, and Mrs. Squiff not nearly warm yet. *Jer!* Jer, guess how this fire happened? "

Jer, master at last of all details of the adventure, gazed at Squiffy with concern, at Rowley with respectful dislike, and lastly at Mary with love.

" I've had an awful afternoon too," he told them.

They sat on a bench, all three together, Mary in the middle with Rowley's hand against her wrist telling her, through all Jer's chatter, how helpless he was, how much he loved her, how secret was their adventure together, and again, how much he loved her. She heard Jer vaguely through it all telling of the intricacies and niceties which should govern the conduct of those whose sisters leave them to prepare so holy a resting-place as a bedroom for a Bishop.

" He had to have your room—you knew you were being turned out? It's positively the only bearable room in the house, bar Aunt Edythe's. Well, Maeve said to me, Have a look round and make sure it's all right. So I opened a drawer, and there it was full of quite the most immoral lot of nighties I've ever seen—gave me quite a cheap thrill to look at them."

" Jer, they're *not* immoral! Why, they're all nicely monogrammed—every one."

" I don't see any diff-differerer-difference."

" Well, it's in case I ever forget myself."

" Oh, Mary, naughty! "

Keep Jer talking. The palms of their hands were flat against each other now—giving one to the other helplessly. Keep him talking, and she could sit near

Rowley for another devil of a moment. " What else did you find? "

" Well, I found a rope of pearls hanging on the end of the bed.   Looked damn fast lying about in a Bishop's room."

" Bishops *must* be human—I knew one who had twins."   It was Rowley's contribution.

" Don't believe it."

" True, all the same."

" Well, the Bishop who's going to marry you is the best Bishop in Ireland.   And he's such a good person you'd wonder how he could rise so high in the Church."

A silence followed Jer's remarks, a silence in which Rowley took his hand away from Mary's and she felt absurdly that the most cruel thing in the world had been done to her.

" The Bishop who's going to marry you . . ." She heard Jer's voice again, while the firelight in the hut died down, the tindry sticks fading to loose white ashes.

Jer got up.   " Fire's out, Squiffy's dry, Mary's tired, and it's past tea-time," he said.

They walked up to the house all three together, and Maeve, standing on the doorstep waiting for them, heard without excitement of the adventures and calamities that had befallen since she parted company with those two adventurers, Squiffy and Mary.

" Mrs. Squiff never had any brains," she commented, " but it's quite easy to get down to the Tinkers' Hole if you just go round the poplar tree." She reduced the episode to silliness.   " Mary, you awful child, you must change, you're so dreadfully wet. Chaps, come to tea."

Rowley, following her across the hall, hated each step he took, loathed himself, railing against the thing he had done, yet which for the life of him he could not wish undone; in that snatched moment with Mary had been more uncapturable rapture than he had ever known with Maeve, or guessed at with others less good. He cursed and blessed Jer's interference. He was hungry now, and Maeve, sitting behind her teacups, lovelier with happiness every day, was the perfect stone he was to take instead of bread. He had loved her, would, he guessed, love her again, and in doing her wrong he had hurt himself not less. But oh, God! the tangle, the hopeless messes, the poor helpless things that life makes of us, with her devilish opportunities!

Maeve, who loved to hear him talking, especially when she was the subject of his thoughts, said softly:

" One penny."

" You couldn't buy them, darling Maeve, they're too expensive."

Maeve looked at him for one shy second. " To-morrow, Rowley, I'll be rich enough."

" You darling! You are such an utter darling! Why do you love me? I'm a swine! "

When she held out both kind hands to him, Rowley for an instant put his forehead against her cool arms. There was comfort, but not enchantment; virtue, he knew, came from her touch and blessed him. But he didn't *want* virtue.

Jer came in with an open telegram in his hand, and a moment after him, Roguey came forward from the door and looked round the room for Mary.

"Three people," Jer thought, "*savagely* in love. Poor Rowley! I'm sorriest for him. No, I think I'm sorriest for Mary. For once I don't think she'll get what she wants. There's only to-night, and then Maeve is safe. Rowley'll love her again all right—no one could help it."

.   .   .   .   .   .

And as Jer had said "There's only to-night," so Mary, looking in her mirror, said, "There's only to-night. *But* "—and here lay all her conception of adventure—"it's not to-night *yet*; it's not dinner-time, *yet*. There are hours and hours and hours. I win, I always do; I used to think it was dull always winning, now I'm glad."

A sudden sensation of delight in her own self overcame her; yielding to it vehemently, she stripped her body bare, and standing on a wreckage of torn shoulder-straps and poor split cobwebs of madly discarded underwear, she gazed with nearly humble interest at her own beauty. The mysterious thick pallor of her skin had the elfish loveliness of a straight peeled rush; her eyes told nothing, but promised much. Stepping up to the mirror, Mary kissed herself on the mouth.

"You're very nearly nice enough," she said, kindly, "for Rowley to love." Then she laughed aloud and looked about her new strange room, seeking reality again. The sight of her hunting-boots, three really satisfactory pairs of them, standing in a self-complacent row against the wall gave her

115

a sense of the things that matter besides the madness
of love. The memory that all three pairs were still
quite unpaid for, and likely to remain so, following
chill and sourly aggressive, Mary sought comfort
from the warmth of her fire and a dressing-gown,
and advice from Mrs. Squiffy.

"Squiff, you're a *one*, you know! Three illegiti-
mate families you've had, and I love you just as
much. It doesn't make you a nastier little dog—it
does not make any difference to *you*, once you've
been and gone and done it, except that you're never
clever about the consequences. Why should these
things make us different? You get on quite well
with that poor little spaniel of Maeve's. But me—
I'm hopelessly different from Maeve. Couldn't hit
it off with her. Still, Jer is as pure as Maeve, nearly,
and we get on like flames. Squiff, can you tell your
mother why? What plans shall I make about
to-night? I won't make any plans, though, I'll
just do my damnedest. God! aren't things fantastic? Aren't they wild? He *can't* love me to-night
and marry Maeve to-morrow—it can't be *done*. Oh,
well, let's dress. What shall I look? Pure and
holy, or bold and bad? Pure and holy. No, he
might be filled with compassion for my youth and
innocence then. All right, I'll be bad. No, I'll be
demure, or mysterious? How I hate clothes, except
hunting clothes! Squiff, if only he could see me in
my just—nothing-at-alls. Squiff, you immoral dog,
you can always be seen in your just—nothing-at-alls,
that's why you get off so strong."

In the end Mary looked much like herself, her
elf-like self, clothed in a dress inspired to express the

elusive, vagrant quality of her beauty—a nonsensical tattering of silver lace like a lovely regretful cloud hiding for a moment the moon's silvered face. Round her throat she wore a string of baleful opal beads, and her feet gleamed like two slender flames shod by a naughty goblin in mischievous jewel-dust.

" Come in ! " Mary called as Jer's frequent knock sounded once more on her door. She minded his presence so little that she continued to gaze at the enchantment of her own reflection. Had she when Jer knocked been engaged in the unlovely task of washing behind her ears, she would have continued the same undisturbed.

" I suppose, Jer, it never makes you feel perfectly drunk to look at yourself," she inquired, laying down the mirror at last with the grave, satisfied sigh of a child full-fed.

" No, I get t-t-tight enough looking at you. That's a t-t-topping dress you have on you to-night, Mary."

" It's not a dress, Jer, it's a casual garment, an idea, a trappy bit of work, but not a *dress ;* only really nice girls wear dresses—clever ones undress either by design or accident."

" Well, don't be smart."

" I'm *not*, I'm merely nasty. Jer——"

" Yes ? "

" Oh, I don't know. *Jer ?* "

" Yes ? "

" I can't help being me. You're not nice to-night. Oh, God ! I hate myself, really, but I never know *what* I'm doing. You'd always be sorry for me no matter what I did, wouldn't you, Jer ? "

" Always, Mary."

" No matter what? "

" I think you're mad to-night."

" I am mad, but it makes me dreadfully sane at times."

Jer picked up Mrs. Squiffy. " Come downstairs," he said.

Mary twisted her fingers in his as they went downstairs. " I'm in the sort of mood for sliding down the bannisters," she said.

" In those moods, Mary, you're only safe shut up."

CHAPTER XI

DINNER was a thing of the past. Jer, who hated dancing, sat with Aunt Edythe and watched six couples struggling and one couple dancing round the big, dim hall.

It was so like Maeve to have asked people to come in after dinner and help them to forget that this was her last evening. Now things were rather fun. Warm girls with happy eyes were laughing and talking stupidly but cheerfully. Aunts Eve and Amy had taken the floor, dancing in a keep-your-distance manner with the uncles, arms held curiously erect, while they dilated on the extreme simplicity—not to say dullness—of the modern dance as compared to the dictates of Terpsichore which they had followed in their youth. "What the Parson fellas quarrel with it for, *I* don't know," one uncle puffed, pushing his partner before him much as though she had been a wheel-barrow. "Good exercise, that's all—healthy exercise."

Mary passed them, dancing with Rowley. A leaf in a high wind was Mary, dancing—bent before it, helplessly entrapped in movement. Rowley, a good if not an inspired performer, knew that never again would he be master of so much magic. He was swept on a tide, a fierce under-current wreathing lines about him. With her so near to him he was

119

helpless to think. He no longer hated himself—not while she was there, so near, so gravely, marvellously giving.

"Don't look at me," she said once, nearly in a whisper.

"Why? I must."

"*Don't* look at me."

Staring over her shoulder, Rowley found himself gazing into a pair of superlatively intelligent, bright, dark eyes—they were Aunt Edythe's. Was it his imagination, or did she wink like some foul and knowing old bird? If she had, Rowley thought her loathsome, almost obscene.

The music stopped. He was following Mary out of the hall. They were alone together in the stiff, cold drawing-room that the Sorriers so seldom used. A fire, burning bright and remotely, gave no more than a painted representation of warmth. Mary and Rowley didn't know whether it was hot or cold in that stiff, self-conscious room. They only knew that things between them were at breaking point, that nothing mattered to them now.

Rowley said: "I *can't* kiss you here. It's not safe," and kissed her slowly, perilously.

"*Oh*"—Mary leant away from him at last—"what brutes we are! Do you mind me being a brute?"

"You aren't to say that. It's what I make you."

"Oh, darling, don't *boast! You*, indeed. . . ."

Mary was possessed of her frail self again. Rowley knew terribly that it was as though their kisses had never been. She had taken, not given. He could never hurt the stinging, sweet spirit of her; could never make her remember, or ever forget himself.

And as Mary laughed and made up her mouth, her heart was rocked and swayed every way, crying for comfort, knowing that love is pagan and knows not compassion. She knew, they both knew, that there is an utter moment, a brief, lovely interval, which time past, love, no matter how pitifully we bolster up its semblance, trembles and dies. But the utter moment had not come yet. Not *just* yet, Mary thought, reaching towards it blindly, with her lovely head thrown back bravely; a hell of a rake she was, and chanced things gallantly.

" Rowley, I *must* go."

" God! I can't see you dancing with other people When am I dancing with you again? Don't go, Mary."

But Mary had gone, and Rowley's voice repeating her name over was as futile as the voice of one crying in the wilderness. He couldn't think of anything real—hunting or horses or Maeve. Everything of matter in his life had gone by the board. Only one thing remained, and he wanted it so dreadfully. What did he feel about her? he asked himself. Was it love? Well, he wanted her. She was terribly sweet to him. A brave thing. His very own thing. What did he feel when he was away from her? An emptiness that hurt—a gap in life bridged and spanned by the helpless attraction between them. If he had the strength to break that bridge, to send its two ends crashing to a chasm of forgetfulness, he would do it. But it was there—always there. A way that could never be closed until it was crossed. A crooked path, with DANGER flagging every corner, but round each corner a perilous discovery of new

delight. There are few lengths short of which a
man will stop, but a woman's compliance is as
limitless as are her subsequent reproaches. Rowley
knew it—knew he must stop—knew he could not
stop.

God, what a tangle!—his thoughts ran on—*what*
an awful mix-up! Why did he know so well love
died—didn't last? If only he wasn't so sure of
that he'd have risked everything—only fair do's to
them both. No, he could face most things, but not
her loving someone else. Roguey? That damned
ass! He wouldn't have him round her. He
wouldn't have the swine making love to her—his
precious, marvellous. Such a thing to have . . .
Oh, curse it! he must keep himself in order.

She was dancing with Roguey when he went back
to stand with Jer and watch. He was late for a
dance with Maeve, and knew it, and guessed that
Jer knew it too.

Maeve, submitting without interest or dislike to
the partnership of an uncle, smiled at him as she
passed, weathering with competence the seas of a
more than ordinarily rough passage. This, she
thought, must be the most wonderful evening of all
her life. So thrilling to think of the dances she was
going to have with Rowley! He was terribly
precious to her to-night! She looked at the back
of his head with a stilled little shiver of pleasure
remembering when she had kissed it. She was too
proud and shy to catch his eyes again: he must look
for her next time. Soon there would be no 'next
times.' Soon—in a few hours now—they would be
together for always, and each day would be a day

to love each other more. And the nights? But Maeve's nice thoughts stopped short there in a sort of mysterious, hallowed glow.

In the meantime there was poor Jer, not dancing, and wanting, she was sure, to talk to her. She would tell him to come up to her room for a long, last talk when other people had gone.

" No, I *loved* my dance," she said, in fervent refutation of the uncle's apologies, as the gramophone needle ploughed and slowed. " I did really—I enjoyed it. Yes, of course I'd love to again. Missing four? But *I'll* remember." She went up to Rowley and touched his sleeve.

" Darling, don't look as if you'd seen a ghost—only me. Were you cross with me for cutting that dance? Please say I'm forgiven. Anyway, I don't think you're in form for dancing to-night. You're looking *rotten*, Rowley. Darling, I'd love you to go home and go to bed. I feel it'd be good for you."

Rowley smiled at her unsteadily. Why *was* Maeve so perseveringly, unbearably sweet and kind—even letting him off the dances he was dreading with her? Everything in him and round him was terrible. Only one person lived. He said, loathing himself:

" I hate dancing with you when I'm dancing badly. And you're quite right, I *am* in shocking awful form to-night." God, if only she'd let him *alone !* If only she wouldn't stand there looking at him. Jer came surprisingly to his rescue.

" You'll do something for me, Maeve? "

" Jer—of *course !* "

123

" Well, give me Rowley's dances. I want to talk to you terribly."

When Maeve had assented above Rowley's faint protests, and had turned away, Jer said to Rowley—there were savage tears in his voice—" I know you're in a hell of a hole. But you've *got* not to let Maeve know." He didn't even stammer. He walked away from Rowley's side, looking furiously neither to left nor right.

" Jer, Aunt Edythe wants you, dear." It was Aunt Amy's gentle admonition. " She's been beckoning to you for quite a long time."

" My young friend," Aunt Edythe said, laying her gem-laden claw of a hand firmly in Jer's moist palm, " sometimes, y'know, people should be left to their own brutal ways. Such things cure themselves best. Human nature's not kind. She's wicked—and dam' strong. *Leave 'em alone*, Jer."

" I'll not have Maeve hurt," Jer said, nearly crying. He sat down beside Aunt Edythe, looking into her cruel, understanding old eyes. He hated her knowing. He didn't want her beastly advice. People—divine amusing people like Mary, competent, undefeatable people like Rowley—must control their brutal selves; should not hurt his Maeve.

" What am I to *do* about it? " Jer asked miserably.

And Aunt Edythe replied with unflinching decision :

" Leave them alone, Jer. Mind you, I'm old, I've seen a bit of life, and I know what I'm talking about. Those two are past ordinary pales, because they're not afraid of anything. And when you fear nothing for yourself you've no pity for other people."

Aunt Edythe hoisted herself on to her feet. "Good-night, my dear. Time I was snug in me bed."

Jer accompanied his ancient relative to the foot of the staircase and watched her mount with finicking laboriousness. Down towards her with long, flying steps came Mary. She seemed to move with a purpose that refused to think, her long limbs carrying her on. She did not look like her own self. Her very white face was a tired, drawn mask; her eyes were as blank as pieces of black velvet. He did not want to see any more. He turned away, knowing at last his utter impotence to help either of the two people he loved.

Aunt Edythe peered greedily over the bannisters at the silver storm of Mary's flight. She breathed excitedly. Almost, she snuffed the air that youth had breathed. Regretfully at last she straightened her back and resumed her tottering climb of the staircase. "H'm," she said to her naughty old self, "I may have been a bit above the odds in me own young days. But that child"—she chuckled delightedly—"I wouldn't trust her a yard, not if it was sixty degrees below zero!"

Under a lorn and hopeless moon—least efficient of chaperones—Rowley and Mary met again. She ran into his arms blindly, like a child at the end of some thrilling game. And when he lifted her into his car, she laid her face against his shoulder, stifling helpless laughter.

"I'm in bed, Rowley. What are you doing?"

"On my way there." Rowley changed into top and trod heavily on the gas. "Are you ever going to forgive me?"

" Darling."

" Darling? "

" There's only one ' once ' in your life. I'm having mine now," Rowley said.

" But, *Rowley* "—there was all adventure breathing in Mary's voice—" we haven't had it *yet*, darling. Darling, not *just* yet."

Much later in a strange dim room, with low lights or no lights, Mary in her stormy silver dress stood on the edge of shadows, with lost eyes and lovely apt words. Mary with such love to give as Maeve, giving everything, would never guess it. Mary so serene in her helplessness. And then a strange, hopeless voice, a travesty of Mary's, was saying, " No, no, no. . . ." A struggling, yielding voice. A voice dying on warm silence.

. . . . . .

Back in another life, cast up once more in the grim chill of her room at Sorristown, Mary stood again in front of her mirror. She couldn't say now, " It's not *yet*, not *just* yet." But neither would she say, " It's over." She looked slowly into her own tired eyes and slid out of her clothes. In bed at last, after an age of futile delay, she lay entranced in a stillness of content. A surge of utter peace invaded and possessed her body. Conscious only of the fan of enamelled flowers that spread slowly open and shut across her spine, she waited, quiescent, for the sleep that was falling surely about her, shutting her close with her love.

CHAPTER XII

MARY built a bridge between a night and another night; and across the bridge walked people who were as unreal as if cut out in paper, whose doings she saw, and in whose talk she joined, but she was as unreal as they—that was how she looked back on the day of Maeve's wedding as she lay again between cold sheets, staring into herself, lost in a hopeless void, realising the utter remoteness of passion fulfilled. She wondered how Rowley felt about it all. Did he hate her? Yes, she felt decidedly he must. Her own attitude towards him she could not define. Purposefully she had left it blank because she was afraid to fill it in.

Walking back over the bridge of her thoughts, she refused to cross further than her awakening that morning. The hopeless, sullen feeling towards herself, that was not shame, but curiously allied to shame, was with her almost before memory, swooping, told her why. Later, when Jer came to her room, Mary, more than half-dressed, had snatched almost guiltily at her dressing-gown before she let him in. She who had loved her body, had never cared who took pleasure in the sight of it, being not so much immodest as unselfish on the subject, hated it now. It had let her down and tricked her and made a brute of her again. But at the back of the self-sickness (which she had known before and knew would go) was another thought, a thought she stifled and strangled in her mind. It was the consciousness of how terribly, how possessively she would have loved her own beauty if it could have belonged to Rowley really and for always, not for one short moment of lust; had it been to him something most priceless—something to keep. But because it wasn't that to him, because their love was an ugly thing, illicit and hidden, she loathed herself more intensely for the knowledge that came to her with a certainty as real as pain that he, and only he, could raise her again to an agony of self-worship.

Mary snatched her fingers open and shut in the darkness, and thought back, between horror and laughter, over the fantastic pageantry of Maeve's wedding. How lovely she herself had looked!—that thought came first of all, her utter beauty crying imperatively beyond Maeve's delightful sweet looks.

Maeve, regally, triumphantly bridal, almost unbearably happy, had gone through the ceremony and its attendant ritual with elaborate enjoyment. Everything she did and wore, every single word she spoke, was woven through with the bright, intense glamour that endues only the actions of those single-hearted and respectable virgins who have journeyed circumspectly down the happy canal of uneventful maidenhood to the lock whose first name is wed.

Mary thought that was rather a clever way of putting it. She repeated the idea over in her mind, and wished she could tell Rowley how bright she'd been to think of it. "But I must never tell him anything again," she thought. "I will never ride

a hunt with him again, probably never see him
again. I didn't know, I'd no idea, one could feel
so damnably alone—alone for always. I wouldn't
mind half so much if I thought he minded, but he
can't. The best I can hope is that he'll forget even
what a brute I was."

In church, she remembered, he'd looked most
depressingly ordinary: much like most bridegrooms
—even nervous. And he'd been perfectly adorable
with Maeve. Just exactly the right degree of loving
protectiveness in his manner. Just the right sort of
speech he'd made when the cake was cut and healths
were drunk. And Mary, too, had gone through it
all with an abandon that had not even funked
looking at him and talking to him with a careless
coolness that was the next thing to reality. Only
when, at the merciful end of things, he shepherded
his bride down the steps and into that big car, something, which she had not known about before, broke
in her, and she knew with gasping suddenness that
there are some losses (generally of things which
don't belong to us) that only a just God can give
us to bear.

After that, doings had been simply mad. *Perhaps*
she'd had too much champagne? She remembered
they'd gone out to the yard, and she'd ridden a
horse of Roguey's, still in her bridesmaid's dress and
a fur coat: ridden the brute awfully well too—
she remembered that. And then there was a rabbit
hunt in which Mrs. Squiffy distinguished herself
gloriously, and more cocktails and dinner. All the
evening Roguey had been beside her, and Aunt
Edythe's eyes had been upon them both, eyeing

them with joint disapproval and sympathy. Then she had danced marvellously and profanely, and had more to drink, and a bet with Roguey—something about going naked to the Bishop's room at midnight. She'd have done it too, only Jer restrained her by force. After all, it would have taken him some time to find the matches—she'd been sober enough to recollect that. Such a ghastly night it had been! And now, at three o'clock, painfully sober, hopelessly awake, she lay, trying so hard not to remember.

CHAPTER XIII

AFTER all, Roguey and Jer did not find Sorristown so lonely when Maeve went away. The ten days since she had been married and gone away had not really been bad days. Jer remembered to feel lonely sometimes when he passed her door; or when Roguey was particularly nasty to him; or when Mary lingered too long in her bath; or when Aunt Evie forgot that he always had an egg for tea after he had been out all day shooting. But, except on these occasions, the excitement of Mary's presence lent a glamour to the days.

The fact that Jer more than Roguey was her friend and intimate robed him, for the moment, at any rate, with fictitious favour in his brother's eyes. Roguey hated to feel shut out from intimacy with Mary. He felt if only he could gain further ground with her she would come to realise what a hell of a person he really was. He wished terribly for her to say the silly, unimportant things to him that she said to Jer. If she would even borrow his handkerchief when she lost her own, as she sometimes did Jer's, or pinch his ties, or let him come and sit and talk in her room at night, life would be a bit more worth living. As things were, the fringe of friendship that she allowed him to hold was sorry warmth for

Roguey, whose young stormy soul grew cold with unhappiness at the dull thought of her going.

She must go soon, he supposed; and, wondering how soon, he determined that she should see him ride the devil of a good hunt before she went. At least he would disprove Jer's lies about him, and show her whether or not he was any good to ride. She had said to him the other day, when he had taken her out schooling:

"I've no judgment about these fences. Now, is that jumpable?" pointing out an uninviting-looking stone-faced bank. And Roguey, feeling all the time how foolish he was to do it, schooled out over the place, and gave the young mare he was riding quite an unnecessary fall and an everlasting distaste for banks of that description. Then, because he loved her, he jumped back again into the field where she sat on her horse, adorably interested in the proceedings, and for this act went up two in his own estimation, whatever he did in hers.

Mary, realising exactly why he had done it, thought him a silly, but quite a nice silly. She knew he had hated jumping the place really, and no one but an ass would have done it. She had not asked him about the fence in a daring spirit, but because she wanted to know. Jer or Rowley would have said at once: "I wouldn't care to ride a green horse over it," and would have thought no more about it. But Roguey was so unsure of himself that he had to show her he was not afraid. Riding beside him, Mary knew that she did not care even to know more of Roguey. Not that he bored her—she liked looking at him, as far as that went—but he meant nothing to her. The better she knew him the less progress he made in her interest. Really the thing she had liked first, she still liked best about him, which was his leg for a boot. That was good. Another thing she valued was the fact that one could spend almost hours in his society without having to speak more than half a dozen words. They would ride out together on some such schooling expedition as this, and her thoughts, taken away from their futile, fugitive expeditions in forbidden directions, and centred on the horse she was riding, were nearly careless again. Roguey was more than content to have her there to look at. He took her some wonderful rides too, like to-day's, up and along lean, low hills, skirting the straggling gorse coverts that held a hardy breed of mountain fox. Roguey said they had right sport hunting here. " It's the nicest sight in the world to see hounds hunting up and down these hills."

" But all this gorse "—Mary looked round her distastefully—" it must just sicken hounds. Do you ever get a fox away from these hills? Now *I* like to see "—her eyes met Roguey's with for once an affinity between them—" a real snug gorse covert that you know for certain must hold a fox and he *must* go, and you're in for a good hunt, and you must mean it from the first yard or not see it at all."

" She only hunts for the ride," Roguey thought. They had not so much in common even on that holy subject of hunting as he had hoped. Not that he really cared; you can thrill to the same chord in different ways.

They turned off the hills and descended by rocky

133

laneways that were mostly water-courses to the road, where the low evening sky stooped to flatten its yellow light against the dark windows of little clustering houses, and back towards lordlier Sorristown. They cantered across the wide demesne fields, with pauses to open the well-hung bridle gates, their horses reaching at their bits and going kindly home. As they rode up the avenue, Roguey suddenly said one of those illuminating, exciting things that open up warm vistas of imagination. Yet all he had said was:

"*Foxes*, Mary. Good word that—dam' good word."

And Mary, with the Sorristown woods full of them about her, and a good horse under her, felt that it was so. Fox-hunting, with its difficult science, its ritual, its hardness, is the one thing that stands alone in life for those who love it—the one thing that cannot be shared or halved; and if the spice of it live in you, never can you lack forgetfulness of all else in life beside it. " I've loved Rowley and made a brute of myself over him; but thank God that is separate from him," she thought. And when she got off her horse in the stable yard, and Roguey, giving his own horse to the groom, came to take hers, she smiled gravely into his eyes from sheer gratitude for the lift he had given her thoughts.

But how was he to know why she had smiled? In the warm, clean loose-box, Roguey put his cheek to the mare's shoulder (the most perfect thing to touch—a horse's shoulder) and swore, forgetting all else, to love Mary and mount her the best always;

so God should give her to him to love and cherish. "She looked rather white to-night, too," Roguey thought, anxiously remembering the last half of those instructions to which he had listened so recently.

He went on to the house, picking up the letters which had arrived by the afternoon post from a table and carrying them to the light of the open hall door. Three he read, one of these a baldly blissful note from Maeve. The fourth, addressed in a handwriting of copy-book illiteracy, he tore across in its envelope and flung unread into the hall fire. Roguey hated reminders on matters dead and past.

Remembering that Aunt Edythe was to-night removing her august presence from Sorristown, Roguey decided to honour the aunts' tea-table with his company. It was a pet affectation of his not to care whether or no he teaed, therefore his presence on a last evening might possibly be accounted to him for virtue. Not that you could ever tell with Aunt Edythe? The sight of you might even annoy her. Anyway, Mary would be there, and he hadn't seen her now for quite twenty minutes.

Mary, when she came down to tea, looked at Roguey with new friendly eyes. What was there in that ride of theirs together that had warmed her interest towards him? She felt so tired now, and he would have minded that. In her soft indoor clothes, dully pink, with her white neck creaming gently into the curve of a silk collar, and her hair shining against the dark cushion behind her head, Mary eyed Aunt Edythe covertly across the table.

Aunt Edythe had been a one in her own youth, just
as Mary was one now and Squiffy and all people
who mattered. Were there some things one didn't
forget, some people who don't pass out of our lives?
Did one grow old unbeautifully like Aunt Edythe
if one's ways have been more adventurous than
circumspect? Even Mrs. Squiffy was getting a little
haggard. But that was hunting: all day at Sorristown she never stopped hunting rabbits. Mrs.
Squiffy, lying in an acute, strained circle as near as
possible to the fire, undid herself from somnolence
and jumped stiffly to Roguey's knees. She loved
Roguey because he showed her sport. Mary suddenly wished we were made so that we could love
those who show us sport. So easy would it be then
to content oneself with Roguey in lovely Sorristown.
And with the firelight and the lamplight shining
dimly to illuminate Aunt Edythe's glancing old
face, and the other aunts, kind and placid and
anxious, sitting round the table, Mary's eyes again
met Roguey's softly, and she wished, almost with
pain, that Rowley had never been in her life. Then,
reproaching hands clutching her heart, she knew
she must always be glad he had been.

But oh, if only she could have loved him long
ago!—that their love was lapped over in a dim kind
past, a wonderful thing, forgotten. If only it would
stop being alive and hurting! Why wasn't love a
thing like hunting? Something to tear you up at
the moment with a live, wonderful lust; something
to leave a clear, stinging memory, a warm delight—
not a hurt like this?

Looking at Aunt Edythe, Mary wished with

sudden vehemence that. the nine-o'clock train
departed at six-thirty. There was something ugly
and penetrating and understanding about the way
Aunt Edythe looked at one that was sickening to
her—as though she said: " I was like you once—I
know all about it. It tickles my old wicked senses
to see a naughty girl. But I won't tell. I never
spoil fun." Her chuckling, unspoken insinuation of
lewd comradeship penetrated Mary's armour of
aloofness, making her feel, so she put it to herself,
her head bent low over darling Squiffy in her lap,
a grimy little slut. Ah, no—quickly she reared a
defiant chin—nothing grimy about *that* night:
there had been no other way. But when you looked
at Aunt Edythe, and considered how she had been
once what you were now, the dreadful thought that
one day you might be even as she hurt and oppressed
unspeakably. The only thing to do was to escape
from Aunt Edythe and her leering intimacy, and the
other Aunts with their pleasant wholesomely boring
conversation, and take refuge till dinner-time came
in your own room, apart from the others, alone with
this new tiredness of body which made you glad to
have no more exacting companion than Mrs.
Squiffy and the vague unrest of a memory the reality
of which fell shorter even than the memory of some
kisses fulfilled.

But Aunt Edythe, once she had found worthy
play for the quality of her wit, was not easily to be
escaped. It was just before dinner that Mary saw
her again. She and Roguey, standing together
before the blaze of the big hall fire, were drinking
their cocktails Roguey, inexpressibly tall and fair,

delightful to look at in his blue dinner clothes, mounting his hunt button, stood, one foot on the fender, looking down at Mary, who spelt so much wonder for him, before he lifted his glass. "Happy days!" He smiled at her. She liked him almost as much as Jer. "Naughty nights and no regrets." Mary finished the old toast, laughing. She was her own defiant, undefeatable self for the moment.

Straight on top of Roguey's laugh came Aunt Edythe's old croak from half-way down the staircase: "None if you're lucky! He, he,—if you're *lucky*," she repeated. Then, gathering her dignity about her again, she passed them by and went on her way towards the drawing-room.

"Ribald old witch!" Roguey commented. "She's taken a tremendous fancy to you, Mary."

Mary put down her glass carefully, because her fingers were shaking about its long, slim stem. She felt sick, diseased. Not fair, to play with Roguey, who was clean, anyway, if a fool. Supposing, just supposing—not that it was possible, of course—that you *weren't* lucky? Then what about it? Mary's tight dress clung for a sick moment to her damp skin as the thought hesitated in her mind. Good God, no! *You* were all right. Careful, anyway. Gulping her cocktail, she felt that the adoration in Roguey's eyes was at any rate about the safest insurance policy she could take out.

CHAPTER XIV

" THAT's not the road, Jer."

" Shortest way."

" Rot! Half a mile shorter to go by Garryowen Chapel."

" Since when? I've gone this road to Ferristown all my life." Jer changed gear decisively, the car roaring up a steep hill in second.

Mary screwed her head round to take a look at Roguey in the back seat, his silk hat in its box beside him, the big collar of his brown coat turned up to meet the old felt abortion on his head, hiding the thick white of his hunting stock. The red of his coat showed in gleaming slits as he searched, his hands diving into side pockets, for cigarettes.

Mary straightened round in her seat again, displeased with the peaky, strained expression on Roguey's face. She hated people to look cross and frightened on a hunting morning. She herself never felt like that, although this morning a new hat seared a band of agony across her forehead, squeezing the sides of her head together with hot iron fingers. Still, one didn't spoil one's perfectly good bun by paying attention to such matters—at least Mary didn't, or never had up to this morning. But to-day there was something imperatively sickening about the way her hat hurt her. Her answers to

Jer's remarks grew scantier. Quite recklessly she pushed her hard hat off her forehead, tipping it back against her little shining bun of hair. That was better—for just an instant. Then, helplessly wiping off a sickening moustache of sweat that found its way through the powder on her upper lip, Mary found a small gulping voice and said: "Stop, Jer. I'm going to be sick—out loud."

Mary never said what she did not mean. She was sick, neatly and efficiently, behind a furze-bush. Then, returning to the car, explained, through the boys' turmoil of sympathy, how much better she felt. Restored indeed almost to gaiety, she bade the hesitant Jer continue, and, fortified by frequent nips from Roguey's flask, arrived at the meet in a state bordering on exaltation.

"Mary, darling," Jer said, "you've smudged your lipstick, darling; and I *can't* allow you to get out of this car till your hat looks less drunk."

"You're right, Jer, I must sober up. Roguey, take your beastly flask away. No, thanks, I really *don't* smoke. I *may* be drunk, but I never forget myself."

Shadowed by Jer and Roguey, Mary got out of the car, striding in her small, queen-like way amongst led horses, and horses ridden, and cars occupied and unoccupied, to where Paddy Doyle and an underling fussed and chided round Roguey's three horses.

Mary looked about her in a sort of cold maze of interest. She thought the horses as a lot showed less quality than did their riders. The cobby stamp predominated amongst the horses, and in a field of perhaps forty the girls outnumbered the men.

And most of the girls rode astride, turning themselves
out well: good boots, good breeches, workman-like.
Mary approved. She liked the men who laughed,
bent in their saddles and talked to one another;
especially one, an extravagant exquisite in a pink,
cut-away coat, who bade an unaffected farewell to a
female of surpassing gauntness and beauty who stood
beside her car, frailly, defiantly with child; promising, if she might see the first covert drawn, to go home
in time for lunch. Yes, and to lie down till tea-time
too. Yes, Toby, darling.

"Oh, God, how safe, how divine!" Mary
thought, and turned to mount her horse, her hands a
little clumsy as she picked up her reins.

And all who looked on Mary, sitting so straight on
the game little Moth, both of them showing their
breeding, thoroughbreds with no two ways about
it, felt that Roguey was a luckier man than his
deserts, should this peach, this queen among women,
be his for keeps.

A big car drew up, out of which there stepped a
little red-faced man, shedding a leather coat,
terribly intent, speaking to Roguey for a moment,
with a "Ha are ya"? but no smile for Mary.
This was the Master. His wife, a fair-haired girl
of smooth bulk, in a habit of blue, masterly exact-
ness, was kinder, not uninterested.

"I must get on my horse," she said, as the hounds'
greeting to her spouse, their huntsman, clamoured
on the heavy morning air when he rode up to them.
"I do hope you'll have another good day with us.
Roguey brought you out to a right meet, anyway."

"That's Peter Countless," Roguey explained.

" A champion. She's talking to Prudence Sage now——" a snatch of Peter's conversation with the lovely pregnant one reached them.

" Darling, how rash and awful you are ! You know it will be born in a gorse covert one of these days."

" Oh, Peter, wouldn't it be marvellous ! Darling, isn't it ripping to think he'll hunt all his life *and* before it ? "

" *Wonderful !* Anthony's just going to scold me for not being on my horse. Do send some one for me if you feel ill."

" Are they sisters ? " Mary asked.

" No, just great friends."

" Oh, how *topping !* "

" Hounds, please, hounds," and mild confusion while horses fretted, their heels to the hedges, and hounds, looking fine-drawn and hard-conditioned even thus early in November, came in all their gallant unity down the road.

" Thank God there's something left in the world," Mary thought, as the Moth, fidgeting at her bits, her head up and her back up, with keen eyes on the jogging pack, carried her down the grey road, saying with every live muscle in her body, " If I wasn't a perfect lady, I'd buck, I would. Perhaps I will— I *will*. I have ! Still quite happy ? H'm. More than I am. . . . Nasty job in the mouth that was you gave me. Well, I bought it."

Roguey, riding beside Mary gravely and possessively, apologised for the Moth's sorry lack of manners. He thought it must be the side saddle, but in any case it was only play.

Mary smiled like a child. She loved riding far

more than she loved hunting. Hounds were to her
no more than a necessary excuse for jumping fences,
and every moment of a day's hunting was a glorious,
exciting adventure. To hear Mary recount a hunt
was worth gold. " Oh, *marvellous !* " she had been
known to say. "We only checked once, and that
was to cut wire."

To-day she stayed gravely by Roguey's side, and
smiled at him, and rode the mare nicely and carefully
like a little girl on her pony. And Roguey, looking
down at her, realised, like a giant renewed, his utter
confidence in himself, in his horse, in his re-acquired
will to be there, and all because of this gallant
little silly, this Mary, who was always to ride his best
horse as she was doing to-day; who was not of
matchless competence like Maeve, but must be seen
safely over each fence, and in due course taught not
to say, " *We* went to ground," when she meant to
convey that hounds had marked their fox to ground.

Jer, following in the car, and even Mrs. Squiffy
straining out her long fine neck over the door, seemed
the trivial people that those who do not or cannot
hunt appear to those who do and can. Roguey
felt happily how infinitely Jer in his plus-fours must
recede in Mary's esteem, and as he rode beside her,
in the crowd, with what sun there was glancing
from bit bar to stirrup iron, the important flash of
hounds on ahead, good and bad horses ridden
pridefully by their owners, while courage was unwanted, Roguey felt that love and fox-hunting were
the two finest things in the world. But Mary knew
savagely that love hurts, and hunting, being a greater
thing, is incomparable thereto.

Never will Roguey forget that day, that utterly perfect and wonderful day. It was like a day straight out of the box of good days that God keeps for us somewhere on a high shelf; none of our own little doings can influence its charmed happenings. Things just come our way, that's all about it. Things came Roguey's way; he knew they would from the moment when his own lifted hat told of a good fox viewed away; while Mary's only-just-repressed squeal of excitement was squashed by him, with a severity that she might have found attractive had she had time wherein to consider it. But there was no time to consider or take in anything. Herself, her horse, Roguey's back, and the hounds (last of all) flowed and overflowed and re-charged with a fresh delirium of excitement Mary's whole being. Again she knew that this, this glorious triumph of the body, is the end to which all who love sport bravely are bred. It is the one, the only thing. Rowley was to her now not even a memory; Roguey was just the world's best pilot; her horse and herself alone mattered, alone were one.

And Roguey? Roguey, they said who knew him, had never ridden a hunt so well and never would ride one better. For forty-five minutes, with a scent laid on like butter, hounds ran, and took a bit of staying with over a country that was now too choice to ride. Forty-five minutes making a six-mile point before they caught their fox fair and square in the open, a brilliant finish to quite a brilliant performance.

Mary, who knew not whether it had been brilliant or not, content only that each moment should be more exciting than the one before it, was presented with the brush and, nearly crying with excitement, held Roguey's hand while hounds broke up their well-deserved fox.

The Master's wife said afterwards to her lovely friend Prudence: " That girl of Roguey's is a proper bit of stuff. In fact, I think she's a real live human being. Roguey worships her. She doesn't care a dam' about him. She'd have suited Rowley down to the ground."

" Why? "

" Because they're both absolutely brutal and absolutely attractive.

" So's Roguey—awfully attractive."

" But he's not brutal, and only brave in snatches, like he was to-day, when I must say I never saw a man ride a hunt better."

Roguey knew it. He knew that if Mary did nothing else for him she had given him for one marvellous day utter self-mastery and the rest in strength that comes in its train. When, in the evening, they found Jer waiting for them in the car at an appointed cross roads, and, getting off their horses, found too the nearly exquisite comfort of warm coats and warming drink, and Mary, her pale, poignant face a note of tired exclamation against the dark close fur of her collar, turned to him to say: " Roguey, it's been past words—I *can't* tell you . . ." he picked up her hand and, pulling it out of a dirty glove, kissed its warm, thrilling palm. Mary said faintly: " Oh, chaps, how ghastly it all is! " and let him; while Jer, furiously silent, pushed past Roguey towards the car.

" Here! get out of it—to hell out of it—I'm driving this car home."

" I'll, I'll, I'll——" Jer's face flamed white with anger.

" Oh, Jer—*so* tired! Don't fight, chaps, I'll cry if you do. Jer, darling, take care of me—it's your turn. Roguey's been most marvellous all day."

Mary, how white and sweet she was!—her bare head leaning back hopelessly tired, the hard line of her stock wound so primly round her throat, emphasising the soft underneath of her chin: in the droop of her pale, unpainted mouth, sadness unspeakable. Jer, sitting beside her, thought: How marvellous she is! how impossibly I love her! how lonely it is without Maeve! Maeve, *Maeve*, what care you used to take of me! Roguey shan't have her. If I die Roguey shan't have her. I'll tell her what a rotter Roguey is. To-night. She's as straight as a bee-line. She won't have him when I tell her. I'd like to kill Roguey with my two hands. Damned swine. And under the comfort of a rug of close, sliding fur, Mary's hand found his and charmed him excessively, though her fingers struck a chord whose top note was something near to tears.

Mary, staring through the windscreen past Roguey's shoulder, thrilled Jer almost unconsciously, for her thoughts had escaped from their warm content, and now circled sadly forward to a joyless bath, to nights never quite perfect, and to a fear, to a fear that grasped her heart terrifyingly—a fear of what might have been the most romantic excitement, pain for which she would have put her two bare hands under the feet of a kind, safe God, were her lot cast for her less fantastically.

" I *can't* know yet," she told herself, sudden panic licking her round. But, my God! how awkward if it's true—how *too* awkward." What, on these occasions, did one *do* about it?

Back again at Sorristown, in the stately gloom of the hall, Mary picked up her letters, and went slowly across to the fire to read them. Not very interesting. Two duns, more firm than polite, and the third from her brokers. Mary opened this last and read it once. Then she tried to read it again, but failed. Curiously blind, she felt, hot and helpless. Things like this don't happen, not in real life. Perfectly good investments shouldn't turn out flat, even if nations are divided against themselves—after all, it's *your* money. But the bank will always do something for you: Mary grasped vaguely at hope. The manager of your bank was such a dear; he'd be helpful about it when he understood that you simply *must* overdraw a bit more. Can a girl live on nothing? Certainly she cannot. Mary read her broker's letter again; this time she realised more clearly what it regretfully conveyed. But this was awful! What do you do when you have *no* money— practically? Not enough, not nearly enough to pay your debts—all of them screaming on different notes of intensity to be paid? And a fear, hourly approaching to reality, consuming your mind so that you could not think. What do you *do?*

" Roguey, Roguey, isn't it awful? All these China things of mine have come smash."

" What? " Roguey, with visions of broken pottery

clattering about his brain, took the letter that Mary held out to him.

" But, Mary "—he was a little dazed—" darling, you haven't got any money at all—practically."

" Oh, rot, dear! I always have some money, somehow."

" But you haven't."

" Oh, *Roguey !* "

Roguey stood frowning over the letter near the light of a lamp. The light shone down on his bent fair head and vivid profile, striking patches over the shoulders of his red coat. When the Demon came importantly into the hall and bestowed himself neatly in the crook of Roguey's arm, he received almost less than no attention.

" *Roguey ?* "

For answer Roguey came towards her, inevitably, possessively nearer.

Oh, quick! *God*, what was one to *do* about it? He mustn't kiss you. He mustn't touch you. . . . Oh, well, *not* so bad if you could keep your face close against the thick stuff of his coat; but some-time, sometime you must raise it. Fair do's, after all. And Mary, whose chief fault was rushing rather than funking her fences, lifted her face and before he kissed her said: " Darling not *quite* so tight—hunt buttons are, barring all jokes, *quite* the most painful sort I know. Oh, darling! "

. . . . . .

It was two hours later that Jer found Mary in her room, with one boot off and one boot on. They were new boots, not the boots she had worn all day, and Jer looked at her with amazement verging on horror.

Mary talked rapidly.

"My dear, these boots are too *marvellous*! I put one on and simply loved it. Then it was tea-time, so I had tea in one boot, and *tried* to put the other on, but it simply wouldn't go. I nearly cried. And now I can't get the first boot off. No powers will move it. Imagine what the rest of my life will be like, spent in one lovely hunting-boot and wedlock with Roguey."

"Mary, are you going to marry Roguey?"

Mary, in one boot, with her stock off and yellow flannel shirt gaping wide at the neck, looked most forlorn.

"Yes," she said, "I am, I am. Go away now, Jer. Please go away."

"Oh, Mary, please tell me. Do you c-care about him at all?"

"Oh, God, yes, in a way. No, of course I don't— but I must."

Jer swallowed something in his throat with quite overpowering difficulty, and as he attacked her boot with clumsy desperation, said: "Cheer up, darling! He's a hell of a good fellow, really. Yes, you'll l-like him. He'll grow on you, don't you make any mistake about it."

And when he had gone—dear, kind Jer—Mary rose to her feet and considered the immediate future without hope or courage or one thing that helps. I won't think—I won't, I won't! her mind shouted, and above the clamour an undefeatable conscious-ness spoke, saying: "There are kisses *and* kisses, and then *some* kisses. So far it's only been kisses. How much more can you stick?"

Mary, facing herself with knowledge and dislike, answered: " I'm not so dam' clean, I'm not so dam' particular. I may have sold my soul to the devil, but if I did I've sold him a pup. What happens to me doesn't matter; but I'm sorry about Roguey—oh, I'm sorry, I'm *sorry* ! " And she fell to strained laughter, and from laughter to tears—or were they tears? It is unknown who cried: it couldn't have been Mary, for that was a thing she never did—too proud. But two handkerchiefs, outsize silk ones, were soaked through once and once again. Mrs. Squiffy, having licked her mistress's face and wet neck many times over with a tongue like a dry rasp, finally retired on the water-jug, the contents of which at least were not salt. A bad business.

CHAPTER XV

JER was all alone at Sorristown now, and in a queer way he liked it. He looked after himself touchingly, changing his socks when they were wet with an odd pretence in his mind that Maeve was there to make him do it. He felt he must live very orderly and carefully through his days if he was to keep back the wild horses of unhappiness that mouthed and reached their necks out towards him.

You got out of bed promptly at half-past eight when White called you, shoved your feet into slippers, and looked out at the sad early winter morning, its thick breath hanging chill over the river. Down on the dark green lawn, so far below, the Demon and Mrs. Squiffy were taking their first morning walk; Mrs. Squiffy, hating it sourly, stood still with little shivers and walked forward with delicate steps. The Demon, foolishly elated even thus early, galloped round in purposeless circles, ready for anything. The paths of his foolish goings and comings showed darker where the mist was brushed off the grass. Silly Demon! He would be in Jer's bed, drying a wet tummy on the sheets, when Jer came back from the bathroom.

Jer's company was better than none at all; even the select Mrs. Squiffy thought that, and flattered him a little, but not with any real liking. With the

Demon she would attend him dourly when he came downstairs, watching him with tiny groans as he lifted the heavy silver lids from the hot breakfast dishes and fed in silence, his back to the fire; while all the ancestors stood away darkly on the walls, and the morning light came in grey and spacious through three tall windows.

White would appear later to know whether Jer would be home for lunch, and Jer almost always said No; sandwiches. For he shot nearly every day, leaving Sorristown far behind him. He liked to get away—there was a brooding on and about the house that made him melancholy. There was a fire in the study for him, and one in the dining-room and, in the evening, in his bedroom, and those seemed the only rooms in the big house that lived and cared to comfort his loneliness, and Jer was very lonely.

When he had fed the two small dogs he would step out on to the lawn, take a satisfactory look at the yellow pallor that sulphate of ammonia had spread upon the tennis court—his doing, that. And perhaps he would see Roguey's horses coming out of the stables, their blue sheets turned back from their shoulders, going out for exercise—a man riding one and leading one. What brave men they were, Jer thought, giving them full marks, riding those beastly, sickeningly fresh horses. Jer wouldn't have done it for a hundred pounds given into his hand. The sight of them as they came out in the field below the lawn, appearing suddenly from the sunk lane-way that led to the stables, bright and wicked in the pale air, made Jer feel as faint and silly as if he really had to get up and ride one of them.

" A very poor fellow I am," thought Jer, returning to the house to put on his greasy heavy boots by the study fire, to pocket his sandwiches in the pantry and then to meet Paddy Byrne, the gamekeeper, waiting for him with his dogs outside the gun-room window.

There was Binty, Jer's black retriever bitch, the only dog in the world with any real love for Jer, and with a respect, too, that hoped on always even in the days when Jer shot less than nothing for her to retrieve. There, too, was Rony, the disobedient spaniel and living falsification of a well-known proverb.

" I makes him carry his own whip," Paddy Byrne would say, indicating the spaniel's heavy collar, " but for all me correction there's a charge o' shot due for him one o' these days."

Jer would look at the delinquent with sorrow, and hope that, like others who erred, he might be spared his dues.

To-day Paddy Byrne and Jer turned their backs on the house and demesne and their faces to the bogs that coiled so endless out before them. The light was not of the best, and, worse still, they would have the wind in their faces all the way up the narrow bogs, twisting and turning as they followed the course of a tiny river. They both knew well how much more difficult snipe are when taken up-wind. But that would be in their favour coming home.

Walking quickly over the places that long experience had taught them did not usually hold, they came suddenly on a two-acre stretch of bog where the rushes had been cut. Little tufts of whin were scattered here and there in a way that did not make for easy shooting. Jer took the right and Paddy Byrne the left.

Scarcely had they entered the bog when two snipe went away wild and disappeared behind a furzy bank. Ignoring these, they pushed on quietly till —squeak! went a snipe that got up almost between them.

Jer fired, and dropped him successfully. The very essence of satisfaction, Jer thought, it being his snipe. So much more often his birds continued on through the swift, cut zigzag of their flight, uninjured.

A second bird got up at the shot, and succeeded in dodging Jer's left barrel. Then a whole wisp rose from a miniature pond in front of them. Paddy Byrne scored a splendid right and left, while Jer dropped a cartridge in the wet in his haste to reload.

That ended matters for the moment, except for a tiny Jack snipe which fluttered up at Jer's feet as he stooped to pick up a bird. The Jack, after the manner of his kind, went off more like a big moth than a bird. Jer missed him.

Now Rony, the riotous spaniel, having dashed off incontinent at the first shot, reminded them of his existence by a series of agonised yelps as he raced after a rabbit which had been lying out in a snug bunch of furze.

Alarmed at the idea of having to carry a rabbit so early in the day, Paddy Byrne watched Jer raise his gun, yet almost half hoping that he might shoot the dog, so close to the rabbit's scut. But Jer, with a muttered " Damn the dog! " lowered his gun, and

watched with some brutal satisfaction the adminis-
tration of justice through the buckle end of the
collar, applied with a severity which made that
hardened sinner Rony yell aloud.

This much accomplished, they proceeded to the
next likely spot.

Fewer snipe this time, but lying better. Jer missed
two easy shots, but was successful with a long one.
Paddy Byrne, as usual, scored. His bird fell in the
middle of a clump of furze and, search as they would,
they could not find him. Binty was at fault, and
Rony interested only in rabbits.

"Must be stuck on top of a bush somewhere,"
Jer said at last. "You go in and have a look."
But an extensive and prickly inquisition revealing
nothing: they were forced to abandon the search,
loth as they were to leave a dead bird behind.

Thus they went on shooting throughout the
morning. Few words passed between them. Talking frightens snipe almost more than shooting. Jer
loved snipe-shooting. Was it the fascination of the
bird himself, with his strange, harsh little cry, his
tiny body and peculiar flight? or what was it? The
bogs, with their pale grass and wine-dark water—
this indescribable faint smell, the very incense to
sport—God, it was good! Here was effort, and
forgetfulness.

It was one-thirty when they sat down to eat their
sandwiches, selecting a dry hummock with plenty
of furze to protect them from the cutting wind that
carried with it a rare, tiny flake of snow.

Unloading their guns, they sat down luxuriously
on the hard and knobby furze stumps. Paddy

Byrne produced sandwiches from a special pocket of the game-bag, and then tumbled out the snipe.

They counted them: two, three, four and a half couples and a Jack snipe. Not too bad. They should have had at least two couples more, though. As they munched their sandwiches they looked from the huddled bundle of snipe—beaks, wings and legs sticking out in all directions—to the cold pale bog and the colder sky.

When pipes were lit, Paddy Byrne produced a biscuit from an inner pocket, gravely throwing pieces to the wet, expectant dogs, that had lain, their huddled, shivering bodies tense in disciplined expectation, while their masters ate.

But now they must collect themselves with an effort and move off, stiffly enough at first. They had reached the top of this line of bogs, and light would not serve them so very much longer. On their way over a hill to shoot the bogs below it towards home, they got a couple of pigeons that had been gorging on indigestible turnip leaves. Their crops were so full that one of them burst on falling.

These bogs they were to work down were drier and more intermittent. Still, many of the snipe which had been risen in the morning were wont to light there. They would be wilder, of course, but they had the wind in their backs.

In an hour they had shot another three couples. Then the light became rapidly worse. Even Paddy Byrne missed many more than he killed. Still, they wanted to get their ten couples, so they pushed on, faster and faster, though they knew it was time to give in.

By four o'clock a flash of white and a squawk were all that betrayed a rising snipe. They had finished their snipe loads long ago, and were almost out of number six.

When they reached the bridge that marked the end of their shoot they had still only nine couple, yet as they trudged the road together it seemed to them that things were well enough. Seemingly tireless, Paddy Byrne strode on along the tiny curling roads towards home, and Jer, walking beside him, would not, for the world and all, have admitted that his feet were pinched and sore and his back ached just a little.

.   .   .   .   .

Now Jer was home at Sorristown, walking through back ways and long, clattering passages to the front of the house. The first thing to do when he got home was always to look at the post, with a hot anxiety to know if Mary had written, and a surer confidence that if Maeve had not written yesterday or the day before there would be a letter from her to-day. But first you looked for Mary's letter, and there had not been one from her yet, but it was coming one day, Jer knew. And to-day it was here: here to tell him with perfect baldness how she fared on this honeymoon of hers and Roguey's.

> Gerald Sorrier, Esq.,
> Sorristown House,
> Sorristown,
> Ireland.

And a foreign stamp on top of her queer, exquisite writing. Mary, darling one! Jer's excitement

157

almost hurt him. And then below Mary's letter
was one from Maeve too, large and promising, and
full, he was sure, of comment on Mary's and Roguey's
swift, unaccountable marriage. She would have
had just time to get his telegram and letter telling
her of it.

Instead of reading his letters at once, there in
the cold hall, Jer thought how much, how intensely
more delightful it would be to keep them unopened,
storing them until he had changed—even bathed,
perhaps, and had his tea. What comfort they would
be in the long evening that stretched before him!
Yes, he would keep them. And so he went into the
study, where the little people greeted him reproach-
fully, yet with a hauteur and a faint smell of cutlet
bones that suggested rather than proclaimed:

" Yes, you *did* go away and left us behind. But
we had quite a good day with our friend the cook.
Life has its little compensations."

Jer planted his two letters behind Roguey's cards
of hunting fixtures in much the same spirit as that
in which the Demon planted his moist cutlet bones
behind the sofa cushions: " I give you up, though I
yearn for you immediately. And why? That I
may enjoy you more intensely in the near future!"

All the time he was picking at his bootlaces with
numb fingers and discarding sodden stockings.
When he was soaking his body back to blessed
warmth in a hot bath, and trying not to bolt tea
too blatantly for his own self-esteem, Jer's excitement about Mary's letter rose and mounted in him.
Do you know, he asked the world—for which he
cared not now—I've had a letter from Mary?

D'you know? She said she would, and she has. It's wonderful. Past words. And he remembered Mary's good-bye when he saw herself and Roguey off on the boat—as far as that on the way she had insisted he was to come with them. Funny, she'd been; acting almost as if she was in love with Roguey. "Good-bye, Jer; such a help you've been—*darling*."

"Do-on't let Roguey keep you away too long," Jer had said, in the hopeless, jocular way one says these silly things.

"*Oh!*" Mary's face was suddenly blank and wild; she seemed a creature seeking escape indeed. He saw her eyes on the quiet sea, and madness sprang in her eyes, as if here she had found a way out.

"You're to come back quickly," Jer said, "to *us*, you know. We'll be waiting for you, you know, *Mary*." And Mary had understood him. The look of sudden wildness had died from her eyes—in them instead was not so much as hope, but less despair.

"I'll be back soon, Jer," she promised, "and I'll write and tell you, shall I?"

She seemed such a dim, caught creature, that Jer, though he knew better than anyone all her sad sinfulness, was filled with a wild championship for her unhappiness. "Good-bye," he said. He had to go. It was like saying good-bye to a dream. It was like leaving a child in distress. . . .

But now she had written, and Jer's excitement over her letter was the next thing to rapture.

In the study the fire blazed and his chair waited for him, a very expanse of comfort. With his two

letters in his hands he sat down, tearing her letter
open, awkward in his eagerness. And it was so
little; told nothing, nothing at all. " I might have
known," Jer reflected, " I might have guessed,
because what is there she can tell me? "

Disappointing things, letters are. You open
them, hotly expectant for the very self of the writer
and they give you almost less than nothing. He
read Mary's over again.

They were in Paris. She would see that Roguey
did not bore her there. Soon, now, they would be
home. How was Jer? She and Roguey were getting
on like flames—the ranks of the godly matrons was
not such a bad place, after all. (He heard Mary's
laugh in two crooked exclamation marks.) " I will
soon be back. I *know* you will be sweet to me.
We will have fun.

<blockquote>
" Darling Jer,
" Love from
" MARY."
</blockquote>

Well, rather a nice ending. He was comforted.
He read much that Mary had not written into the
meaning of her letter before he put it down and
opened Maeve's.

" MY DEAR JER,
" Rowley and I were so surprised to hear from
you about Roguey and Mary Fuller. How very
surprising it is! I hope Roguey won't be dis-
appointed in her. But I am sure she is very nice,
though I never liked her *quite* as much as you did.
I do hope they will get on well. You know you can

always come and live with Rowley and me at Castle
Fountain if Roguey doesn't want you at Sorristown
now that he is married. I am sending you a little
book of photographs. We have seen all these places.
I am so glad Aunt Evie is coming back to look after
you. When does Roguey come back? I haven't
heard from him, but of course he must be very busy.
We get back in about three weeks. It will be nice
to be hunting again. I hope your asthma has been
all right. Give my love to Aunt Evie when she
comes.

" Love from
" MAEVE."

What a nice letter! How sweet Maeve was! Of
course, she hated Mary really. Why should she like
her? Why, indeed, should anyone like that sad
and selfish nymph? Jer wondered. He thought of
the evening—so long ago it seemed now—when he
had gone to her room to tell her, somehow, something that would break matters up between her and
Roguey. A very mean idea of his it had been, too.
But that night his whole self was mad with nervous
temper and jealousy of Roguey. And he was fit to
cry like a child, he cared for her so dearly.

How dearly he cared he only knew when, with
blinding, dreadful enlightenment, he had realised
her need of Roguey—the absolute necessity to her of
Roguey, and of their immediate marriage. Jer had
said : " He's a—oh, hell of a fine fellow! . . . Yes,
you'll like him, Mary." To Mary one gave, not
necessarily the best of oneself, but all one had. And
in men's love for her the good went with the bad.

161

But to-night Jer was so tired. His two letters, read now, added more to his loneliness. They gave him so little of the great deal that he wanted. Their comfort was slim indeed. With a sigh for himself, Jer picked up the day's papers and read them, and slept, and read again. The evening stretched out vastly. Mrs. Squiffy, curled morosely in the chair opposite, regarded him with polite contempt. To her he seemed a very poor sort of creature. And with her low opinion of him Jer was in entire agreement.

CHAPTER XVI

IF winter had come to Co. Westcommon, all
thoughts of spring were shunned with loathing by the
greater portion of the community, of the right and
proper community who thought in terms of hunting,
and then of the greatest possible number of days
which could be fitted into the five possible months
of the year.

Already there had been that great run from
Kilooly covert, with its seven-mile point and hounds
rolling their fox over by the light of a rising moon,
no member of the field there to make a lifelong boast
of having lived with them till the end. Such a
scenting season it had been, since the curtain rose
on a bright opening as remained barely in the
memory of man. Anthony Countless, the master
and huntsman, who had shown sport for two seasons
under exceptionally bad scenting conditions, at last
came into his own. He was the best in the world
now, best huntsman, best man in Ireland. And
Anthony, outwardly taciturn and unapproachable,
was warmed and glad about the heart, for his
hounds' sakes. Not much of a lot to look at yet, no.
But they could kill foxes.

Nor was this great season the only excitement of
the countryside. There had been—besides Roguey
Sorrier's sensational marriage with the lovely

unknown, his sister's bridesmaid, a marriage con-
summated with a neglect of detail so sweeping as to
leave the obvious conclusion so obvious as to be
negligible—the birth of Prudence Sage's young son,
an event which threw the county in a ferment for
close on three days, Prudence being one of its best
loved and hated amusements. And now Maeve
and Rowley Fountain had returned to their hunting
from the honeymoon they both grudged the con-
ventions, and were duly expected to provide diver-
sion for their neighbours at Castle Fountain, a place
that had lacked a mistress far too long.

.   .   .   .   .

Maeve was at Castle Fountain. She was mistress
of Rowley's house. All her plans and dreams were
coming true. Her new clothes hung in ordered
precision in the great cupboards of the bridal chamber, where countless Mrs. Fountains had loved and
slept. Her photographs and scent and new tortoiseshell and silver were gleaming afar off on the bow-
fronted, slenderly vast dressing-table. Micky, her
black, sweet spaniel bitch, slept in her green basket,
caring nothing for her change of dwelling, so she
might sleep and eat and do an odd spot of work,
and not too much of that.

Maeve lay very quiet and still in bed, watching
the moonlight pacing slow slants across the floor,
listening to Micky breathing in her basket (she
couldn't hear Rowley breathing beside her); listening to the faint click of the dead fire in the grate.
Wide, wide awake and quite still. Thoughts rushed
through her brain, keying her up to vivid points of
memory or decision, regret or hope. . . .

Your honeymoon—you thought vaguely of your honeymoon all your life: of its joys or horrors, as the mood took you. But what you had never visualised were its dreadful moments of boredom, moments when you delivered yourself of words with travail unmitigated. You, whose look had been a flame, whose whisper of love had served for wit and wisdom, you found yourself suddenly unable to compete. It was as though a link had fallen out of a sure chain. You were left. Something you had relied upon within yourself to the extent even of not realising its presence was gone from you. You might pick up the ends one day, when you ceased to love so terribly, when you had learnt to love intelligently.

Still, things were good, were rich with interest and delight. The horses especially — Rowley's horses and her Old Tranquillity, rugged up as she had been when Maeve ran out to see her the morning after their return, her lean head dropped pleasantly over Maeve's shoulder, telling she was pleased with her new quarters, happy—at home. Such things are mercifully unalterable. Maeve had turned her back on the warm, airy box, with its good pungent smell, to watch a boy jog out a young horse for Rowley's inspection.

Rowley, standing there away from her across the yard, for the first time for weeks utterly occupied with something that was not herself—Maeve was suddenly, blindly aware of him almost as of a stranger. He had loved her and possessed her, and he was a stranger. How excellent his shoulders looked in that admirable and decaying tweed coat!

how aloof his square, pliant hands! how cold was his eye on that young horse going lame in front! how curt his dismissal of it to its stable! "Shall I come over and stand beside him?" Maeve had thought. "Shall I? shall I?" and then, "How awful it is how one can't forget love! Shall I go over now?"

But at that moment Jer had arrived—Jer, his dear, ordinary self, accompanied by the Demon and a small little, sour little string-bodied terrier that Maeve recognised after hesitation as Mrs. Squiffy.

"Hullo, Jer!"

"Hullo, Rowley! Had a g-good——" Jer found his best stammer and blushed.

"Slap yourself, Jer. Yes, we had a lovely time, darling. But I'm terribly glad to be back. Micky was nearly mad with joy to see me again. She hates Rowley worse than ever."

"Maeve, you look t-t-topping! T-tell me all about it."

"No, tell me all about Mary and Roguey."

They wandered off, leaving Rowley, his head bent, savagely intent on his horses, visiting each box in turn, his words of thoughtful admonition falling unheeded on the ears of his old stud-groom, who confided afterwards to a friend that marriage had made great wreck o' the major; he was as cross now as ye wouldn't believe.

Maeve remembered Rowley's difficult silence and premeditated questions at the luncheon that followed. That and dear Jer's stammer had had a most crushing effect on the general timbre of their intimacy.

The right impression of Mary and Roguey's
sudden love and marriage Jer utterly failed to get
across to his sister. Maeve, sitting serene and
chastely fair at the foot of her husband's table, old
oak the background for her grave yellow head, said
she simply didn't understand it.

"Of course, any girl might have fallen in love
with *Roguey*," she admitted; "but I shouldn't
have thought Mary was quite his type, that's
all."

"Roguey's had a d-dash at most sorts," Jer
reminded her. "Type's nothing to Roguey. Besides, Mary's wonderful. G-God! she's —she's——"

"Slap yourself, Jer. Rowley, is she really
wonderful?"

But Rowley, carving beef at the sideboard, had
not heard.

"Rowley, do you think Mary's frightfully attractive?" Maeve repeated, gravely insistent on an
answer.

"Don't know. Is to some people, I suppose."
Rowley shrouded himself once more in silence,
and left it to Jer's halting tongue to blunder
on the inexplicable rock of Mary's hold over
men.

"Well, I do wish I could see it; I must miss a
lot," Maeve complained gently at the end of Jer's
speech. "I've always thought her pretty and
attractive in a queer way (even if you don't, darling);
but she's so silly and untidy and helpless about
things generally." Maeve rose to juggle dexterously
with a coffee machine. "She'll *never* be able to
look after Roguey. Coffee, Jer? Sugar and just a

spot of coffee—that's right, isn't it? Darling, may we have the cherry brandy? Jer's a perfect whale on it."

Jer, cherry brandy and hot coffee percolating comfortably through his system, felt anew the total warmth and sureness of his love for Maeve. His love for Mary, different and strange and exciting, had met now its inevitable end; no, it was not ended, because he loved her still, though with confusion and disappointment in the place of trust and dimmest hope. He looked forward to her return to Sorristown, and hoped, with reservations, that she would be fairly happy with Roguey—unhappy enough, that was, to find out the useful strength of a brother-in-law's devotion.

After lunch they sat in Rowley's study, a charming place, its dull walls crowded with old prints: admirals of the fleet, ships, horses and hunting scenes—its leather chairs worn to an extremity of comfort. A glass-fronted fishing cabinet took up one wall—a wonderfully satisfying piece of furniture. Maeve, lighting her cigarette from a taper stuck in an old iron rushlight, spoke of doing up the room. She mentioned chintz and creamy paint and those Snaffles and Lionel Edwards pictures they'd had for wedding presents. Rowley, with Mrs. Squiffy established like a limpet on his chest, agreed unenthusiastically, till, as he saw Maeve curled down in the corner of the wide, deep sofa, he said, with sudden savagery: " Yes, I'd *like* this place changed; it's awful as it is. We must do something about it, Maeve."

Jer, looking from Rowley's hooded eyes to Maeve,

sweet and comfortable on the sofa, knew with sudden and intense understanding why Rowley wanted this room changed as entirely as might be. He saw Mary standing there in half darkness, half afraid and wholly adventurous, her silver dress dripping like moonlight; Mary trembling and waiting, Mary whom you looked at once wondering whether she was pretty, and twice to know that she was so lovely that you must take a third look and love her to distraction and sacrifice for ever after. He thought of Mary when she, too, loved and—no, he could never blame Rowley. But Maeve, poor Maeve!

" It's a bad thing," Jer thought, " to care about people so much that you learn something about their natures. The more you know about them the more afraid you are of them. Maeve is getting like that with Rowley. If only she'd crash along and be herself, and not study him. I wouldn't like to bet on her being happy now. She's got a terrific handicap to play off."

Aloud he said : " Mary's sent over bales of stuff for Sorristown. She'll have Roguey far more broke than he was over the new loose-boxes."

" Oh, Jer, I'm so glad ! I was afraid she wouldn't worry about the house. And I did like Sorristown to be nice. I hope she won't change the new chintz I put in the study before I got engaged to Rowley, though. It was such an uncommon design, and a grand background for dogs' footmarks, I think. I might get it for this room, Rowley. Would you like it, darling? "

" Don't remember it, Maeve."

" Oh, well, we'll look at it this evening, when we drive Jer back."

" I've got to go and see old Malone about having those earths stopped along the river." Rowley put down his paper. " I'll drop you and Jer at Sorristown and come back for you later."

Maeve sat in the back of the car with the dogs on the drive to Sorristown. Jer, an enthusiast about cars, occupied the seat beside Rowley, and in his interest almost forgot his stammer.

Back at Sorristown, Maeve had felt at once entirely alone and aloof, a sense of not belonging that amazed her. To return to the house of your youth after an absence of weeks only and find it antagonistic to your mood is a strangely unhappy experience. Impossible to define just whether Sorristown failed her or she failed Sorristown. Maeve, wandering about the house and stables with Jer, felt enormously how little she now belonged to the happiness of the place.

Aunt Evie in her month of ministration to Jer had faithfully resurrected many of the idols of her previous reign—idols whose heads had long been laid in the dust by Maeve. Of these, a yellow shawl draped chastely over a screen in the drawing-room was one, while another, a singularly unappealing photograph of the three orphans—herself, Roguey and Jer, ages varying from eight to one year— annoyed Maeve from its place of honour on what had lately been her writing-table in the study.

" Thought I'd burnt that." Maeve looked at it distastefully. " But oh, *Jer !* How could you let her? " The cry of horror was called forth by the

170

sight of an inevitable wedding group—herself, serene
and smiling, Rowley an almost inanimate droop,
flanked by girlish bridesmaids and chubby train-
bearers, which stood well in the centre of the mantel-
shelf. Maeve picked it up distastefully and put it
down again. Why, she could never have explained,
but this sudden sight of her own wedding seemed to
sever her from the intimate life of Sorristown, putting
her firmly and quietly down in her own new life,
where she was still so lost and buffeted about that
she could see no way clear before her.

"Well, Jer, my dear—— Why, *Maeve!* back
with us again! How nice! Now tell us all about
it. And did you enjoy yourself?" . . . Aunt Evie,
not having Jer's stammer to fall back upon, coughed
instead long enough to enable Maeve to forget to
answer her last question. "Well," she said, "you
look *blooming*, perfectly flourishing. I've just come
in from the garden, and what about tea?"

Tea was difficult. Maeve just remembered not
to sit behind the tea-pot, and ate brown bread and
honey and chocolate cake (giving the icing to Micky),
and answered Aunt Evie's questions, feeling suddenly as though she had returned to the schoolroom.
Finally the conversation lapsed into Aunt Evie's
remarking three times on end that it was odd
of Rowley to be so late—could the motor have
punctured?

It was in the warmth of the study after tea that
Jer got his first real sense of Maeve as she used to
be—the Maeve who had played with him patiently
all her life, before this tide of marriage had washed
her to a far, indefinite sea where perils, hidden from

her eyes by swathing mists of glamour, hemmed her narrowly round, threatening her dully on every side. Jer forgot this sad Princess Maeve as he sat beside his quiet and confidential sister, roasting and eating Spanish chestnuts in ash-smeared friendliness. No gold hair was ever half so crisp and smooth as Maeve's, no hand ever so dexterous with a chestnut, no mind ever so ready to embark on the great problems of life—such as the selection of one, out of the many possibles, as husband for Binty, his retriever bitch, the infertility of ferrets, or the application of sulphate of ammonia to the tennis courts. And Maeve, sitting in the firelight talking without brilliance and without restraint, knew for a fleeting second something like wild regret as they both heard the unmistakable note of Rowley's horn at the door.

Yet later she knew again that it was past words, away altogether beyond speech, to drive home with Rowley, together, alone. At least, so it should be, with the fogged rim of a moon shining for them behind dark hills, the warm gloom of the big car round them, and between them the love that impelled her suddenly to slip an arm through his and lean up to kiss very gently the back of his head.

" I love you," she whispered, leaning closer. " Say you do too, Rowley—say it, darling, *please !* "

" Silly little one. Silly, darling Maeve." Rowley spoke with a stiff lack of meaning in his voice as though to a doll; but he did not kiss her as though she were a doll.

The rocks that Jer had seen threatening and surrounding Maeve were hidden in the mist again, because when you loved you hadn't time nor wish to think. Things just were—till they were over; and you lay, as Maeve was lying now, quiet, quiet, still between your sheets, your mind flaming helplessly with the words Rowley hadn't said.

CHAPTER XVII

ON an evening in January, at the hour of seven-
thirty, the lovely room which Mary had evolved from
the refined discomfort and distinguished ugliness of
the Sorristown great drawing-room was empty.
Hushed in its warmth and scent of flowers, it waited
with inconsequent confidence the arrival of Mary's
guests, who were to feed at Sorristown before
proceeding to a hunt ball.

The drawing-room at Sorristown, with its high
walls half panelled in teak wood, had come under
Mary's hand to beauty. For longer than any of the
family could remember, the room had been considered impossibly and undefeatably repellent.
The upper half of the walls, papered brown to
match the panelling, held in murky indistinctness
the high-busted, *décolleté* portraits of the ladies of
the family. The tall bow windows that lighted the
room from one end only had been immemorially
curtained in sickly though rich yellow brocade,
looped up at regular intervals by pale green loops.
The perfect floor had long kept its boards virgin
beneath an expensive green-flowered carpet, and all
available space had been studiously filled by tables,
cupboards and chairs, some hopeless, some priceless,
all in their wrong places.

Now, under Mary's guidance, the room, like a girl

of accepted ugliness dressed suddenly in the right
clothes, had acquired an exciting beauty. To-night
long curtains of wood-smoke blue and rainbow flame
swept a soft chord of rich colour, shutting out the
thought of the night. The wide oval of a gate-
legged table stood in its mature grace across the
outcurved bow of the window-place; violets in
shining silver bowls blotted their colour and scent
against its dark wood, and illustrated papers, in
layered, gaudy profusion, kept their even, vivid ranks
upon it. Two wide low sofas of impossible depths
and redundancy flanked the enormous wood fire
at the precise angle for warmth and comfort, their
hollows wadded by loose cushions covered in silver
and blue and flame-clouded silk. The heterogeneous collection of furniture that had been vomited
by some god of disorder about the room was gone.
Grave, lovely pieces laid their quiet images in still
reflection on the bare dark floor, cupboards shielding
rather than showing their treasures of china and glass.
From the walls, warm cream now above their panels,
the ladies Sorrier deceased looked down with
smirking appreciation on the scented warmth of a
room in which their *décolletages* were at length
appropriate. Dull blue rugs were peaceful flats of
colour on the rich floor; and banked high against
the wall in one mass of feathered sweetness, yellow
freesias poured out their honeyed souls. The lights,
clouded through amber and iris and pale water-green
glass, shone on a confusion of lovely personal
possessions of Mary's—a jade box, a broken string
of amber beads, an immense brilliant bag—on a
dog's collar of vivid green leather (this vulgar

oddment belonged to Mrs. Squiffy), on a little wry-faced terrier dog (Mrs. Squiffy herself), curled, the image of contrariety and standoffishness, in a sunk corner of the largest armchair. But with a fresh, open fox-bite on her little scarred muzzle, Mrs. Squiffy might (being the heroine of the house and hour) do as she very well pleased, and very well she knew it.

Presently Mary came through the open door and slowly down the length of the room, criticising and enjoying its arrangement. She stood near the fire in a white dress that fitted and flowed from her body, and wore Roguey's pearls with priceless carelessness. Her small, squarely lovely face was grave under her paint, and her eyes as she looked round the divine room of her creation were almost serene. She switched off a distant light, and as she waited looked down on her hands with their heavy load of rings.

She smiled as Jer, having at last defeated his white tie, came into the room.

" All bugged up, darling? Jer, you look smashing, awfully good! "

" So do you, now I come to think of it. Oh, as an expectant mother you're past—past words! "

" Only two months gone, after all," Mary said carefully, straightening his tie. " Couldn't you forget it, Jer? You'll be talking about my interesting condition soon."

" Darling, am I ever coarse? "

" No. I'm so frightened of to-night's party. I shall have to cling to your neck all night, Jer. May I? "

" Oh, Mary, do! I've really washed it."

Roguey came importantly into the room. In his red evening coat he was a sight to thrill any really young girl.

"Now, you're not to stand about," he said to Mary, "I told you, Jer, she wasn't to stand about, and wherever I go I find her standing about. *Sit down!*" He picked her off her feet and with an arm under her knees sat her on the sofa. "I can't stop you hunting an' drinking an' dancing, but I *won't* have you standing about." He placed himself with his back to the fire and looked with enormous pride at Mary, sitting unprotestingly where he had put her. "Now I've seen to everything. I've seen to the drink," he announced boastfully. "And it's far too good to waste on these people. I saw to those oranges, too. Now, who's coming, Mary? Rowley's coming? That's right. Grand fellow, old Rowley! Rowley and Maeve, and who else? Tony Countless and Peter. That's right; got to have your M.F.H. to dine. Must talk to him, though; he's hunting down the other end too much—tell him to give us fair do's. Are Prudence and Toby coming? Now Prudence is a hell of a woman——"

"Shut up, Roguey! You've got verbal diarrhœa and a dam' loud voice to have it with—considering they're in the hall now." Mary got up and went across to the door without looking near Roguey. It hurt him, she knew, but then he shouldn't be so pestilently annoying.

Jer, listening to Mary's charming, anxious voice talking to the arrivals in the hall, was, well as he knew her complete nerve, struck to wonder by her calm on this evening when, for the first time since her return with Roguey, she and Rowley were to meet with enforced intimacy. Did she realise how difficult it was going to be? The situation was, to Jer's mind, impossible; and that the two people he loved most should be involved made it the more repellent, the only matter for thanksgiving being Maeve's utter ignorance of any situation at all. Knowledge could only defile Maeve through compliance or break her on inevitable disaster.

Mary's return to the drawing-room with four of her guests put a momentary end to Jer's misgivings. He must exert himself to talk, and talk was to Jer indeed an exertion.

"Jer, darling"—Mary rescued him from a nightmare hiatus in his greeting to Prudence Sage—"about those cocktails, old man?"

Thankfully as Jer departed on his mission to the dining-room, he would have given a good deal not to have been so complete a witness of the meeting between Rowley and Mary. He had expected it to be awkward, or bridged by overdone carelessness. But he had not expected it to be painful. As he came back to the room behind his tray of glasses he saw, as though a stage were set, Maeve and Rowley, the last arrivals, and Mary coming forward to greet them.

They might have managed it better, those two. Rowley's dark face was so void of expression that a fool—any fool, Roguey, Maeve, even—might have seen there matter for thought. And Mary? Under her paint her colour flamed up pitifully. She was still helpless.

The ringing crash of two cocktail glasses were

Jer's alleviation of a situation which, as a matter of fact, appeared strained to three only of the company—two of which were Rowley and Mary, and the third himself.

" Hullo, Rowley! " Mary was saying. " Awfully glad Maeve succeeded in dragging you here at last."

" Oh, he came one day, Mary "—Maeve wouldn't have her sister-in-law hurt by any seeming carelessness of Rowley's—if she could guess the struggle to get him to this party to-night!—" but you were out, you know."

"Yes," Rowley said, suddenly tired of being accounted for, " it was a bad show, missing you. I've *wanted* to see you ever since you came back." Then, because Mary looked at him with as much expression in her eyes as you will see in two glasses of cold water, he added, shaken by an unreasoning wish to hurt: " You and Roguey were away such months, weren't you? "

" Yes,"—Mary looked with shy affection to where Roguey was standing explaining to Prudence Sage the correct method of bringing up babies—" we had the *devil* of a honeymoon."

That was one up to Mary, anyway, she decided, as she collected people to go in to dinner. This desire to hurt was a new dreadful thing, born suddenly in her because of Rowley's nearness and hopeless distance, his competence to keep a hard line drawn between them. She wanted that line there, too—of course she did—but it must be drawn by herself alone. What possible right had Rowley to look at her with eyes that said: " I have no interest "?

Love died—she knew that. If you are an optimist you begin it again with someone else, but never can you put the clock back with the same person. No, she didn't want to, she didn't *want* to; but after everything there must be more between them than this difficult sufferance, this ragged, hurt feeling of defence. Dead love is a kind, quiet thing; it regrets, but gently and with a smile. That is dead love. Mary, looking suddenly towards Rowley sitting on her left hand, and deep now in talk with Prudence Sage, felt immediately and devastatingly afraid. She felt in danger—there was no safety for her in the hold of beautiful stable things. Sorristown, that she was making so gracious and lovely a house; Roguey, who was so terribly, utterly happy with her; Jer, who loved, if he did not trust her—if only these things had their hold fast rooted in; but they had no hold. Nothing had any hold. Everything broke away. You were incomplete. Shivering and forgetting, Mary plunged into a splendid conversation with Anthony Countless, the M.F.H., who sat on her right hand.

Maeve, across the table, shuddered with pity for the totally marvellous things her sister-in-law had to say about fox-hunting. But Anthony, with lovely Mary to look at, enjoyed himself very much, and found in her an intelligent if illiterate seeker after truth.

"Yes, *I* remember"—Mary recalled a hunt—"we ran across those fields at the back of Castlerellis and jumped the most awful fences, and finally we went to ground in a rabbit-hole, do you remember?"

"You and I together, Lady Sorrier? How *ripping* of you!"

"No, but I remember that smug-faced, pug-faced, snipe-nosed hound—d'you know the one I mean, a whitey hound? Well, that hound was *marvellous!*"

"B'gad, you're right, too." Anthony swallowed his soup quite excitedly. "Woodlark—a grand bitch! Yes, she had a line of her own that morning, carried it across a bank and threw her tongue in the next field and put them all right. She's a *hell* of a bitch!"

"Yes, and so awfully nice for you to have one different from the others—one you can always know—isn't it?"

"Yes, most convenient." Anthony was solemn.

"Why, I knew her even——" On the sacred subject of hounds Mary was simply indefeatable. Anthony was quite sorry when they wandered therefrom, via subsoils and kennels water-supply, to his hostess's bathroom—the latest room at Sorristown to be recreated by Sorristown's new mistress.

"Green and amber," Rowley heard, ceasing for a moment from his efforts with Prudence, "an' bath salts to match—Roguey bought me nearly a ton when we were in Paris——"

When they were in Paris! And Rowley had shut his mind to any thought of Roguey and Mary in Paris or elsewhere. He remembered the moments, drenched in nearly terrible regret, in which during the past months he had tried to forget what he had done to her. How he had sweated blood, blood and loathing of himself, and pity for her (poor rash, lovely her!). Now to realise that she was indeed one of those rare women, who can look on love as an episode—an artistic achievement bought, as he very well knew, at one price only—the highest price of all, disillusionment. This, which he had not even hoped for, he now hated in her. Meeting her narrow eyes, listening unwillingly to the hesitating, husky voice, Rowley realised something else, something which again complicated their relationship to one another. She was now to him so unattainable that her very aloofness constituted a challenge daring him to forget. She was now far less his than if he had never had her gift of love. Love was no longer there between them. But there was something else—an insurmountable difficulty of approach, a deadly interest that kept them apart yet refused to let each go his own separate way. He did not say it to himself. He would never own it to her. He must be strong, and kill without hesitancy that which rose up in him, proclaiming against any odds that they two belonged. He might love her or hate her, but his feeling for her could never reach that stage of light tolerance which is a man's defence against a woman he has loved too much.

At any rate, Rowley decided, farcical as things between them might be, there was no point in rendering their difficulties apparent to others. He leant towards Mary, just an instant after his wife had noticed their silence. " You've done wonderful things to Sorristown," he said, conversationally.

"What, Rowley? I'm *still* jus' a little deaf." Mary's tone was one of apology. " Oh, to the house? Yes. Roguey likes it awfully. I suppose

Maeve's been making herself hated at Castle Fountain in the same way." She faced him with level eyes, furious with herself because she could not feel indifferent.

" I love *change*," she said, and looked down at her hands again, hoping now that he would not realise the indifference she had meant to convey.

" We're in the middle of doing Rowley's room," Maeve struck in helpfully, " aren't we, darling? Do you know it, Mary? It's that dreadful old hole that looks out at the back. Rowley won't even keep the old sofa there, and it's the *most* divinely comfortable thing in the house. Everything has to be changed."

" No, I don't think I know it, do I? " Mary looked from Maeve to Rowley with a hopeless lack of interest. Rowley, his eyes stubbornly down, saw her whitened knuckles gripping the edge of the table. Suddenly he knew that he couldn't bear her to be hurt; that Maeve was a damned fool to go on rubbing things in; that—curse it!—something had to be done about it. He must speak to her. To-night.

But Mary was beyond Rowley. He could not compete. All at once she grew into the life, soul and centre of the party. Every one was round her, but none could get near her. It was a sudden way she had of doing things that defeated the rest; a silly story she told Anthony that no one else quite heard; the vagrant rash way she stirred champagne with a fork and drank, laughing and lifting her eyes to Roguey. Roguey was drunk with her—adored her, any one could see that. Jer said: " Mary, shall I

183

do this or that?" "Mary, what shall we do about
the other?" The two brothers were so sweet in
their ways with her, telling stories that centred
always round what Mary did or said or how she
made a fool of herself. She was Sorristown's radiant
treasure—lovely and honourable and theirs. Rowley
saw her, after dinner while he waited in the hall for
his car. She stood half-way down the dark stairs,
wrapped preciously away in white fur. Roguey
came down behind her and stood over her for a
moment, possessively, without a word. He did not
ask for anything. That was enough. Mary called
up to Maeve, who was still upstairs: "I'm going
on. Roguey is taking me, after all," and they came
down, past Rowley in the hall, gave their joint
instructions to old White who stood at the door, and
went down the steps of their house together. Rowley
saw Roguey put his wife into the car and take the
rug from White to wrap round her, saw him drive
her away into the night; and, turning, found
Maeve, who had never yet kept him waiting for
anything, standing, beautiful and secure, beside
him.

. . . . . .

Maeve, on her arrival at the house where the
hunt ball was already in progress, found Mary in
the cloakroom, making a scene about her suspenders,
which had, it seemed, played her very false.

"But I drove here with Roguey," Maeve heard
her tell the rest of the party when, at last restored to
safety, she joined them round a fire. "So he can't
pretend I'm not an honest woman. Can you,
Roguey?"

184

Her speaking eyes refused to admit any really scurrilous import in her words. But Rowley in a dead white voice said to Maeve: " Come and dance," and took her away at once. They were dancing before Maeve's blush had time to die on her white neck.

" Oh, Mary, aren't you—oh—aren't you awful! "

" Don't care, Jer. Let's dance. Shall we? "

" D-don't care—slipped up on the t-tarmac," Jer reminded her sombrely as they reached the crowded floor.

" Well, don't let me down on this floor, darling. Roguey'll half kill you if you do."

" I'll never l-let you down, Mary, or give you away, or anything else."

" Oh, Jer, you are sweet! Such a help, you are! You almost make me believe in myself sometimes."

" Don't hurt yourself, Mary. Who's worth it? "

" You can't help yourself when you're me," Mary said, with solemn eyes. She stiffened helplessly in his arms as Maeve and Rowley passed close to them, and Jer knew she was hurting herself again—as she always would. As only he knew she would. Those who suffered because of her might think of Mary that she hurt others, herself she could not hurt; but Jer, knowing her better than those who had loved her more closely, knew that she hurt herself perhaps most deeply. A puppet pulled on the wires of her own helpless emotion, she was; defiant of the world; shrinking with despair from her most critical audience—herself. Maeve, with her staid principles and sure affection, searching her own heart for the cause of unhappiness, would never suffer as Mary, taking all with both greedy hands, would still know suffering.

" Jer—and you never *used* to dance! " Maeve's tone was almost one of censure as she met her young brother at the conclusion of his dance with Mary.

" Well, I only dance with Mary," Jer stated in awkward extenuation.

" Oh! " Maeve felt forlorn. This Mary—she'd spoil Jer, with her beauty and her low stories and everything about her so strangely unlike the companionable things she and Jer had enjoyed all their lives together. Maeve, watching Mary's slender, strong body, knew that had she herself been expecting a child she would not have rushed about to dances, or bought new intoxicating dresses which would certainly be out of the question before they could be worn three times. No, she'd have stayed at home quietly with Rowley and worn any old and comfortable dress.

Roguey touched her on the arm. " Hullo, Maeve! We must dance. Isn't Mary looking marvellous to-night? By Gad, y'know, she's wonderful—marvellous! Oh, you don't *know*. Maeve—look here, Maeve." Roguey sat himself down determinedly, turning up the tails of his coat. " God, y'know, I do want a drink. She hates me drinking whisky, though. Y'know she *is* looking crashing to-night—only woman in the room worth looking at. She shows me all her dresses—asks me which I like. And, mind you, she's not one bit extravagant—buys her garters from Woolworth. She has an innocent *mind*; but she's so *wild*—do anything you dared her to. Little tiger to ride——"

" Are we going to dance? "

" Oh, well, y'know, I only dance with Mary these times."

" Why don't you go and *dance* with her, then? " Maeve was unspeakably hurt.

" Oh, rot! Can't do that. I'm not going to leave you alone, Maeve, dash it! Well, I'll just see if she *is* dancing——" Roguey moved off.

Left alone, Maeve gazed for an inattentive moment at the throng that danced past her, each couple so solemnly intent on movement. She didn't see Rowley among the crowd of red-coated men. But Mary she saw, dancing now with Anthony Countless. Anthony (whose dancing even his adoring wife, Peter, did not encourage, it being of the more aggressive fox-hunting type, elbows and legs its predominant elements) appeared to be having the evening of his life. Anyway, he loved dancing with Mary.

" Maeve "—Jer came up to her—" won't you dance now, Maeve? "

" No, thanks awfully, Jer."

" I'd love to d-dance with you, Maeve; d-d-d-*oo*——"

" Slap youself, Jer. I will later on. If you really want to."

" Oh, Maeve! I—I'll come over and see you to-morrow. Mary and Roguey are hunting."

" Yes, come, Jer. Rowley has to go to Dublin."

Jer contemplated the prospect of a day with Maeve with entire satisfaction. " I'll tell you *all* about Roguey and Mary," he volunteered.

" *Do* tell me."

187

" Well, y'know, she's *marvellous*."

" I *know*," Maeve sighed.   Had it all got to begin again?

" Well, but, Maeve, d'you realise Roguey's stone sober to-night?   But, dammit, it's the first hunt ball for years he hasn't been t-t-tight.   Well, isn't it? "

" Rot! "

" S'not *rot* "—Jer was huffed—" 's'truth."

" Well, I always knew Roguey could take a pull on himself if he wanted to."

" Well, and who made him want to?   M'm . . ."

Jer's triumph was somewhat spoiled by his fruitless efforts to produce the name of the witch who had brought about this happy state of affairs.   Neither Maeve nor any other should fail to acknowledge all the vast of good there was in Mary, his beloved. Even Maeve must be brought to realise that Mary had to be forgiven everything, always.   It was her right, given to her along with her charmed ways.

" Does she look after you when you have asthma, Jer? "

" I never tell her."

" Well, she might see for herself."

" Oh, dear——" Jer feeling it all to be most painful, sighed and ceased.

.   .   .   .

Mary and Rowley were dancing together.

Maeve, disliking Mary to the helpless point of wishing Rowley would not dance with her, had, after a struggle, trampled on her own feelings in the matter and suggested, during a lull in the party's hilarity, that he should do so.

" Haven't been able to get near you all the

evening," Rowley explained, aware of a sudden shock of expectancy in the silence. " Am I too late to improve things? "

" Well, second extra," Mary said sweetly, after a grave consultation of her programme. How great an effort it had been to swamp the sulky desire (fit only for a slighted maiden of seventeen) to say : " So sorry, *absolutely* full up," only she knew. Oh, Rowley, *why* did he make you feel such a kid? So useless and unhappy and full of that horribly girlish excitement. It wasn't *fair*. Remember, *you* were lovely and broke hearts. Remember— you must remember—and keep yourself safe.

And now they were dancing. And it was worse— or was it far, far better—than either of those two had thought it could be. All the strain between them dropping suddenly away as they were alone, close together, they fell to talking, strangely intimately, ridiculously.

" Why did you look at me as if you hated me? All night you have. Yes, you said it as plainly as if you'd spoken. Didn't you? "

" Rowley, Rowley. No, I never meant it."

" Are we friends? No, really, are we? "

He wasn't making love to her. They were closer together than that. More in intimacy and at peace than on that last evening when they had danced and loved each other. Why had it come so suddenly, this feeling of still content, when for months now the thought of him had been a twisting hurt in her mind, and he had known the thought of her and Roguey choking him nearly with intolerance, sending his blood hammering and raving through him?

She shouldn't have hurt him like that—not fair.
But now they were together again, and he must see
more of her. Must. Had to. So he said again, his
eyes trying to meet hers: " We're just the best
friends in the world, aren't we? "

And Mary, knowing as well as he did how sublime
a hoax is that much-abused form of friendship, but
how useful a purpose it may serve, meaning as much
or as little as the players in life's most entrancing
game may admit it to mean, said:

" That's right, Rowley. Best pals in all the world,
we are, darling." Knowing then, with pain like
sudden blindness, that he didn't want to be friends—
knowing that what he wanted was something else,
but no responsibility—she said, with seeming irrele-
vance that nevertheless bit and stung as she had
meant it should:

" But there's Roguey now, and Jer and Sorristown—oh, I can't explain! But they've been so
good to me."

Rowley said sombrely: " I've got Maeve—Maeve
is the most wonderful wife in the world."

And their little, bolstered-up pretences shrunk
away, leaving them each so much alone that it was
frightening. Just why is it so appallingly difficult
to get what one really wants from life? An hour
ago Mary had known that all the light in the world
was gone because Rowley, she thought, no longer
loved her. Now she knew he loved her, but to what
end? Selfish swine, men were. Why must he
have flooded her whole being again with need of
him if after that all he could do was to talk about
Maeve, his wonderful wife? No, it was better to

end things—end them here and right now. No more
of this divine, precarious intimacy.

" I'm going to have a baby," she told him, without
preamble.

" Not *mine* ? " There was a glory and an intimacy
alive now in his voice. Suddenly the thought of
what might still be came helplessly on him.

" No, oh, *no !* " Mary lied primly. " Roguey's."

" Good luck to it, darling."

She had done it. Rowley had in one moment gone
as much as a hundred miles away from her. Well,
he could go. He might stay with his wonderful
Maeve. Mary had Jer. Mary had Roguey. Mary
had a baby coming (that would never be born now
if by hunting she could help it)—a baby the idea of
which she'd rather liked up to one wild minute ago.
Oh, God! the cruelty, the pain, the brief, brief
happiness. Who is able to compete with the things
life does to you all in a moment, before you can
draw breath or change your mind?

" Roguey, I'm so *tired ;* take me home, darling,
will you, please? "

Mary's whole mind was a stiff blank, as cold as
her body; her throat hurt her in a queer, terrible
way, as though she was going to cry. If Roguey
argued with her she knew she would cry, and if he
took her away she would cry because everything
was so hopeless, because everything shrieked and
hurt. Because her dance with Rowley had ended
on such a note of sick uncertainty. Because things
could never be any better.

But argument was far, far from Roguey's mind.
To get the car and take her away and have her by

himself was all he asked, ever. The moments when
he slammed the door on her white fur back, leaving
behind all the people whom she charmed so excessively, and who came even superficially between
them, were the moments he prized highest among all
their hours together. Her long, casual silences he
loved; herself; her lovely clothes; her sufferance
of his love-making, sometimes a little weary as if she
dared him to thrill her. To-night, all the long drive
back to Sorristown, he supposed her to be asleep,
and when they arrived home would have lifted her
out of the car and carried her indoors, but she was
out and stumbling stiffly up the steps, in her high-
heeled shoes, before he could get round to her.

Half an hour later Roguey, a barbaric figure in
flaming pyjamas, came into their room. Mary,
standing over a dead fire, still in her white fur coat,
looked at him with frozen eyes.

" Mary, why aren't you in bed, darling? Aren't
you terrible? God! you're as cold as ice. Have
you got a chill? *Are* you feeling cold? "

" Oh, I'm so *cold*, Roguey." Tears slipping under
Mary's eyelashes, slipping down her face, blurring
her beauty. Her hands, damp and blue with cold,
her white feet stiff and shiny—no wonder Roguey
loved her. Rolling down the mist of her silk stockings, his mind fumbling at the intricacies of the
scented, soft rainbows that covered her pale body,
Roguey put her at last into her nightdress that lay,
crushed and sweet (she had slept in it for two nights),
on her turned-down bed, in which at last he laid her.

Heaping her fur coat across her over a purple
eiderdown, he dosed her with much brandy, and

held her in warm and kind, not passionate, arms until, with tears now drying in salty tracks round her mouth, she slept at last.

Roguey loved her to-night past bearing. Because she was shaken from her difficult, estranging beauty to tears that he could comfort, she made him a king, a very hell of a fellow. With vain self-vauntings he rehearsed in his mind the words which should convey to her in the morning his unalterable decision that she was not to hunt that day.

CHAPTER XVIII

JER turned his little car round on the gravel sweep in front of Castle Fountain and walked under the stone canopy, wide enough to allow a carriage and horses to drive beneath it in the old days, into the house. Maeve was standing in the hall, with a basket in her hand, and was calling the dogs as if bent on some excursion lengthy enough to justify exercising them all. Jer thought she looked a little white and strained; that might have been owing to the dance the night before, but whenever had a dance eclipsed Maeve's radiant and unalterable health? She was lovely, though, coming down the hall to meet him. The original Henry Heath hat shaded her deep eyes with becoming gravity, if its lines did belong to a mawkish yesterday, when people wore different hats for gardening from those they wore for any normal occasion. Maeve wore, too, a loose jersey and a jumper with a bright pattern round the hips and woolly bobbles at the neck— her white neck, that had the same strong, pure lines as a bird's throat.

"Hullo, Jer!" Maeve picked up a reddy, fawny silk handkerchief, knotting it round her throat, and slid her large, graceful hands into cavernous gloves. "D'you feel strong enough to walk? Have an apple?" She gave him, after careful selection, the

best one in her basket. " Because I have to go up
Coolcarry Hill with a message for Rowley."

" Can't I drive you ? "

" Oh, let's walk. I want to take the dogs. I
promised Rowley I'd exercise them."

They started on their walk in silence—down a wet
avenue shaded by heavy beech trees, the afternoon
sun showing patchily through their black, shiny
twigs and silver branches. The little dogs, longing
to be off hunting, but fearful of missing a better
draw than the home coverts, kept circumspectly in
sight, coming when called with misleading obedience.

" Mrs. Squiffy is a funny little dog," said Maeve
suddenly. She thought it really rather a subtle way
of bringing the conversation round to the subject of
Mary. She hated talking about Mary, but she also
hated not talking about Mary.

" Yes, she's a queer one," Jer assented, adding :
" She bites me, but she'll go anywhere with Roguey."

" She didn't come with you to-day ? "

" No, she stayed with Mary."

" I thought Mary and Roguey were hunting with
Toby's harriers to-day." Maeve slowly began to
feel pleased that Jer had removed himself from the
charmer's society to her own.

" Well, she was g-oing to, but Roguey made her
stay in bed—she was bet up after last night."

" Of course she shouldn't hunt," Maeve said in
a flat voice of disapproval which disposed of the
subject. " Rowley's hunting to-day, too. Toby's
mounting him. It's too far to send a horse on.
But he wanted to have a day with Toby, so he put
off going to Dublin."

" Yes," Jer said politely. They walked single file
up a deep lane with half-dead brambles crushed by
rain masking its banks—a wet, stony, winding way
with a soft, heavy sky above, and sometimes when
the banks were lower a glimpse of dark, wet hills.
Two white goats, smelling dreadfully, clanked
solemnly before them till they found a gap through
which their couples and spancles would allow them
to go. The little dogs, sometimes shrill with excitement, pursued their own devious, important paths.
It was nothing extraordinary in the way of a walk,
but Jer, remembering Mary's warm, complicated
room where he had so nearly stayed, felt suddenly
happy to be walking with Maeve—a mild, suffused
content which had something of the peace that
rewards virtue in it, because he had *wanted* to stay
with Mary.

Maeve's message accomplished, they walked back
again. A different way this time, through a wood
in which there ran a deeply sunken stream; across
this obstacle it was important to see which dog did
the best jump. Naturally this delayed matters,
because two dogs, Maeve's spaniel and a buccaneer-
ing outdoors terrier of Rowley's, jumped it at once,
and immediately proceeded to hunt rabbits, while
one timid lady could not be persuaded to throw her
heart over and herself after it, in spite of every
blandishment and encouragement. When at long
last the horrid feat was accomplished, neither sign nor
sound of the two hunters was to be seen or heard.

" Come on, it's past tea-time, and they'll be back
before us, probably," Maeve said at last, after much
unavailing calling and whistling.

Half-way home through the wet, dark wood she wheeled round to Jer with a sudden movement that startled him.

"Jer! I quite forgot Rowley wanted to shoot this to-morrow; he'll be furious with me for taking the dogs through—disturbing any pheasants there are. What a *fool* I am!"

"Don't tell him," Jer suggested practically; "he won't ask you where you've been."

Maeve said nothing, but her silence conveyed quite enough disapproval to embarrass Jer.

When, half an hour later, Rowley came in to tea, full of the pleasant importance of one who has seen a good hunt while others have remained at home, Jer was hardly even surprised that almost Maeve's first words were a confession of her misdeed.

"Oh, that's rather a bore!" A swift shade of annoyance clouded and settled in Rowley's eyes. He said no more about it, and Maeve, Jer could see, was proportionately miserable. How absurdly difficult things were! Jer thought, looking at Rowley, who had nothing to give either of the two Sorriers, but sat in his old leather chair, being sweet to the loving little dog who shared it with him. Rowley, with his charm and his strength and his selfishness, his strange attractive face that could light up so marvellously for Mary, who could not bore him, and his voice, so helplessly cold to Maeve and so full of changing kindness for his little dogs. Jer's thoughts swung suddenly to Mary at Sorristown; Mary so brilliant and so unsuccessful, so rich with love and so incomplete. *She* wouldn't have cared two hells if she *had* annoyed Rowley. She wouldn't have

drooped over the teapot or fussed about the toast;
she'd have said something hopeless and uncon-
tradictable about it, or more probably never
admitted the offence at all. And Rowley, with her
there, would have been different altogether. It was
sad, Jer thought, and though he tried to cherish
anger against Rowley he couldn't do it. Rowley
had acted like a bounder, to Jer's mind, but he had
not acted in character. No, it is hopeless to vex
oneself by sorting the good from the evil with
charming people of no principle. Because, having
no motive, they act from impulse, and never fear
results, either for themselves or anyone else.

But Jer feared—he more than feared—for Maeve's
happiness. Maeve had given all she knew how to
give of love to Rowley. And, dimly as Jer knew it,
love is the frailest globe that can contain utter
delight. If you are a wise woman, you hold it
carefully in your two hands, keeping it apart from
yourself. So only will it endure. Do not crush
love to your heart, giving it with a wild generosity
all that you have and are. All that you have is
taken and taken again, but the gleaming distant
entirety of love is spoilt, and Passion swoons, and in
dying pierces the breast where it has lain in stilled
enthralment.

But Jer, eating his toast and jam and drinking hot
tea, only knew that things were so difficult already
between those two, that his presence as a third party
was certainly welcome to Rowley, who even roused
himself to the extent of talking with charm and
interest on subjects fit for Jer's limited intelligence.
That is to say, he did not talk about hunting or

horses, but, with his shoulders sunk back into his chair and a cigarette hanging between his fingers, he caused Jer to inform him on many topics of importance : such as the numbers of snipe in certain bogs, the number of miles Jer's Austin Seven did to the gallon, the alteration to Jer's gun, lately completed, and kindred matters.

When Jer said good-bye he felt more than ever the strain between Rowley and Maeve. Maeve, he knew, was only longing for him to take his departure, so blind was the trusting assurance that her love gave her. When he was gone, Rowley would kiss her in the firelight and breathe her name : " Darling Maeve——" and all would be very well. But Jer knew that Rowley had no impatient desire for lovemaking. There was none of that " get out of it, for God's sake, and let me have her to myself " look, that came so often into Roguey's eyes (unless Jer was marvellously circumspect), in Rowley's long-drawn-out farewells. On those occasions at Sorristown Mary would be either utterly unconscious or a trifle amused, but always she made things easy. That was her great gift—making impossible things easy, and difficult places silly or funny. Maeve could never do that. She loved. She had. And what she had she gave.

Now, when Jer had at last gone, she stood beside Rowley in the dusk of the porch, slipping a hand into his. Rowley patting it, gave it back to her, and announced absently that he must go round to the stables. " I'll come." Maeve's mind reached towards a battered old fur coat hanging in darkness.

" Oh, no, why bother? I shan't be five minutes.

It's beastly cold." Rowley's voice was so determinedly dissentient that Maeve slipped away from
him quietly, and when he had gone—hurt, wounded
and with a dry, unapproachable fear curling up her
heart—she stumbled twice over familiar rugs on her
way back to the fire. Kneeling there, her yellow
head bent down, her heart was shaken out of all
proportion, because Rowley had not asked her to
go with him. It was absurd. It was ridiculous.
But struggle how she would, Maeve could see no
reason why, no way to meet this cruel matter.
Rowley hadn't wanted her.

.   .   .   .   .   .

In Mary's room at Sorristown Roguey sat, importantly discussing the day's hunting. Mary was
sitting up in bed, her hair feathering up round her
head, her smooth arms bare to the shoulders of
severe satin pyjamas. Spread out upon her purple
eiderdown was an ordnance map of the county, upon
which she was endeavouring to measure a point,
and to reconcile the map and Roguey's statements.
Argument relative to point, place and time she found
difficult, especially as Roguey preferred looking at
her to looking at the map.

" Well, if you *must* hear about this hunt, at least
let me kiss you at the checks." Roguey slipped his
hand between the warm firm pillow and Mary's
warm smooth back.

Life was good, too good. To have had a day
like this one; to have ridden that hunt as a good
man should with quick decision and sure judgment; to have forgotten everything but the glory
and interest of the hounds and their work—this

was to Roguey a fierce fulfilment and a hallowed satisfaction.

When he came into her room, tall and superb, still in his breeches and red coat, Mary, with appreciative eyes for his long lean lines, and a little lonely owing to Jer's desertion, had been kind; pleased when he kissed her, his face cold with the cheerful chill of a day spent in the open.

Roguey, hotly contented with the day's sport, happy and tired, sat by her blazing wood fire with Mrs. Squiffy on his knee, lulled by the scent and colour in her room and by the sight of her, so precious, so wonderful to him, adorably interested in his doings. God! it was worth anything, *any-thing* to have her there.

Now, leaning over her, his head bent down beside her cheek, he waited a stilled second, then pushed away the map she was still pretending to study. " Love me," he whispered quite low. " I—love you so *awfully*——"

" Look out! " Mary slipped away from his arms, frowning at him as Jer's hasty knock sounded on her door. " Come in."

" God *damn !*——"

" Oh, sorry! C-can I sp-eak to you, Roguey? "

Jer was still in his big coat; his hair stuck up untidily at the back of his head, and in the dim shaded light of Mary's room his face looked queerly pinched and white.

" What's up, Jer? " Two little bright sparks of colour sprang into Mary's cheek-bones. Something *was* up, she knew.

" N-nothing "—Jer fought down his stammer—

" only Paddy Doyle wants to see Roguey before he goes home."

" Oh," Mary said. " How's Maeve? "

" *Are* you coming, Roguey? "

Jer stood in the open door, very still, ignoring Mary's last question. Urgency was in the air.

" You'd better go and see old Doyle," Mary said from her pillows; " but come back when he's done with you." She joined the tips of her fingers together thoughtfully and shaped her mouth to a kiss for him. Then, remembering Jer was still there standing in the doorway, she blushed and turned her head away. She hated Jer to see her at any of those light tricks of love, which were so much a part of her that she could no more help using them than Maeve could help flinching from the thought of Rowley perhaps not loving her.

But Jer, when Roguey at last rose and followed him from the room, had far other things to possess his mind than the thought of Mary, although the thought of her was indeed at the back of all this trouble.

" Where's Doyle? " Roguey asked.

" It's not Doyle——" Jer opened the door of the bathroom and waited for Roguey to follow him inside.

" Now, what the devil's the matter? " Roguey began wordily. " I don't see the point of all this mystery. Why couldn't you say whatever you wanted to say in Mary's room? Now for God's sake slap yourself, Jer, and don't start that damned stammering."

Jer hardly seemed to hear Roguey; he looked

rather white and sick, and fiddled helplessly with the hot-water tap, his head bent down. When at last he spoke it was in a stream of words, his stammer almost eclipsed. As Roguey listened to him, his young careless face grew curiously blank, then horrified, incredulous, and lastly obstinate.

"I won't go," he said as Jer ended. "Too damn late. Too cold. Too tired. Can't leave Mary. No, dammit, why *should* I go?"

"She's *dying*, y'know," Jer said.

"*Dying?* Well, the whole place'll be rotten with priests. *I'm* not going."

"*Roguey*"—Jer was nearly crying—"Jerry Conroy says it's, it's, *it's*——"

"For God's *sake* try and say what you mean."

"He says it's not like a person at all." Jer rushed out the words in dreadful sick confusion. He sat down on the edge of the bath, his hands sweating against the cold china.

Roguey's lips felt stiff and slimy; his whole being was shaken as if by sickness. He cleared his throat painfully, trying to find a voice, and said at last: "What do you think you mean?"

"I'm telling you, damn you. Your beastly bastard's a beastly deformity, and the girl's dying. Is that plain enough for you? There's the end of your dirty rotten ways." Jer was sobbing now with rage. He had lost his temper to match Roguey. "You swine!" he sobbed.

"Shut up!"

"Shut up, yourself, you—you—— Are you going down to see Jerry Conroy?" Jer asked, catching desperately at calmness.

" I'm not."

" Some one's got to."

" Why in hell should I? Where is he? God, I can't see him! I can't deal with this." Roguey looked wildly about Mary's lovely bathroom. " God, y'know, this is more than any fella can stick! " He sat down, his shoulders bowed together, his young face broken up by suffering. Jer, meeting his eyes, felt suddenly terribly sorry for Roguey; for his careless rottenness that had brought him this ghastly thing.

" *Mary*," Roguey said suddenly, and all that mattered in this world was in the way he said her name. " Doesn't it—— If she heard—*God*, the way she is, it might make her—make it—— Jer What's it *like ?* " Roguey's voice was terrible.

" I don't *know*." Tides and waves of understanding were sweeping through Jer's mind. If he'd had *that* fear for Mary he'd have gone mad. Thank God, he was delivered from it by his knowledge of her child's father. She had about as much as she could stick without that.

" Take a pull, Roguey," Jer said. " Come down and have a drink. You've got to see the fellow sooner or later. You may as well do it now. The sooner the safer."

" Is it alive? " Roguey's mind went horribly back to that awful thing.

" For God's sake, come down and see Jerry Conroy."

Jer walked across the bathroom and snapped off the light, heard Roguey curse and fumble his way out of the dark room behind him.

With his mind in a sort of dull maze that held at bay the sickening onrush of his thoughts, Roguey followed Jer downstairs. Dumbly he passed him in the dark doorway of the study, pushed the door open uncertainly and walked in. Suddenly his breeding came to his rescue. Generations of his sort had done as they pleased. Well, he'd see the fellow damned first and come down handsomely later. He'd——

Roguey looked round the room, most arrogantly, his head high. But Jerry Conroy was not there. He had gone, leaving in the centre of the mantelshelf an envelope addressed uncertainly to Sir Ralph Sorrier, Baron Knight; with tall, spindly, slanting letters forming the word " Private " across one corner.

" He's gone." Roguey raised his voice. " He's gone, Jer."

" Well, he's left a letter; shall I get the car out? "

" Wait a minute. I'll tell you." Roguey was opening the letter slowly. Watching his face as he read, Jer thought that it would have been better perhaps for him to have heard the whole brutal truth from Jerry Conroy himself. Once, at a circus long ago, when he was a small boy, Jer, who hated snakes, had turned his back on the ring when two snakes were brought in writhing and curling. Looking behind him into all the ranks of eyes that saw what he could not look at, he was conscious of a reflected horror so great as to sicken him. It was worse than looking at the real thing, this fascinated reflection. Now, his eyes on Roguey's face, Jer knew exactly the same feeling.

Roguey folded up the letter at last, looked helplessly about him for a moment, then crossed over
to a window and, leaning out into the cold night
air, was violently sick.

"Mary can't know," Roguey said at last. "I'll
do anything, *anything*, Jer; but we can't let her
know. It'd be worse than killing her if anything
happened to her—you know, her baby."

Jer picked up the letter. "What does he say?"

"It's—— Oh, for God's sake, put the damned
thing in the fire."

Roguey folded his arms against the mantelshelf,
leaning his head down on them. Looking at him,
at his strong young body, Jer found it nearly impossible to believe what Jerry Conroy had told him
of this child of Roguey's begetting. It was fantastic, out of order, totally unreal. Instinctively
one turned away from such thoughts even, and now
to face such a matter and deal with it in hideous
privacy was appalling.

"Are you going to see her?" Jer asked again, not
peremptorily this time.

"No, I, I *can't*, Jer." Roguey's voice was more
helpless than obstinate. He sat down in a chair,
lighting a cigarette with shaking fingers, threw it
away and got on to his feet again. "It's Mary,"
he repeated; "if she hears—— My God, Jer, I'll
do anything, any mortal thing, to keep it from her!
I wish to God I'd never been near her! I—oh, it's
hell this, y'know."

Jer looked at his brother. He was angry, sick and
sorry, but most of all, sorry.

"Look here," he said. "Don't know much about

it, but, y'know, it was drugs and trying to do away with herself and all that sort of thing that did it. Oh, don't let's *talk* about it! It's so beastly. And you can't let him blackmail you over it, Roguey."

"I can't let Mary *know*." Roguey's voice was finally and utterly obstinate.

Jer, realising the futility of further argument, said no more on the subject.

"Have a drink?" he suggested.

"My God, I will!"

In the dining-room Jer heard the once-so-frequent sounds—the rattle of a decanter and hiss of a syphon, stilled now for months because "Mary hated you drinking whisky."

Realising that it wanted only a quarter of an hour to dinner-time, Jer turned slowly upstairs to change. No more could be done to-night, in any case.

"Jer," Mary called as he passed her door, "come in. Where's Roguey?"

"Changing, darling."

"What did Doyle want?"

"Wanted to see him about one of the young horses that was kicked out at grass," Jer improvised hastily.

"Oh!" Mary looked at him with faintly mocking eyes from her pillow. How white she was, how unhappy those mocking eyes!

"Mary, are you feeling all right?" he asked anxiously. He picked up her arms; they were damp and sweating, and her mouth suddenly went all anyhow.

"No, I'm in awful pain." Mary spoke in a small, stunned voice, her words gritting out one by one.

"You can't help me, Jer. Go away, please, please. . . . Oh, *God!*" Her hands were clinging in his, her eyes wild. "*Get* me someone," she implored; "it's that stuff I took, you know— Jer, *Jer*——"

.   .   .   .   .   .

"It would be all right now," the doctor told a tired, white-faced, stammering Jer, late that night. A near thing it had been, though. Oh, over-doing it, of course, that was the trouble. Hunting, he understood. Well, it was criminal. In plain words, that was how he would describe it. Oh, rest. Care. No exertion for the present. She'd be all right. But you should have someone in the house besides yourself and Sir Ralph—someone she'll obey, someone to look after her. Another woman, of course, he meant.

Jer, smiling lop-sidedly, indicated that such a one would not be too easy to find.

"H'm, she has the pluck of the devil—highly strung, though." The old doctor had known Jer for a long time. "Keep worry away from her, Jer. She's not too happy. No need for me to see Sir Ralph before I go? I'll be along in the morning. Good-night."

In the study, Jer, going wearily in to turn out a last light, found Roguey. A decanter of whisky three parts empty stood at his elbow and a dead syphon beside it. Roguey rose to uncertain feet. He was maudlin and full of words, especially argumentative on the subject of occupying any room other than his wife's.

Jer, having conveyed him to his own bed, remembered with a faint stir of hope that Roguey had had nothing to eat since breakfast that morning, which would in part account for his beastly lapse.

Outside Mary's door Jer paused and listened. He could hear her maid moving about ever so quietly inside, but not a stir or sound from Mary. Presently the woman came out and went down the passage with a tray.

" Her ladyship's asleep," she whispered to Jer.

Jer nodded and moved away. He wouldn't even look in on her for an instant so fearful was he of waking her.

With his mind almost blank from tiredness, Jer undressed. " I'll think about it all when I'm in bed," he decided, shivering in a cold, unaccustomed room. " I've got to think what I can do. Mary matters most—Maeve darling, I do love you, but I can't let Mary hurt herself." But once in bed he fell into a warm, dreamless sleep, a merciful break in the tangle of his thoughts.

CHAPTER XIX

MARY stood on the steps of Sorristown waiting for Jer to bring round his little car and take her for a drive. It was her first outing since she had cut down the doctor's orders of a week in bed to forty-eight hours and, fraily but unalterably defiant of Jer, had proceeded on the usual rash course of her days. This afternoon, Roguey having gone out on some vaguely described business, Mary had assented to Jer's proposal of a drive to Merlinstower, the home of Toby and Prudence Sage. It would, Jer thought, at least keep her quiet, and perhaps give him the opportunity of reaching under her reserve at some sort of understanding of her unhappiness. He saw her, as he brought the car round, run down the steep flight of steps and across the lawn, exquisitely accompanied by a red setter whose movements and beautiful shape typified exactly the same measure of undirected carelessness that was Mary's attitude towards the things life does to you.

" Hullo, Jer! " Mary called, waving one hand to him, the other fast in the collar of the straining setter. " Squiffy is hunting a rabbit! " She had a view of the rabbit bolting across a corner of the lawn, and her voice lifting Mrs. Squiffy to the place was the most perfect thing. Jer, who was always seeing fresh angles in Mary's beauty, was suddenly filled

almost with awe by the swift enchantment of her.
She was wearing a thin, slim, brown tweed—
almost the exact colour of the setter, who was pulling
her weight now against the thrown-back strain of
Mary's hold. Her little close-fitting green hat
squared out her peaky, upward-curling face.
Simply, she was past words. How could one talk
sense to one such as she, who could face issues of
birth and death one day, and the next hunt a rabbit
with a serious keenness that was almost exasperating?
Jer decided to be severe, but doubted whether the
opportunity would be given him. To find an
opportunity for severity with Mary was as difficult
as holding an eel in your fisted hand, so easily did
she evade rebuke.

The rabbit hunt concluded, as most unpre-
meditated rabbit hunts are concluded, by Peter
Rabbit taking his pick of a dozen unstopped earths.
Mary retrieved Mrs. Squiffy and took her place
beside Jer in the car.

All the way to Merlinstower Mary said little. She
leant against Jer's shoulder in a manner which
cramped his style round left-hand corners and
smoked thoughtfully.

Jer himself was so busy hatching conversational
openings that he let the miles slip by with nothing
said, and only realised when they got to Merlinstower that this had been because she had wished
it so. Few people had her trick of unassailable
remoteness.

At Merlinstower, Prudence Sage, that gaunt and
wayward beauty, welcomed them with distinctive
and careless friendliness. Jer was a friend of hers,

Mary she already liked. Her husband, Toby, drifting into tea later, liked Mary too, but his eyes were all for Prudence, the mother of his son.

After tea—a cheerful almost ribald meal—Prudence went up to fetch their child from his nursery. She left the room a girl, a leggy almost hoydenish thing of immature angularity, her short red skirt anyhow, her fair hair rough from ragging with Toby. She came back a Madonna, her bowed head crowned with all the love in the world because of the thing that she carried most preciously, the thing that stirred and lived in her arms.

Jer saw Mary watching with a queer bated look in her eyes as Toby and Prudence strove not to fuss or appear concerned over this marvel, this hell of a fellow, this son of theirs. She looked at the baby— it was so young as to be quite indescribable—with faint awe, touched it as though to make sure it was real, and when she saw its curling feet, gave a little gasp for wonder at its completeness. A minute afterwards she rose to say good-bye. " May I come and see you again? " she asked Prudence. " I like your young son—he's got a look in his eye——" She bent for a second over the faintly sweet creature, and then hurried almost dumbly out of the house and into Jer's car.

. . . . . .

" Don't cry, Mary darling, it *will* be all right," Jer promised her faintly, when they had driven upwards of two miles. He stopped the car and reached over the back of the seat for her fur coat. " Please don't cry; it's so bad for you." He wrapped her in her coat and looked into her eyes. " Listen, darling,

you've *got* to talk to me about it. You can tell me
anything, because I do know."

"What do you know? You can't know what a
mess I'm in—Jer—Jer——"

He held her hands, pulling her gloves off and
holding them up to his cheek.

"I know about Rowley," he said.

"Yes, I know you do. Don't, don't measure me
by that *altogether*, Jer. I've done my best since.
Jer, *please*. The worse I am, the more I like you.
Listen! I shouldn't have married Roguey; I
knew——"

"You're twice too good for him," Jer put in
savagely.

"Oh, 'good'! That would have been *nothing*
if I'd liked him. How can I make you see? I love
you. I love Sorristown, now. I didn't mind this
baby so much, even, till——"

"——till you saw Rowley again, darling?"

"Jer, listen. I must tell you now, because I
never will again. I love him so terribly I nearly hate
him—no, not him, it's myself I hate. Nothing would
hurt me if he loved me: I'd have this child of his;
I'd do anything—I swear I would. It's his not
caring about me that makes me feel *cheap*—dirt
cheap. I can't live with myself. I hate this kid, I
won't have it. Roguey's more than I can stand.
Oh, *Jer*!"

"Steady, darling. Listen to me—but you must.
Mary. Now, Mary, be good. Precious, you'll like
it all right when it's born."

"It never will be." Mary's words were small,
desperate, and utterly meant.

" Not if you buy Epsom salts by the pound and gin by the bottle, it won't." Jer was holding Mary's narrow wrists in a strong, disapproving grip that almost forced her to take hold of herself. She gave a little gasp and, dropping forward, leant her forehead against Jer's sleeve.

" Jer? "

" Yes, darling, I confiscated it; but that won't stop you buying more, I know. You've got to *promise* me not to. Remember how you hurt yourself."

" It's no good me promising, Jer." Mary's was the voice of a penitent child protesting against an impossible exaction. " When I've forgotten the pain I'll do it again." She was as firmly, unreasonably obstinate as a child.

" But, Mary, it's—it's horrible of you——"

" Oh,"—Mary wailed a long, thin whisper of a cry—" you don't *understand*. If only Rowley cared about me—just a little for myself, just enough to want me for keeps—it'd be all right. I'd go on with this rotten pretence to Roguey—*anything*."

" Mary, darling, things are worth while," Jer urged. " You have Sorristown, and hunting, and me to look after you. And Roguey's not half a bad sort, either, you know. Bar all rot and jokes, we'll pull things together somehow. Precious, you know you won't always be in love with Rowley. It dies—*really* it does." They were sitting close together, Jer's arm firm round her shaking shoulders, nothing but concern and sure affection in his hesitating voice. He cared for Mary's hopeless self so much that he would never trouble her with the love that was in him for her enthralling body. " Does Rowley know about this baby? " he asked thoughtfully.

" Ye—es. I told him it was Roguey's. At the dance the other night, Jer, it all started to happen over again. No, it's *not* his fault. It's not my fault. It's just when we're together things are hopeless. I know he must stick to Maeve, and I'm going to stick to Roguey. And just snatching at love together wouldn't be bearable : I know I'm a rotter enough to do anything, but I can't sit down in cold blood and plan schemes for deceiving Maeve and Roguey."

" *Dammit*, Mary, you don't think Rowley would either? "

" Yes. That's the only way he wants me. *He'd* call it something nicer, but that's what it comes to, and I can't bear it. That's why I ended things by telling him it was Roguey's baby. ' Good luck to it,' he said. I said, ' Thanks awfully, darling. I'm going to be terribly happy.' And he looked at me, Jer, half relieved, half disgusted. That's the way he loves me, Jer—not really."

" If you think of him like that, darling—what I mean is, why worry? "

" Oh, don't *talk* about it any more, Jer! You *can't* understand. If he was the most utter bounder I'd love him. Other people don't exist for me. He and I are the only people that *matter*."

" Doesn't his baby matter? "

" If he loved me, Jer, I'd die to keep it—I didn't know how much till I saw Prudence and Toby with

theirs just now. But without his love it's just—
beastly. And Roguey for its father—it's all so too
sickening."

" Mary "—Jer's mind fumbled hopelessly among
difficult words—" *don't* you realise it's not yourself
you may hurt, but the poor little brute may be
born—queer or something——"

" Oh, no, it won't," Mary said, in a voice of such
unemotional certainty that Jer's heart felt cold. She
was so quietly, desperately in earnest.

" What do you want? " he asked her, almost
impatiently. He was leaning forward, his thumb
on the self-starter. Really, Mary down from her
own remote heights was a thing that tore his heart.
He had asked for her confidence, and now was at a
loss to cope with her.

" I want *Rowley*," she said, in a crying, despairing
voice—the voice of a child that sees no reason but
unkindness in the hopelessness of the way its heart
is set.

" You want a hell of a lot too much, Mary,"
Jer told her helplessly.

" I do, I know, but it's amazing what one can do
without." Mary sat up straight, staring into the
night: out before her on the dark, wet road. " Go
on, Jer, step on it," she said. And as the cheap self-
starter blenched and whirred: " No, I'll drive, may
I? Thanks; you're the world's tonic, darling."

Jer, changing places, knew that his moment of
broken confidence with her was dangerously, incon-
clusively finished. They had arrived at nothing.
He saw less than no way out for her, and nothing but
unhappiness near those who loved her. His eyes

went from her thin, ungloved hands on the wheel to her dim, rash profile.

" You'll get fifty out of her if you really try," he told her with an effort at sarcasm lost indeed on Mary.

" I'm all out," she said briefly, as the night rushed past them. " I hate these cheap cars." She drove dangerously well.

.   .   .   .   .   .

Back at Sorristown, preceded nimbly by Mrs. Squiffy, Mary, her hat bruised under one arm, her hand almost unconsciously pulling her hair back into set waves, walked across her lovely room to the rose-and-blue glow of its fire. If beauty could help it was hers; all round her, outside her house and inside, and herself the keystone of it all. If bravery could help, and the strong, honest excitement to do with horses and hunting could help. If the keenness and the darling ways of little dogs could help, she had all these things. If love could help her at all to forget love—Roguey rose from the depths of a chair near the fire. His face was flushed and surly and anxious.

" Where've you been? " he commanded.

" Merlinstower—seen the Sage's."

" Now, why? " Roguey demanded truculently.

" *Why?* " Mary stared at him.

" Wanted see old Toby meself—only fella in the country worth a dam. Had hell of an afternoon with—these—damned—h'm——" Roguey subsided into his chair, unconscious of Mary's eyes growing chill with dislike upon him. Turning her back, she went slowly out of the room.

" Roguey's tight," she told Jer in the hall.

217

He watched her going up the wide, dark stairs, her slim legs toiling from step to step, her hand pulling on the bannisters as though she felt the weight of her swinging fur coat to be more than she could carry.

Jer's thoughts flew to a girl in a silver dress, proudly, rashly, carelessly taking life at the very flow. He had seen her coming down these stairs swift and unafraid on her one hopeless, passion-driven night.

Jer retired to the drawing-room, there to cope with Roguey who was not so drunk as to be insensible of Jer's wounding suspicion of his sobriety. He was, however, either unable or unwilling to give an account of his afternoon's dealings with the family of Conroy. Going up to change for dinner, he walked carefully through the colder gloom of the hall, and half-way upstairs paused in his unsteady ascent to warn Jer in an uncertainly hectoring voice to mind his own qualified business. Jer heard him go straight to Mary's room, heard the door open and shut and a pause ensue, just long enough for a salubriously smart reception, then the door opened and shut again. Roguey's advances, if any, had been promptly turned down. Jer, wandering past the open door of Roguey's dressing-room, saw him, five minutes later, standing quite strangely still, his eyes fixed with a sort of numb despair on the wall between his room and Mary's. Jer passed the door indecisively; turned on his heel, and went back. Roguey had moved over to his dressing-table, and was contemplating his hair-brushes with the same hopeless grief.

" Roguey——" Jer began.

"Now what do you want? Now, for God's sake, what do you want?" Roguey swung round his sad young face, distorted with grief and temper. "Oh, get out of it, to hell out of it!" he snapped, his voice breaking.

Jer got out.

CHAPTER XX

It was one of those rare, gleaming days that come sometimes in January. Every hedge takes on depth of black and purple in the pale kindness of the air. Pools of water are peaceful plashes of wintry gold. Young oats, spearing the dark earth, are like broken veils of jade. Thrushes swear vehemently that spring is here, and strong, sturdy crocuses open their brazen hearts to the deceiving sun. But the woods are dead still, as dead as the wet, leathery piles of leaves they wore last year, and in the dull, short-cropped grass fields water lies blue in the cut crescent of a horse's hoofprint.

Maeve and Rowley were standing together in the last slanting warmth of the low sun; it shone into the black glass of the windows of Sorristown behind them, and dazzled across their eyes as they watched Mary riding a big, bright bay horse round the field below the gateway where they stood. She did not see them even when she came quite close to where they were standing, so intent was she on what she was doing.

Her horse, fresh from his stable, was not a particularly easy or pleasant ride, nor was Mary riding him particularly well. Her small, wild face looked pinched and determined; and as, with a peculiarly nasty backward glance at her stirrup, her horse gathered himself up till his whole back seemed accumulated directly under her saddle, she let her heel into his ribs, surviving the plunge which followed more by good luck than good management.

" What's that she's riding, Maeve? " Rowley asked sharply.

" I don't know the horse, but she can't *ride* it, whatever it is. Oh, *look* at that! "

Galloping now round the outside of a series of schooling fences, they saw the horse's dirty swerve across the wing of one in a determined and successful effort to cut short a corner of the field; saw Mary give him a job in the mouth only just in time to save her leg on the wing; saw him put down his head, stiffen his neck, and hook it with her for a couple of laps round the big field in a way which could only be described as damned unpleasant.

" She can't hold him," Maeve said at last, with a quiet obviousness that was not unacquainted with pitying criticism. " She can't stop him, Rowley," she added, as Rowley said nothing.

" She's dam lucky if she keeps him in the field." Rowley's eyes were helpless on the small, straining figure of Mary, tired and crooked in the saddle now. " What the hell does that bloody fool Roguey put her on such a swine of a horse for? "

Maeve looked at Rowley—so intent—sideways, for once not quite lovingly.

" I should think poor Roguey has very little to say to what Mary rides. I think her dog had better stay with us." She picked up Mrs. Squiffy, who came swiftly and delicately down the muddy cart-road to the gate where they were standing.

"Thank God she's got a pull on him at last!"
Rowley, with less than no attention for Maeve's
doings or sayings, went quietly down the field to
where Mary, with her horse now pulled into a rough
jog, was coming towards him. He caught her rein
and led her back towards the gate without a
word.

Mary, her wind gone, speechless and nearly sick,
with a scarlet face and hair sticking against her wet
neck, her arms hurting and slack after the strain,
her knees useless round the pummels of her saddle,
leant forward and laughed.

"Oh, Rowley, wasn't I a *silly*?" She reduced
the reins bunched in her hands to some sort of order
and looked down at him, relieved and daring him
to scold her, like a child who knows that the awful
result of a forbidden escapade will be considered
punishment meet for the crime.

But Rowley didn't scold. He was hardly a wordy
person, but, even had he been, you can't scold
people when your heart has been shaken cold because
of their danger only a short minute before.

When you've known desperately that everything
in the world that matters is to be snatched from
you, or in any case to be frightened and bruised
and unspeakably hurt; when you have that thing
safe again, knowing with a terribly renewed intensity how much it matters to you, you don't say very
much.

Maeve came up to them, her face, when she
stopped and spoke, almost a continuation of her
beautiful slow walk, and said to Mary: "Where did
Roguey get the broken-down race-horse?" her eyes

first on his legs, fired and patched up, and then
dwelling in meditative approval on his grand lines.
" If you gave him four new legs he'd be worth a lot,
but he'll never be a horse for you to ride, Mary.
Roguey ought to know that."

Mary said immediately: " Oh, the horse is all
right—if he was half ridden. He's only been in the
stables three days, an' I'd better take him back now
before Roguey knows I had him out. I don't
know where he bought him—from a man called
Conroy, I think."

" Oh, that play-boy! " Maeve looked at the
horse again distrustfully and just a little worried.
" Oh, really. Well, if you don't mind my saying
so, I don't think he's *at all* the thing for you to ride."
Her voice was so flatly, uncontradictably disapproving that Mary nearly giggled as she answered without
rancour:

" No, I don't a bit mind your saying so. Roguey
and Jer went off in the car about an hour ago;
they'll be livid at having missed you."

" Where have they gone? "

" This horse'll be coughing to-morrow if you
keep him standing around in the cold much longer."
Rowley was furious and impatient with Maeve and
Maeve's slow, unhurrying disapproval of darling
Mary and her ways. Couldn't she see, now that the
colour had died out of her face and the excitement
was gone from her eyes, how white and beaten and
spent Mary looked?

" Where have they gone? " Maeve repeated,
painstakingly refusing to notice Rowley's interruption.

" Oh, to see Aunt Edythe—she's staying at Kilronan." Mary sat round in her saddle as she rode
her horse away, calling to them over her shoulder,
" I'll meet you at the house."

But when she came through the hall and out on
to the steps, ten minutes later, she saw only Rowley.
No Maeve, no car. Only Rowley. Not fair. Not
when you were feeling so rotten, and frightened
still rather, after that beastly ride. She said:
" Hullo! Where—where's Maeve? " and knew as
well as anything from the way Rowley said " Gone
to see Aunt Edythe," that Maeve and Rowley had
just had one of those sickeningly acrid and personal
contests on the subject perhaps of Aunt Edythe,
perhaps of herself; nothing much said, probably,
but a very ravine of difficult estrangement suddenly
flung between them.

" Well, tea, I suppose," Mary said. Her heart
hurried her, and she was tired—oh, tired and
shaken!

Rowley, following her into that blue room of hers,
watching her thin, unreal-looking legs with Jhod-
purs gartered below the knees; those unsteady feet
in soft brown shoes, high tongued to take a stirrup
iron; her narrow hips and shoulders set, it seemed,
almost to music; that small and passionate face,
ancient as frailty, with its hot mouth and cool,
estranging eyes, knew that she was his—that was all.
There weren't any other facts in life that mattered
beside that fact. And then, as he saw her souse
herself into a chair, utterly tired and done, her heels
dug into the rug in front of her, her chin dropped
to her slackened shoulder-blade, and her hands not

thicker through than the hands of a sick child, he
remembered why it was that she was now, for the
present months at least, utterly, most sacredly
another man's.

" Let's have some tea," Mary said at last. There
is something almost unbearably, disconcertingly
familiar in long silence, if you care enough for the
person with whom you are silent, that is more
defeating to the best of resolutions than any number
of dangerous words. So Mary got herself out of her
deep chair and poured out two cups of tea in a
jerky, unromantic fashion, as different as could be
from the graceful, informed, mysterious ceremony
that Maeve made daily behind her teapot and kettle
of shining silver, and thin china cups, her hands
ivory acolytes at the altars of domesticity.

No longer did rich and abundant teas flourish at
Sorristown. A meagre plate of sandwiches Mary
ordained, and if, when they had most unashamedly
raced for the last of these, Roguey and Jer ever
sighed for more, they never dreamed of implying
criticism of Mary's housekeeping to the extent of
demanding more.

To-night Rowley and Mary drank their tea
because it was there, but the only person who
benefited by the sandwiches was Mrs. Squiffy.
Darkness came heavily and inevitably on them, as
they sat there together, still quite apart. And
when Mary moved across the room and put on two
lamps that reached palely through jade and cyclamen to dispel the lovely intimacy of the unequal
firelight, the inevitable only closed round them each
more nearly.

" Cigarette? " Mary said. To smoke—that was the normal thing to do. That would help. Rowley lit hers and his with careful precision, put the match-box back in his pocket, took her cigarette out of her hand, and laid it down beside his own in an ash-tray.

" I don't want you to smoke."

His eyes were on her far more imperative than words. Mary, all resolve failing and falling from her, came to him, wordless, helpless. Nothing provoking about this love of hers. Her eyes, when he kissed them shut to ecstasy, demanded it as selfishly as did his own.

" Oh! " Mary, waking, turned from their love in surprised dismay, her white face bent on her crossed arms, her body flung suddenly away in a distant corner of the sofa to be by itself. And she was alone. Those men who kissed you and made nothing of you, and left you, nobly fighting their own damned devils, gazing out into the night as Rowley was doing now, how much or how little did they guess of the devils they raised in others! Not fair. . . . Nothing was ever fair.

Rowley was standing over her now, looking down at her, twisted miserably in her corner of the sofa. His eyes were calm, miserably repentant and almost shy, like a little boy who has done the wrong thing *again*. Those lines of helpless selfishness were gone from his face. Contradictorily Mary wanted them back, loving him for everything he'd done to her. God, how much she loved! Stretching up her hands to his coat to pull him down beside her, her cheek against his arm; near, very near; words so easy

226

now in the quiet room. He wasn't to sigh like that
—not done, she laughed.

"Oh, *God*, darling, I *don't* know. I—shouldn't
love you. Mustn't."

The light played sharp tricks with the curved
back of her soft head. He leant down and kissed
her neck under her hair—the most perfect thing in
the world, shivering and sweet to kiss. She turned
back her head slowly, slowly. He was so dear, he
was so much hers. Nothing was stronger than their
love: their love that hadn't died, that had survived
even fulfilment.

Rowley said, "There isn't long. I mustn't tell
you what I want. But I want you to *promise*——"

"Oh, I *know*." He shouldn't break dreams by
telling her what she knew he wanted. Of course he
should have it. Once, a lifetime ago, a mad girl
had thought of curious inanimate things like Sorristown, and the feelings of people who just weren't—
like Roguey and Jer, and Maeve even. As though
such insubstantial obstacles should prevent what
only mattered. Now she knew that she was there
simply because Rowley, selfish and sullen, needed
her so dreadfully. And what, anyhow, was her love
if it could not give him all he wanted and ask nothing
more than that he should take? So she said again,
"I know what you want, darling," staring down
through her eyelashes at his strong, fascinating hands
—Rowley's hands—hers. She kissed his palm,
fitting in her lips slowly, and raised serious eyes to
his face at last. She was not shy.

"You are absurd. Listen to me. I *mustn't* kiss
you now."

"Well, how too unkind, darling!" Mary's shaken heart was her own again, but she would not flirt with love now. No time. "Well, tell me what?"

"You've got to *promise* me to stop doing mad things like riding that horse to-day. I don't want you to be hurt. Darling, the—it—may be someone else's, but you're *mine*; I want you to know that." Rowley held away from her, and caught her close, whispering again, "*Promise*," and "you *know* you are."

"Yours? Oh, my poor girl!" Then, suddenly grave: "Listen, darling—swear you won't think me awfully careless—Rowley"—it was a bigger thing than she thought—telling him—"Rowley——"

"Not—*ours*?"

"Best word in all the world—that—Is it your first, Rowley? I swear it's my one success."

"The success is mine, sweetheart: The failure's yours. *Pleased*, darling? Hell, it's *wonderful*! But you—Mary, *what* a thing you are! How did you stick it, precious? Tell me. No, *don't* tell me—I can't bear to think what I've done to you. Darling! And I haven't been one minute happy either." He held her close, his cheek on her hair, staring out across her shoulder into the fire. Then all the months between their love, all the hopeless tangle of people and things and places, difficulties insuperable before their further love, came to his mind with sudden overwhelming force. Maeve? Castle Fountain? And Mary, almost a wraith of a thing, her thin knees crossed, her eyes enormous, who was she that he should throw down his household gods,

228

shattering them at her feet, his frail idol? And
Mary, stirring uneasily in his arms, answered the
question with a confession that showed him exactly
what she was and quite how dear.

"Darling, I must tell you—I tried to kill our
baby. Would you believe? Because I thought
you didn't care—because I got *desperate*, couldn't
stop myself loving you. Now "—she sighed and
came close again—" I *loathe* children, but this is
yours—and then the *pain*." He felt her body flinch
in his arms and her forehead wet against his mouth
thinking of it. It *was* all theirs—the love, the child,
everything. He wouldn't have her hurt. This
very minute he'd take her away if it could be done.
All his life given to her could never make a blank of
those three months of hell he'd given her, too.
Again Maeve? It was definitely less cruel to desert
Maeve than to desert Mary. Maeve had solid
pillars of support—her calmness and strength and
love for others; Mary, with the love of all men
perilously near her, was his own alone. Her frantic
ways were still, with him. In his her nervous
hands lay quiet. Her eyes, trusting him, forgot
their cold, glancing ways; she was a wild thing
completed, yet won only in snatches from her pale,
unresponsive, pagan heights. And for her everything he had was not enough for Rowley to give up,
with love. "Mary," he said, "listen to me. I
don't want to rush you, but——"

But Mary was on her feet laughing, a little confused, still without any ugly guiltiness ; and as Maeve
and the two brothers came into the room she was
smoking, a new cigarette, seated on the hearthrug,

playing Rowley one up through the pack—a shilling
flutter for which her passion was well known. " I'm
six up—play! " Mary exclaimed as Maeve moved
across the hearthrug to warm her hands at the fire.
" Look out! chase Mrs. Squiffy off the cards."

" How can you be six up? " Maeve asked, her
eyes on the scattered cards, " when Rowley has a
pair of Aces and King, Knave, ten, nine. You
haven't got anything higher than eight out yet! "

" Oh, Mary — cheating, oh, cheating! " Jer
stumbled across the rug, jumbling the cards still
more.

" Cheating? Doesn't that spoil the game rather?
Can you give me a cigarette, Rowley—I think
you've got mine. Thanks." Maeve looked about
her for an ash-tray, and then said to Rowley, in a
suddenly bruised and shaken voice, " I think perhaps
we ought to be making a move. Good-bye, Mary.
Good-night, boys."

" Oh, no. Rowley "—Jer was stammering madly
—" I—— Oh, my God, am I g-going to sta-ammer?
—I want to show you this rod I got. It's t-too
heavy for me."

Rowley got up, mystified and sullen, to follow
Jer through the hall and into the untidy limbo of a
rod-and-gun room.

" The fact is—— " Jer began unhappily, " I
suppose you'll tell me to mind me own business." He broke off, staring in miserable discomfort at the tops of his stockings, while words
joining in fantasy and pageant in his mind resolutely eluded utterance. Rowley's eyes were not
sympathetic; but Jer, in his hurrying discomfort,

could not have seen that it was because they were
so unhappy.

Suddenly Rowley said: " And about this rod? "
—in a voice which made Jer's rod the only matter
in the world fit for discussion, entirely forbidding
him, as it were, to approach any nearer than the
length of a sixteen-foot salmon rod. Then for ten
minutes Rowley gave to that matter the most
earnest and painstaking interest, which restored Jer
almost to calm and intelligibility. But at the end
of the ten minutes Jer could no more have broached
the subject of Mary than he could have handed a
religious tract to a fellow-traveller in a first-class
railway carriage. Coward he was, coward he
remained all the way back across the hall to the
drawing-room. And there, in the warmth and soft
lights where Mary and Maeve and Roguey were
sitting, he remembered with a sort of shock how
easy, after all, it would have been to have spoken
and told Rowley just how matters stood. How
sensibly and clearly he could have put it! And
now it was too late.

In the doorway Rowley paused to say: " Can you
shoot with me to-morrow, Jer? Kilooley, ten
o'clock. Right! By yourself, I mean." His eyes
stopped, resting on Roguey, handsome and garrulous, holding forth noisily on the iniquity and gal-
lantry of Mary's ride of that afternoon. " Not that
fool," Rowley said quietly, and Jer could see how
he strove to avoid looking near Mary.

Roguey said in a sudden pause: " Aunt Edythe's
gone to the devil entirely. Do you know what
she's been up to, Mary? "

Mary shook her head. Aunt Edythe, who had seemed once like the shadow of an ugly future, did not now interest her.

" Well, we've asked her to lunch to-morrow "— Roguey was staring at Mary in an avid, provoking way he had—" and you won't know her when you see her."

" Why ? " Mary's curiosity was only of the faintest.

" *I* think it's the first sign of her mental decay," Jer struck in. " D'you remember how she always would try to be with us instead of staying with the old ones like herself ? "

" Jer's being optimistic," Roguey sneered. " We all know what a pet he fancies himself to be with her. You'd better look out, Jer, she doesn't marry again and leave it all to a young husband."

" What's she *doing ?* " Rowley asked.

" She's rejuvenating—she is, though, bar all jokes." Roguey was solemn. " You'd never be-lieve what three months' hard labour and all that money behind it have done for her. I hardly knew her. She looks an awful old tart——"

" *Roguey !* " Maeve hated that.

" *Oh !* " Jer gabbled the air in his disapproval.

Mary, tired and bored with Roguey's discourse, played unkind games with Mrs. Squiffy in one corner of a chair.

Again no one's to love or scold, herself and her adoring, snarling little dog the only two people of distinction, they reserved to themselves the right of finding others inadmissible to their confidence. And last Jer saw Maeve, and darkness and pity for her

came over him like a blinding sheet. Darling
Maeve, who had loved so kindly, why should all the
peace in her life be rooted up and flung out? He
saw her suffering dumbly, unreasoningly, waiting
perhaps with pathetic confidence for Rowley's love
to come back to her. Not knowing how in their
brief life together there had been much pity, a little
passion, but the love all hers. Because Rowley and
Mary were so strong and brilliant, so passionately in
love and so passionlessly selfish, Maeve had to
suffer. Hideously unfair it was, without reason or
faintest pattern of hope. More bitter and lasting
than death, Jer thought, is love when its time comes
to fail, then turn and glow for another. The best
to be hoped is forgetfulness; but, before forgetfulness, comes for some such live pain as passes
belief, and forgetfulness itself is an empty loss for
these poor, constant ones.

Maeve was in the hall, in the old hall of Sorristown
that Mary had not yet found time to change from
its decorous inoffensiveness to unnatural beauty.
It was still the same as it had been all Maeve's young
life, when she had gone out through it every day to
fish or hunt or to shoot rabbits with Jer, or just to
do nothing in particular. How unaware of it she'd
been in those long, unaccountable days! how deep
and kind and sheltering it seemed now when life
had suddenly taken her by the throat to shake her
into a realisation of all that was most ugly!

"Good-night, Roguey," Maeve said. Roguey,
dear Roguey! Never should he be hurt if Maeve
could help it; if *anything* could be done.

"'Night, Maeve—Rowley." Roguey went back

to the drawing-room where they had left Mary, and
Jer followed Maeve out on to the cold step.

"Good-night, darling—see you to-morrow, p'raps."

But Maeve didn't answer Jer. Deep in her heart
was a wordless conviction that Jer *knew*. Jer knew,
and his calf-like sympathies were with a wicked
woman like Mary, if his pity was for her. Pity!
Who wants pity?

Maeve, sitting beside Rowley all the familiar
miles home, was afraid—deeply and miserably
afraid. Slowly, fighting for its birth in her, was the
knowledge of how little she knew Rowley, how deep
was their constraint together. However well he
loved her, he was as inaccessible to her as any
stranger, the more so for their intimacy. And
Rowley did not speak. He drove on, his face dim
and fixed, his mind, no doubt, back in that lovely
room where she had found him playing an idiotic
game of chance—Rowley, who was not given to
indulging in foolish and childish card games; or
further back still, shaken again by the sight of Mary
riding a horse that was too much for a fool the like
of her to ride. And Maeve, painfully jealous, as all
unimaginative women are, and proud as only the
pure in heart are proud, had seen this, and more.
She had seen, lying on a square, flat piece of jade,
two dead cigarettes—their cigarettes, lighted at the
same time, had burnt a moment unsmoked and died
precisely together—stiff, unblushing witnesses to the
helpless call at which Mary and Rowley had laid
them down.

What, she wondered, was there for her to say or do
or think? In actual fact what had she to go on?

Nothing. Was it surprising that the sight of a girl riding a difficult and dangerous horse should have upset Rowley ever so little out of his usual calm? There might have been a thousand reasons besides her own faint scorn of Mary's equestrian prowess to precipitate Rowley's soured dissent from her proposal of going on to see the boys and Aunt Edythe. Fool she was to have taken the car and left him in that mood. After all, Mary very likely *had* cheated over that silly card game—quite the sort of thing she would do; and the sudden untimely death of two cigarettes is not invariably evidence of passion between their smokers. A little sense, Maeve thought, a little patience, and oh, please God! a little less of this dreadful choking jealousy that caught you and held you, forcing the grotesque into your every thought and action. " The difficulties of married life," how the phrase had persisted in every unilluminating book she had painstakingly and profitlessly read on the subject! What was the *use* of people writing books like that, purporting to help, when they didn't know Rowley, or anything about the dreadful difficulties Maeve was in? Nor could they guess (for surely their numbers are not frequent) that there are girls like Mary in the world. Girls—Maeve's hands clung together in her lap, her nails biting into her palms—girls who have no respect for their own slack, lustful bodies; who love and demand and take other women's dear mates; who never stop for fear or for favour; for whom ostracism is not punishment, but an amusement which they faintly deride. Maeve had seen a picture once—what was it called: The Adulterers? A girl and a man tied side by side, lashed to two posts. Stripped they were, and their eyes agonised; while those who passed by leered at them, spat upon them, reviling them for their hateful sin. Those were the days when the sinners were punished, when such special Calvaries were provided for their chastisement. Fiercely Maeve knew that those days were right, that such thieving women as Mary deserved just such a fate. Maeve could see Mary's white back with its shadowy, narrow bones, stooped forward like the woman's in that righteous picture; could see her scornful, tired eyes humbled, and her mouth bruised and smeared—the thought filled her with a kind of fervour. But she did not for a moment see Rowley tied by Mary's side to expiate his share of their sin. No, she saw Rowley far away, alone with herself, careless of everything but love for herself: her own alone, and only hers for always. Dark and blind and silent, Maeve sat beside the real and actual Rowley, as powerless to charm him at the present as she would always be.

Mary, had she known of the fear and jealousy tearing across the peace of Maeve's life, would have stared with lazy audaciousness; and should Maeve have called her by the terrible name that she almost guessed her to deserve, Mary would have murmured probably in her husky, unhurried way: "Fairly *primitive*, you know—two women spitting fire and blood at each other over one man," and perhaps laughed, or perhaps just stared again before she turned away to play with her dog. You could not get at Mary, either to punish her or to love her; but Maeve did not know that. Her own heart cried out

for justice, while there is no justice—only consequences. And consequences are the most inconsequent and incalculable things in the world. They
are just as likely as not to skip over the unrepentant
head of the evil-doer who has brought them about,
and light heavy with calamity on the bowed neck
of a sufferer whose load is already heavier than can
be borne.

CHAPTER XXI

ROGUEY sat alone in the study at Sorristown. It was half-past ten on the same evening, and a very lovely night it was, too, with a faint crackle of frost in the quiet air that went up in a great clean bow straight from the earth to the stars. There were no clouds. But Roguey was not thinking much about the night, except in so far that he hoped quite acutely, in spite of his other preoccupations, that there would not be a severe white frost, for white frost generally meant a rainy day to follow, and rain overhead would spoil scent, which, as to-morrow was a hunting day, would be another damned thing in the list of damned things that possessed what Roguey (and others by courtesy) called his mind— another matter to interfere seriously with his enjoyment of life and his appetite for food, if not with his thirst.

The study was a dull room, the chintz which Maeve had once selected as a favourable background for dogs' footmarks not supplying any very enlivening note of colour. It was another of the rooms on which Mary had not as yet impressed herself to any very marked extent, but it suited the dogs very well, and was supposed to serve Roguey for business interviews and the like, for which occasions (and they were few) it did very comfortably. To-night he sat there because Mary had gone to bed early, and Jer, who was cleaning his gun and oiling his boots, sniffling in the cold of the gunroom, had allowed the servants to let the drawing-room fire go out. At least Roguey could pretty well have sworn its sulky extinction was in some sort due to Jer's stupidity. So here Roguey sat, while his thoughts possessed him even to the length of forgetting the two little white dogs who strove with fitful intensity and lasting jealousy for his attention.

Roguey had indeed food for thought, food so unpalatable that his brain steadily refused to face it or his reason to digest its portent. Easier to think of other things—of his horses, for instance. That chestnut four-year-old would prove the best in Ireland yet. By Jove, but a future National horse! He'll jump anything—jumping is his delight—and he'll go and stay. God! there couldn't *be* a better horse, Roguey thought. Then he thought of the bay horse with fired hocks that Mary had ridden that day, and dwelt sadly on the thought. Always something to play hell with you, and that was the very devil. From the bay horse his mind swung, with sick unwillingness, to the horse's owner, for he had not bought the brute—there were other reasons for keeping it in his stables. Roguey's mind flamed at the thought of Jerry Conroy, and sank again helplessly, as it did twenty times a day. " If *she* was all right, I'd see him at the devil before I did a thing for him. I wouldn't pay him another shilling. I've done about enough for him. But I can't face her knowing it—*anything* sooner than that. Not now. No, *dammit* "—the difficult blood rose insufferably to his forehead—" she must *never* know."

Roguey got up from his chair to mix himself a drink with deliberate concentration. You got like that when your mind was half crazy with worry—you were grateful to little things that obliged you to concentrate even for a moment. You did them slowly, to make the forgetfulness last a little longer, stretching out their comfort as far as possible. Roguey drank and sighed and lit a cigarette, putting off thought just a moment more. But his mind was pinned on a crucifix of remembrance. He could not escape. Mary, he thought of, and her cool, sweet ways. Mary, his brave, darling thing whom no one was to hurt—ever. Now, if he'd guessed she was going to ride that horse this afternoon, he'd have had the brute out and shot it, and damned the consequences. A light, horrid sweat broke out over his body as a vivid memory of her bad riding and complete nerve swept over him. Little champion, she was—his, too, the darling fool. Never must she know the dark, sickening things that had come out of Roguey's careless philanderings. No price was too high to buy silence, even for a time, till she was safely delivered of his child—— The edge of the decanter clattered against Roguey's glass again. For himself he was trying to buy forgetfulness of that other child, and the price of that forgetfulness was just as stiff as the drink he was mixing for himself. God! it did him good, though. It was what he needed. Now he wasn't going to have that swine Conroy coming it over him. No, to-morrow he'd tell him it was time for this nonsense to end. No more of it—not another penny. And he could take his damned race-horse out of the Sorristown

stables. Roguey would have nothing to say to any
point-to-point ramp with a horse that had run under
rules. No, Roguey was a gentleman, and gentlemen—h'm—— Roguey stared before him solemnly,
repeating, with intense feeling, almost with tears,
the fact that he was a gentleman. The thought comforted and sustained him. On the strength of it he
mixed himself another drink—"just a spot." That
was better. He felt grand now; but it was a great
thing to know when to stop. Roguey knew when
to stop. He stopped when he'd had enough.
Enough—— He slid back in his chair, his hair on
end, the flush on his cheek-bones meeting the
stupefied, conscious brightness of his eyes. Momentarily he was growing more drunk. Truculence and
assurance steeped his mind in a glorious riot.
Brilliant thoughts and schemes posturing and parad-
ing within his easy grasp, he felt himself more than
the equal of his slanderers and blackmailers. Rather
glad, indeed, than otherwise, to have them there,
that he might prove by their overthrow what a very
hell of a fellow he was.

The fire fell together, the air in the room grew cold
and stagnant, and the little dogs sniffed uneasily.
It was late—very late; bed-time, Roguey knew.
But, then, the door was such a long way off, and
between him where he sat and his bed lay a remote
infinity of hall and stairs and passage-ways. Roguey
saw it all as a black, impossible desert, but at the
end was the glowing mirage of Mary's room,
where Romance trembled and was still. If he was
there, once there, she would understand how
difficult it had been to win his way to her through

the cold, unfriendly confusion of stairs and passages—
she would understand, and be kind. He loved her
so; it was all wrong, another low trick of Fate, that
she should not be his when he wanted to have her,
when he had—never needed her so much. Proceeding upstairs with due pains and dignity, Roguey
permitted himself a passing censure on the designers
of the staircase; the dash dashers might at least
have seen to it that the steps were of equal height.
No need to add to a fellow's difficulties. Things
were bad enough without that. However, it's a
grand thing to know your way about your own
house, even on the darkest night. Here Roguey
crashed into a spare bedroom, and spent a dazed
minute anathematising its cold naked chill, while he
steadily refused to become rattled, but took his
bearings like a sensible man. A severe mental
effort brought him at last to Mary's door. He
knocked, and came in with owlish importance.

Mary's room was lighted softly by a shaded lamp
that threw flat pools and patches of light across her
smooth, silk-covered bed. Very tidy her bed was,
as though she moved about in it, if at all, with the
greatest delicacy, and she sat up, remote and
deliciously comfortable, a thousand miles removed
from the carnal lusts of Roguey's flesh. His own
bed, neat and inhospitable beside hers—he could not
believe he had ever slept in it. He had never
known about love with this cold girl.

Mary raised her eyes from the contemplation of
her hands that lay folded on the sheets before her.
" Go to bed, Roguey," she said, in her small, un-
hesitating voice, " you're beastly drunk."

Drunk! To be told you're drunk when at least one drink short of insensibility, to be told you're drunk when stone and sober are your second and third names! He'd show her if he was drunk, he'd——

"Don't touch me," Mary said. She looked up at him where he stood over her, between her and the light. Her eyes never flinched nor wavered. "If you do, I'll—I'll kill you with my two hands."

She meant it. Roguey took her words hardly. He stepped back from her bed, a hurt, broken look between his eyes. Mary! Was this Mary? Presumably it was. She stared up at him from her pillows without pity or liking, her eyes bright and sharp, her mouth unyielding. "Go to bed," she said; "you've been making a swine of yourself." She looked over at the door of his dressing-room, and Roguey, like a rated pup, walked across towards it and shut it carefully behind him. He sat on his bed and trembled, the cold night air came squarely in through the lifted sash of his window. Never had Roguey imagined such loneliness and shame of spirit as were his that night. . . .

Later, his poor mazed head shoved into his pillow, and her dog pushing warmly against his shoulders, Roguey slept, unhappily.

CHAPTER XXII

JER'S black retriever bitch sat shaking with importance in the back of Jer's Austin Seven. There was not room in the car for more than herself and Jer's gun-case, yet she tolerated with haughty patience the infuriating fussiness of the terrier people, who, in defiance of many well-remembered disappointments, were determined that the car should not again start without them. This was her day and hour, and well she knew that the dispersal of this rabble was in the sure hands of her god.

Her god came down the steps of the house with his small, stout cartridge bag in one hand and his big slack game-bag in the other, and stowed both away in the back of the car. Picking up the terriers with regretful firmness, he walked back up the steps and put them in at the door. He was just shutting the door on their two imploring faces when Roguey came through the hall and, pushing past him, let both little dogs out of the house again with offensive carelessness.

" Here, d-dammit, I don't want them following me——" Jer flushed with quick annoyance.

" Never knew a dog yet that would follow *you* very far." Roguey stamped down the steps, his wonderful legs exaggerated miracles in his long black pipes of hunting-boots, their light tops shot to

copper in the sunlight, his garters a narrow band
of flakey snow above them. The pale strapping of
his breeches was softer than a glove, and his red
coat—too short for any grace of line—gave a
careful impression of exaggerated workmanlikeness.
Roguey stooped, his whip under his arm, to light a
cigarette from the match in his cupped gloved hands,
and walked off towards the stables without another
glance in Jer's direction.

Jer, hating his brother almost to the point of
tears, once more collected the terriers and, shutting
the door again upon their lamentable execrations of
his tyranny, pushed his arms into a dirty old Bur-
berry coat and applied himself to the difficult task
of igniting a spark in the unyielding bosom of his
Austin Seven. Not till Roguey came past him
again mounted on the blood horse that Mary had
ridden the day before, did Jer return to the yard to
seek the help of an underling.

Roguey rode silently away into the brilliant
morning, his house like a wraith left behind, doubts
and despairs cast off from his mind, his whole being
concentrated on the one important matter of riding
the horse that fidgeted between his knees, its ears
unkindly laid, its back tucked up and coat roughened
in the bitter bright air.

Who said " care sits behind the horse-man? "
It's another lie.

At last Jer was off. He would, he calculated, be
ten minutes late for his " date " with Rowley, thanks
to Roguey's damned interference. As he drove on,
the wheels of his little car crushing cheerily through
the thin rims of ice that lay in each faint pool, Jer's

mind drew back in slow disgust from his
temper against Roguey, and balanced slowly
forward to wonder as to what had caused Rowley
to ask him to shoot to-day. Such an invitation was
a rare grace. Jer felt pleased at it, though unaffectedly curious as to why it had been forthcoming.
Jer never could think why he was ever asked to do
anything. Aware of neither merit nor attraction in
himself, his grateful cogitations as to why anyone
should be nice to him filled half his mind on these
occasions, the other half being occupied with unhappy
misgiving over his own bad shooting.

Rowley's big car was already at the meeting-place
when Jer's Austin came to a sudden rushing stop, all
his brakes, luckily none of them very good, crammed
on together. He let Binty out and went across the
old stone bridge, built in a hollow over a neck that
joined two wide bogs, to meet Rowley.

" It doesn't matter, Jer," Rowley cut in on Jer's
stammered apology for his unpunctuality. " As a
matter of fact, I wanted to talk to you."

Jer was silent for wonder. *Rowley* saying it didn't
matter when he was kept waiting fifteen minutes on
a shooting morning. Rowley " wanting to talk,"
instead of getting on with the job of walking the bogs.
It was all out of order. It was paralysing and
gratifying and quite wrong. Jer nearly blushed
because Rowley was so changed from his usual
distant self. He had always kept himself apart;
this sudden familiarity was below him. Rowley
hitched himself up on the low stone wall of the
bridge. Jer thought his face, looking at it against

246

the pure cold distance of bog and mountains, seemed both bad and sad—his eyes were so dark and unhappy, with no peace in them at all. There was a look about him, too, of unreasoning insistence that reminded Jer strongly of someone—but that was the catch of it—he could not think of whom. Jer, plunging at anything to do in his discomfort, took the cigarette that Rowley offered him, smoking it with awkward dislike.

" Damned queer, you must think this." Rowley's eyes were suddenly shy and pleading—for a second only, though; Jer's mute incomprehension chased that look out of them.

" Did Mary tell you we were going to hook it? " he asked.

Jer's retriever came fawning up, laying her head ridiculously against his knee. " *I'd* go with you," her eyes said, " to the world's end, I would," and Rowley's hands caressed her head with intuitive magnetism. Jer thought of Mary last night in bed, so idly, tensely still, bound up in waiting, scarcely breathing, holding a memory fast to her; so still and quiet as he had never seen. Fool he'd been not to have guessed. He nodded dumbly.

" She didn't *tell* me," he said then, " but I knew, anyway."

" Did you, though? " Rowley was darkly silent. The awful difficulty of discussing the subject broke in on Jer like a flood. Suddenly it washed away his tongue-tying shyness, just because it was so hopelessly difficult and Rowley was shyer than he and he must help.

" If you hadn't, Rowley," Jer said, his eyes fast on
the clean distances of the hills and sky, " I was going
to ask you to! "

" To——? "

" To do something to help Mary. She was out of
hand. D'you know she was trying to kill herself? "

Rowley drew in his breath across his teeth.
" Bad as *that*? " he asked. " A near thing, Jer?
Why didn't you tell me? You knew—about us,
didn't you? "

" I didn't know what a wild one she was. How
could I? " Pity came to Jer and a sort of anger.
" And what about Maeve, I'd like to know? " he
stammered.

" Well, what about her? " Rowley looked at Jer
for advice: it was the most disarming thing. " You
have to look after her, Jer, I'm afraid. God!
I—I *hate* leaving her: she *is* one of the best." He
said it so impersonally that Jer was fairly staggered.
It bore home to him, as nothing else ever would,
how, for Rowley, there lived and suffered one person,
and only one. Fiercely aware of her, he had love,
pity and understanding for her only. Rowley was
strangely limited, Jer thought, and he loved Mary
even only as far as the length of his own selfishness.
She was the chief part of his selfishness, and so he
loved her as himself. One cannot argue against
blankness, therefore Jer spoke no more of Maeve,
only held closer in his own heart to his cherishing
love of her.

" What are you going to do," he asked—" now, I
mean? "

" Do? Now? That was what I wanted you to

help about. Can you bring Mary to meet me this
afternoon? We can drive up to the boat to-night.
That'll be a start, anyhow." Rowley spoke as of
the most natural thing in the world, while Jer's
confused mind saw only difficulties and blackness
all around.

"But, look here, Rowley"—Jer was grasping
and clutching in his mind at the sane and normal,
for Rowley's calmness was not sanity. "Have you
thought? Y'know, Maeve can't divorce you, even
if she wanted to—not in Ireland. I haven't gone
into it, but I've heard people talking—— What
about Castle Fountain? What about *everything ?*"

"No good to me without *her*." Rowley ground
out his cigarette end on the stone beside him and
rose to his feet, the discussion ended so far as he was
concerned. Jer, cold and dumb and powerless to
argue with such absolute clarity of purpose, followed
him down the bridge. What was he to say? What
was he to do, anyhow?

"Does Mary know? About this afternoon, I
mean?" he asked.

Rowley, half-way into his car, looked faintly
worried. "I don't think I mentioned this afternoon—not in so many words, at least," he said.
"You'll bring her along all right, though, Jer."
And Jer knew that he would. The force of
Rowley's will was like a tide, just so strong and
inevitable.

"What time?" Jer asked.

"Time? Oh, three o'clock—here. That would
do, wouldn't it?" Rowley was vague. He was

thinking of something else. " Look here," he said quickly, " how am I to tell Maeve? How *am* I to tell her? "

Jer shook his head solemnly. " I don't know. I can't do it. I'm too fond of her."

" Couldn't you, Jer? It's worse for me because it's the other way on."

" No, I could *not !* " Jer's face grew crimson.

Mary was all right now, Rowley loved her so that all he had was not a price to give for her happiness; and although Jer had waited and wanted for weeks to see that one possible solution of all this tangle, now that his hope was so nearly realised, all his love and pity for Mary turned to an anguish of anxiety for Maeve, and a bitterness against Rowley, who had brought this about. Cad—bounder—swine! he thought, kicking and rubbing his boots together like a little boy, as he stood beside Rowley's car on the muddy road. Yet Rowley, he knew, glancing at his dark, troubled face, was none of these things. He was a brave man and a gentleman. And—Jer knew it—he was a victim. He was Mary's victim as much as Mary was his. They were too strong for each other, those two. They were without the law.

" R-right you are, R-rowley "—Jer stepped back from the car, lifting his head suddenly so that the light fell broadly on his mild, honest face—" I'll have her here—it's the only thing to do."

" Thanks." Rowley nodded. " I'm *awfully* sorry about spoiling your day's shooting," he said. " I'll tell O'Brien (O'Brien was Rowley's keeper) to meet you here to-morrow. I *must* move now, I've got a few things to see to." And in two minutes he had gone.

Jer drove home to Sorristown, Binty, in the back seat, an unquestioning martyr to the caprice of her god.

CHAPTER XXIII

THERE is something strange and surprised, almost unwelcoming, about the look of a house when you return to it long before the hour that it expects to see you again. Sorristown, in the clear yellow sunlight, looked like this to Jer as he drove up to the house at twelve o'clock that day. A cold wind blew through the hall and the door banged shut behind him.

" Where's her ladyship? " Jer asked White, who came out of the dining-room to inquire, almost in a tone of personal injury, whether Jer would be in to lunch. " You *will* be in, sir? Very good, sir. Her ladyship hasn't come down yet."

" Thanks, White."

Jer went slowly up to Mary's room, his heart turning sick and leaden as he mounted each step. Every moment that brought the reality of this thing nearer hurt like a bruise. The excitement of it all died and the Romance. For where is Romance? In a kiss on the mouth? In a wet wood at morning? It is where we are not and in all those things out of reach. But never in a consummation, however devoutly desired.

" Oh, come in, darling! " Mary called. She had just finished dressing, and stood brushing traces of powder off the shoulders of her brown Shetland

252

jumper. The cold wind blew in at her open window, and her untidied room, with its unmade bed, smelt sweeter than a garden.

Jer sat down on the edge of her bed, his cheek pressed against some garment of the smoothest wool that hung over the end.

" Thought you were shooting," Mary said. She paid no particular attention to Jer as she straightened brushes and jars on her dressing-table, with a dream in her eyes and in her rambling, uncertain hands.

" So I was going to," Jer answered, " but Rowley was too busy."

" Oh, did you see Rowley? " Mary said it as though she grudged anyone else that excitement, and picked up a hand glass to satisfy herself of the perfection of the little round bun of hair that shone low on the back of her neck. " Rowley in good form? " she asked. Even to talk about him was mysteriously enchanting.

" Not *frightfully*." Jer leant his cheek nearer to the warmth of that discarded garment of Mary's. He felt too forlorn. " Mary, will you go with him —this afternoon? He wants you to."

" Go? Go away with him? *Now?* Mary turned her back on the vanities of her dressing-table and came slowly across her room to sit on the unmade bed beside Jer.

" Well, will you, darling? I'll drive you. Three o'clock, he said to meet him, on the Kilooly bridge."

" Oh, *Jer*—" Mary's sigh was impatient with indecision. " Jer, tell me, really. What did he *say*? Did you, did you tell him about—you know what about—what I wouldn't promise not to do? "

" Um—that too," Jer nodded. He couldn't look at her.

" What did he *say* ? "

" *Say?* Say? Didn't *say* anything. Took two steps backwards and had a sympathetic pain on the spot."

" Oh, how hopeless you are! Why try to be funny? Can't you *tell* me? " He saw her eyes were staring with tears and her mouth shaken. " Don't you see, I can't go to him if it's only because he's *sorry* for me? Oh, hell! "—her face fell forward into her two hands—" I can't, I can't go! " she sobbed. " Besides, if I do, I'll be being such a beast. What will Roguey do? I don't care; but still, there it is. *You'll* disapprove of me, Jer."

" Disapprove of you? Of course. I'll keep my eye on you—through the bottom of a gin-glass." His voice mocked her with love from Jer. " Darling Mary! " Someone had to be strong, " Listen. He's *not* sorry for you—not a bit. Even if you didn't love him half as much as you do, you'd have to go to him now. You'd have to, simply. There isn't any other way. You might put it off, but what's the use? Only complicate things worse. Bound to happen some day."

" Maeve? " Mary asked again. She loved Jer for convincing her that she had to go—perhaps he could help that thought away too. But Jer could not. He would not speak of Maeve. Save her he could not, but the thought of what they were doing to her was more than he would ever help them to forget.

" Bit late to think of Maeve." He put down Mary's hand that he'd been holding for comfort. " She'll do her part of the show all right."

" Divorce Rowley? "

" *Well* "—he considered—" it's a dreadful business. Can't be done in Ireland, y'know. Means he'll have to give up Castle Fountain. Live out of the country, and so on."

" Does he know *that*? " Mary asked. Her eyes were fixed on Jer, her chin shaking in a queerly tense expectation. " Are you *sure* he knows, Jer? "

" Sure? Certain."

" Certain he's giving up Castle Fountain for me? "

Jer nodded. Castle Fountain was not one half, no, nor the quarter of what Rowley must give up, but he needn't tell her that.

" *Well*," Mary said. She sighed and her eyes shone with bright tears. " Oh, I'm not *worth* being loved like this! All this love is being *wasted* on me. Jer, Jer, how can I leave you? Will Roguey have to give up Sorristown to divorce me? "

Jer hadn't thought about that. " God! " he said. " Well, isn't that the devil? Now how *can* he? He can't afford to. *Sorristown*. What a terrible show, my dear! "

" Well, he's not to." Mary spoke over her shoulder from the dressing-table. " I don't mind living in sin a bit—rather fun. But poor Roguey —he *does* need a wife? Look here, Jer, here are his pearls. Will you hang on to them? " They were in her hands, warmly laid against those strawberry soft, unmoral palms of her hands, lying so close to the flesh as to seem nearly a part of it, as only lovely pearls can. Yet she handed them to Jer quite at random, as careless of them as she was

of honour or of safety. " Those awful diamonds
are at the goldsmith's and silversmith's," she said.
" I must see if the key of my other box is downstairs."

Jer followed her slowly down. He felt like a child
who is being left behind—the same absurd desire
to put out his hand and hold on to some part of her
clothes and not *let* her go. Nothing was so important
as his want of her.

The sight of a strange car, glimpsed through the
hall door as he paused at the foot of the stairs,
brought Jer back to reality again. Was it a strange
car, though? Of course not—it was the Kilronan
car, and—in a second it all flooded back on Jer's
memory—if this wasn't the day Roguey had asked
Aunt Edythe to come to lunch?—Aunt Edythe, to
whom they had paid their dutiful visit only yesterday.
Well, Roguey had forgotten, and he had forgotten,
and Mary was properly caught now. *Well*——
Jer, as the hall clock struck one, felt that matters
were indeed come to a pass. Puzzled and unreasonably concerned, he followed Mary into the
drawing-room, where she would, by now, be shakily
entertaining Aunt Edythe.

Seated composedly in an armchair, her back carefully turned to the light, Aunt Edythe received
Jer's chaste salutation without moving a muscle of
her old stiff neck. Jer met Mary's eyes across the
sable-clad shoulder and nodded mute appreciation
of the hole they were in. Never mind! his eyes
encouraged her, we'll get her off somehow, don't
you worry. And he sat down to talk to the ancient
relative, while Mary, with murmured apologies,
moved over to the writing-table.

"All right, m'dear; posts are like young men—
made to be caught. No, I *quite* understand. Well,
and what have *you* been up to lately?" She
rounded paralysingly on Jer.

Jer, as he gave chapter and verse for his doings
of the last months, could not take his unwilling,
fascinated eyes from off her face and clothes. Last
night, in the half light of the late afternoon and the
kindness of shaded lamps, he had not half realised
how vast was the change that the last few months
had wrought. Goodness! he thought, with a kind
of hysterical mental giggle, how mad she must be,
and what an ugly madness to overtake the old—
this lust for self-bedizenment, this grotesquely
successful aping of fashion! The very restrained
artistry of her inspired make-up, the black hat that
drooped so cunningly, the sable stole hiding, with its
limp, close caress, that dreadful old throat, and the
cobweb fine stockings, through which the bones
of her legs and ankles showed as many angled as
those of a little hungry bird—there was something
ghoulish about the whole that disgusted Jer more
than he could have admitted even to himself. For
whatever things are lovely in old age, to the young
there is nothing but that which is hateful to indecency in the thought that their old should not forget, as utterly as though they had never known them,
the lusts and passions which are to youth by right
of youth. Jer thought, still looking at Aunt Edythe:
Old witch! What does she think she's doing—
dolling herself up like this? He remembered tales
dimly heard of Aunt Edythe's riotous youth. Yet
she had been clever—so clever as to bring things off

successfully in days when light behaviour was not
countenanced. And what had they left her, those
riotous years? Bad enough she'd been as her old
bullying self—bad enough indeed—but now she was
sickening—— Orange juice and violet rays and
massage—— Jer shuddered. The vulgarity of it,
and the pity! Was this all a bright, violent past
left you when your clear mind went faintly cracky
with age? This, and the greedy excitement that
flashed sometimes into old dim eyes and shook in
swollen, gouty fingers?

With sudden terrifying apprehension Jer looked
from Aunt Edythe, scented and powdered and
bedecked, to Mary, her lovely head stooped over her
writing, the back of her neck such a swift line;
unalterably young, her clothes so soft and ordinary
and careless. God forbid that she should grow old
dreadfully like this other, who had been wild and
sweet and witty, and loved to distraction too, in her
hour. Jer thought of something: "Whatsoever
things are good, whatsoever things are pure, whatsoever things are lovely, think on these things."
Could Mary think on these things and save her
life from ugliness? He knew she could not. Such
comfort belonged to Maeve by right of generous
love and unthinking continence. Mary had no
happy right in them; or only a Magdalen's despairing right, and, should she never come to know that
need—— Jer looked at Aunt Edythe again with
something not far removed from terror.

   .   .   .   .   .

  "Jer,"—Mary came across to where they sat by
the fire—"give this letter to White and say I want

it to go at once, will you? It's rather important.
Thank you, darling." She turned to Aunt Edythe:
" I *am* sorry——"

Jer left Mary. He didn't see her troubled, secret
eyes that shifted this way and that way, or how she
glanced from Aunt Edythe's little crooked legs to her
own, lovely and slender, and curled them away
beneath her where she sat.

Jer in the hall was opening the letter Mary had
given him. It was addressed to himself, and had
" Open, darling," scrawled in still wet ink over one
corner of its envelope.

" Will you pack for me like an angel? " he read.
A list followed of the clothes he was to pack for her
—clothes the like of, which his mind had never
imagined. Nor could he ever recognise them, he
felt sure, when he saw them. Surely her maid might
have done it. After all, if she was really going, why
all this secrecy? He read her list again, his mind
clearing slowly over some of its minor details.
Stockings—those he could find all right.

Back in her room, he opened a cupboard. Her
blue tea-gown? His eyes went hopelessly from one
slit of vivid colour to another, where her dresses
hung in close-packed line, their edges neatly showing.
Blue? and a tea-gown? That must be the velvet
garment she wore sometimes for dinner. It had long
sleeves that wrinkled down her wrists and tightly
over her hands, while it was cut away at the back
so far that Roguey's long pearls lay all along her
bare shoulders when she knotted them on the
nape of her neck. Jer pulled it out from where it
hung and threw it on the bed. Could it be all

there? There didn't seem to be anything *of* it.
However, it was a beginning. Now what about
her grey jumper suit with a snakeskin belt and steel
buckle? Well, *what* about it? Jer wondered
savagely, his hands prowling unhappily among her
shelves, his eyes half the time on the door, for he was
most apprehensive of the arrival of that smart maid
of Mary's, a woman of whom he stood in considerable
awe. At last he gave up the search in despair, con-
centrating his energies on the collection of her
washing apparatus, for to travel hopefully without a
tooth-brush and sponge was a lot worse (not better)
than arriving with a jumper suiting, grey with
snakeskin belt and steel buckle. No sponge bag,
of course. Jer sighed, his mind whirling, and
made good the lack with his own, a somewhat
scarred specimen, but still a sponge bag, and not to
be despised. He stowed away Mary's seven tooth-
brushes and various ducks and fish of celluloid, which
it was her idiotic custom to float in her bath, also
a giant pot of cold cream, and ramming two sponges
down on top of the lot, pulled the strings of the bag
so tightly that they broke; so he tied the checked
neck with a pink hair ribbon, and felt that he had
really made a start. Stockings were easy—he had
known they would be. But when it came to under-
clothes he shut his eyes and grabbed a few layers off
every pile of intoxicating rainbow colour that he could
see. Never again, Jer decided as he knelt foolishly
on the unyielding lid of Mary's green leather dressing-
case, would he take a hand in the organisation of an
elopement. An unthankful, unromantic, and un-
entertaining part was his, involving much labour

and loss of dignity. Never, oh, never again! At the sound of the gong he shoved two full cases under her bed and went downstairs.

Lunch was a fearful meal. Aunt Edythe, dieting to misery on patent bread, salad and cheese, looked with hungry eyes at the food which neither Mary nor Jer could make more than a show of eating, and explained to them at length the hideous workings of their over-burdened insides. " If *I* can't eat hot woodcock or make a pig of myself over coffee-cream," she said, her eyes snapping as she snapped her crisped health-bread in her twinkling old hands, " I'm determined not to allow *you* to enjoy them, that's one thing certain."

Not very witty, Jer decided, thinking of his own inside with sudden apprehension, and looking at the woodcocks with dislike. Mary he saw leaning back in her chair, now flushed, now rather white, and knew she had had about as much as she could bear. She only nodded when he spoke to her, and drank cold water in difficult gulps. Jer was terrified that she would cry if she was made to talk, and so directed all the subtlety of which he was capable into his conversation with Aunt Edythe. He had, in fact, a success bordering on the flirtations, and rounded off the meal by pledging her in cherry brandy. Aunt Edythe, rioting from her strict diet, almost smacked her lips over their return to the flesh-pots. When they got back to the drawing-room the cunning angle of her hat had gone slightly askew and there was a heartier flush in her cheeks.

" And when do you expect Roguey home? " she asked Mary, who answered shakily that it would not be till late—very late indeed, some quite unearthly hour she indicated, and looked to Jer for help. Jer's speech staggered and failed him; his eyes were on the hands of the clock, creeping on for two-fifteen. Would Aunt Edythe only go?

. . . .

Oh, the awful, unspeakable misery and fuss of these elopements! Jer thought, as, Aunt Edythe at long last sped upon her road, he hurried his poor little Austin along, with Mary sitting wide-eyed and wordless beside him, as unhappy as he had never seen her.

"Why did I come?" she said suddenly. "Why *did* I come? You made me—didn't you, Jer? Didn't you? I'll only mess up his life, you know. Oh, why did you make me come? *And* I've forgotten Squiffy. What shall I do, oh, *what* shall I do?"

Never had Jer imagined that Mary's nerve, that unsmashable nerve of Mary's, could go so completely and suddenly. "I'll look after Squiffy," he promised. He thought of Rowley almost with pity. In taking Mary was he, in fact, to lose her? Leaving Sorristown, as she pushed her arms into her heavy, lovely fur coat, she had turned her small, hopeless face to him and said: "I will never be happy again any more, you know," but Jer had only laughed, his own heart very sad and doubting and full of dim oppression, and said, though they were already behind time: "Have a drink with me before we go. Yes. D-do you good," and they stood together in the dining-room, with all the unfriendly Sorrier eyes looking blackly down upon them, and drank to each

other. "Here's luck, darling"—they said it together. The drink helped them out of the house
and into the car.

"She'll be all right," Jer kept on telling himself
with confidence, and the more he looked at her the
more he doubted it, so quiet she was, such misgiving
in her silence.

Dreadful apprehension came swooning over Jer.
Was all this of his doing? No, but was it? Honestly
now. His confidence in the finality of Mary's and
Rowley's terrible love and satisfaction in one
another, which had burnt in him as steadily as a
flame, was suddenly nowhere. What is all love but
vanity of the flesh? And what were Mary and
Roguey but very cowards to one another? Oh,
God! Jer thought, and poor Maeve! Is it too
late—is it? Can we still take a pull? Suppose
we've torn things all round for everyone. His
indecision was worse than pain. Was there no way
out?

"Why are you driving so slowly, Jer?" Mary
asked.

"Almost there, darling," Jer smiled at her.
"Mary——" No, it was too late to torment her
with his own doubts and fears. The anguish of the
responsibility must be all his. Besides, again, it
was too late. Rowley's imperative horn (" Five
quids' worth of electricity each time," Mary had
once said about it) sounded behind them—half
an hour after time, he was, and so were they. Jer
pulled up his meek, useful little car so that Rowley
could pass them and stop, and Mary, suddenly wild
and determined as a hawk, wrestled blindly with

the door catch and was out of the car, running up the wet road to meet him.

"Hullo, darling! Baddish starter, aren't you?" Jer heard Mary say, as the two met and Rowley stooped over her swiftly to say something no one would ever hear except Mary, before they walked back down the road towards Jer. What was it that had gone from Rowley's dark face? Or what had been born in it? The restlessness was gone and the pain and sadness. And there instead was a peace that passed all understanding, a completion beyond bounds. And Mary—her small, acute white face would be like a flame for always in Jer's memory. Tears there were behind its gladness— blinding tears for love and gladness for giving herself, and a hopeless lack of concern for the future. And in all three such a promise of peace as Jer had never dreamed of for her.

Her bare hand had flashed into Rowley's hand, and it seemed that he could never get her fast enough into that monster car of his that stood so sullen and powerful and ready to go on the narrow muddy road. "Good-bye, Jer," they said, "darling Jer——" They didn't belong to Jer any more. They were born again. They were no one's. They were each other's. And they were gone. Jer was staring stupidly at the wide tracks left in the road, all that was left to him of something wild and precious.

CHAPTER XXIV

Jer was more than half-way back to Sorristown when he overtook Jerry Conroy riding one horse and leading another. Jer, who never could tell one horse from the next, did not for a moment recognise the big blood bay, leading so badly, as the horse that Roguey had ridden that morning. In any case he would have passed on if Jerry Conroy had not practically pulled his horses across the road to stop him.

" Mr. Sorrier," Conroy called, very taken up with his two horses he was—and no wonder—" I beg your pardon a minute——"

" Well? " Jer got out of his car and came doubtfully round to the horses' heads. He had had too much unpleasant work with Jerry Conroy in the recent past to wish for any further discussion with him. Besides, he did not know how Roguey stood over this last matter. He had been too thankful to keep out of it; and, anyhow, things were finished now. With Mary gone, and when he knew why she had gone, Roguey need stand no more from Jerry Conroy. So, " Well? " Jer asked again, rather more bluntly this time.

" I'm taking this horse back to my own place now." Jerry Conroy spoke in a shamed, crushed voice, as though something beyond measure had befallen.

"What horse?" Jer stared stupidly at both before something familiar about the saddle on the led horse smote him. Do farmers such as Jerry Conroy carry wire-cutters on their saddles? Certainly they do not. Nor do their saddles and leather achieve the hallowed age of those on which he was staring still without recognition.

Suddenly, looking from the horse to Jerry Conroy's bowed head, a hot wave of apprehension, composed more of excitement than anxiety, fell over Jer.

"Where's Sir Ralph?" he asked. "Has he had a fall? Is he hurt?"

"Yes, he's hurted bad." Jerry Conroy raised his head and looked out past Jer to the distance of the mountains. "He's killed," he said with a certain dignity that was not without awe.

"What?" Jer could muster no feeling save a dreadful feeling of surprise. A waywardness possessed his whole mind. Above and beyond all it was important not to laugh. To laugh would shock Jerry Conroy so much. Jer's mouth twisted strangely as he stood there trying to gather himself together, trying to imagine what it all meant and what he should do about it. Jerry Conroy was pouring out words, words that explained nothing to Jer's numb mind. All he gathered was a general impression of Roguey, in his most deadly obstinate and foolish mood. Roguey had said he'd qualify the horse and be damned to it. And that was madness. Jerry Conroy had told him he couldn't ride that horse in a hunt. But Roguey had laughed at him and cursed him. He had never seen him as strange, Jerry Conroy said. And when hounds found their fox

and left the covert with a burning scent, Roguey had
bent the big horse round in a narrow lane and
hopped him out over a high stone wall you couldn't
knock down with a sledge, and with hounds at the
start had stayed with them by a series of miracles.
The fences on which the horse had never put a fore-
foot and usually missed behind, their name was
legion; the river he had jumped with feet to spare;
the narrow bank where he came down, hitting it
and coming over on top of Roguey—poor gallant
Roguey. With the photographic memory of the
illiterate, Jerry Conroy faithfully recalled it all. And
not one mark on him, you could see, he said. " He
met a great death, Master Jer."

Jer nodded. Yes, it was a proud sort of death,
but a bit hard on those who were not the central
figure of the hot tragedy. Yes, a bit hard.

" All right, Conroy." Jer stood back from him
in the road. Hard words came to his mind. " I
never thought you *would* have much luck over that
dirty work," he said, " and you won't."

Jerry Conroy gathered up his horses' reins again,
fidgeting them to start. " Maybe there's others,"
he said, without looking at Jer, " will have worse
yet. And for the matter o' that "—he jutted his
chin dagger-like at Jer—" did I choose what come
to happen? "

" Choice or no choice, you took your w-w-*whack*
out of it."

Jerry Conroy laughed unhappily and rode away.

His anger passing from censure to extenuation,
and finally blotted from his mind by the enormity
of this last happening, Jer got slowly back into his

little car. He did not realise how shaky he was until he started to drive again, then he muttered to himself aggrievedly: " I never did get on with poor Roguey. (Why " poor Roguey "? it made one realise so finally how dead he was.) God! if I'd guessed about this, though, I'd have stood a lot more from him." Then it came over him like a blow that if Mary had known about this an hour before she and Rowley would not have gone away together. And what would have come out of that? he wondered. For Maeve two separate sorrows, instead of one great blinding sorrow almost deadening the other. For Mary and Rowley months of waiting, of stolen love to defile and take the edge off their sacrifice to one another. But the end the same. It could never have been other than that which Jer had just seen, as fore-ordained as the rush of a river to the sea and as calamitous.

The little cheerful roads on which Jer was driving flew by, the familiar miles coiling friendlily out behind him; the afternoon sun shone as kind as it had shone yesterday. The mountains stood bright and sharp against the light sky, and Jer's heart reached suddenly through trouble to hope. He thought with a guilty, delightful excitement of Maeve— Maeve with none but himself to care for her, Maeve with none but him to care for and think of. *Well*— Jer drew a deep breath—what times they might have together when all this was over and done with, he and Maeve. Oh, he'd always loved Maeve best: he had been more unhappy for her, if more frightened for Mary. Already Mary needed him no more;

she was now as much not his as any fairy. But Maeve, his dear Maeve, was given back to him again, twice over his because he had lost her for a time. Jer, hot with the certainty of this comfort he could bring her, trod on his accelerator, pushing the little car along, hurrying back to Sorristown—Sorristown, where trouble lay so heavy now, but where there would be joy one morning. Jer trembled. It was indecent, he knew, but he could hardly stop himself from thinking of the times in store for Maeve and himself together at Sorristown. The long days for fishing and the short days for shooting, and they two together to enjoy them and rest in the evenings after. They might remember sad things, yet be comforted with one another, and with the near thought of good sport on the coming day and the satisfaction of a good day behind them.

Jer turned his car in at Sorristown's great gates with the careless sweep of long practice. The gate lodge woman ran out as if to stop him, then paused unsteadily and turned back. She could not tell him. Rather nice of her, Jer thought. So many of her sort would have rushed at you, ghoulish with such news. He stopped the car, nodding to her. " It's all right, Mrs. Fanning," he said (you must remember and keep very solemn), " I've heard." There was something he wanted to ask, but the words stuck on his tongue. He hadn't realised the certainty and sorrow of it till he tried to ask : " Have they brought him back? "

" Yes, they have, sir." Mrs. Fanning had been crying. " Doctor Foley's car went in with him just

now.   Let you hurry, Master Jer, poor Miss Maeve
is above at the house—Mrs. Fountain, I should say.
Sure I don't know what I'm saying.   You'll excuse
me, Master Jer."

Hurry, hurry, thought Jer.   Get there first.
Before—before what?   He didn't know.   How well
the car was going!   What would it be like?   He
felt quite sick and excited.   He must remember to
go slow round the last turn to the house, it would
never do to run over one of the dogs.   The low sun
smote through the trees into his eyes, making the
whole world seem black.   It was colder now, and
the heavy breath of a fog lay in the river valley on
his right hand.   Jer turned the last corner (not forgetting to slow down for the dogs), and there in
front of the door was Doctor Foley's car, and several
men standing quietly round it.   Indeed, then it was
a real thing that had happened.   Jer walked across
the gravel with mincing uncertainty, as though he
were in church or on the stage, till he saw Maeve
standing on the steps, and, forgetting everything,
hurried on to her.

Maeve was looking past Jer and into the car
standing just beyond the steps.   Hunched crooked
against one corner, his fair head lolling to the
shoulder of his red coat, was Roguey.   Mrs. Squiffy,
forgotten by Mary, jumped stiffly in past the men
standing about, touched his slack hand with her
nose, then jumping delicately out of the car, bolted,
her tail between her legs, for the near darkness of
the rhododendums.

Jer went up the steps to Maeve.

One man whispered: " Master Jer, where will
we put him? "

But Jer did not hear. The mist was washing and
swirling up the river valley below them, like all the
weary sorrow in the world that weighed round
Maeve now, his poor Maeve.

" Darling, come away," he said.

But Maeve never saw his hands that went out to
comfort her.

" Bring Sir Ralph in," she said. And she stood
terribly quiet when they carried Roguey past her
and through the hall, shafts of low sunlight striking
dustily on his yellow head and brave red coat.
When all the servants had gone she turned round
again to Jer, and her voice when she spoke was like
a small, desolate dry wind.

" Now that she has *everything* she wants," Maeve
said, facing Jer, " perhaps you're pleased. I tell
you what, though "—her lovely face and voice were
alike ugly and vindictive for the moment—" she's
not going to keep Roguey's child. That belongs
to Sorristown, and it's coming back to Sorristown.
I'm going to see to that."

Was it Maeve speaking with the vitriolic, futile
importance of a slighted woman? " We've hurt
her," Jer thought, " beyond anything." Then
swiftly it came to him that she had to know everything, better to know everything now than later

" Maeve," Jer said in his low, hesitating voice,
" don't bother them about it, Maeve. It's—it's not
Roguey's——" But her eyes forbade him to go on.
Maeve's eyes—her calm good eyes—hated him, as he

dimly perceived they would always hate him. Because he *knew*. She turned away from him, almost running, hurrying away from him across the hall and up the stairs to Roguey, her unshaken idol.

" Lucky Roguey! " Jer thought, " lucky d-dog! "